THE
HARD
STUFF

DAVID GORDON

A Mysterious Press
book for Head of Zeus

First published in the US in 2019 by Mysterious Press,
an imprint of Grove/Atlantic, New York
First published in the UK in 2019 by Head of Zeus Ltd
This paperback edition first published in the UK in 2020
by Head of Zeus Ltd

9 7 5 3 1 2 4 6 8

A catalogue record for this book is available from
the British Library.

ISBN (PB): 9781838933128
ISBN (E): 9781838933135

Typeset by Alpha Design & Composition of Pittsfield, NH.

Printed and bound in Great Britain by
CPI Group (UK) Ltd, Croydon CR0 4YY

Head of Zeus Ltd
First Floor East
5–8 Hardwick Street
London EC1R 4RG

WWW.HEADOFZEUS.COM

For Matilde

PART I

Joe felt like hell. The last thing he remembered, he was in the back seat of a tricked-out white BMW, riding low to the ground, rims spinning, music thumping, with three Chinese gang kids from Flushing crossing the empty Verrazzano Bridge in the dead of night. Far above him, like the vault of a cathedral, the arches lifted a dark heaven. The cables were strung with stars. He woke up in the parking lot of a diner in the middle of nowhere, the summer sky bluely aglow now, the stars pale, the pink dawn just over the horizon.

"Good morning, sunshine." The driver, Cash, was grinning at him the rearview. The other two kids—who'd been introduced as Blackie, up front, and Feather, in back with Joe—both laughed. They all wore tank tops, black or red, baggy jeans, and Nikes. Gold chains and a lot of ink. Razored hair longer on top and tight up the sides. Except for Cash, who was completely buzzed. Joe was white and unshaven with unkempt hair, wearing a plain black T-shirt, old jeans, and black Converse high-tops. He was a dozen or more years older than them. Though today it felt more like a thousand.

3

He had a black eye that still smarted and freshly dried blood on his knuckles, some of it his own.

"Pit stop, boss," Feather said. "You want to get up and meet the dude? Or just keep snoring?"

"You're louder than the stereo," Blackie said. "If we didn't need your help, we'd have smothered you by now."

Joe ignored them, focused instead on the clicking in his neck as he yawned.

"We're going to eat while we're here," Cash said, cutting the engine. "You want something for breakfast?"

Joe nodded. "Four aspirin."

Feather laughed. "Glad you got an appetite at least. You want anything to drink with that?"

"Yeah," Joe said. "A bottle of Pepto-Bismol."

The guys laughed as Joe got out of the car, slowly unfolding his long frame, like he'd been badly packed for shipping. He stretched and looked around.

"Where are we anyway?" he asked, trailing behind them. Cash spoke over his shoulder.

"Somewhere in South Jersey," he said. "A long way from home." Home was Queens, New York. They were on their way to Cumberland County, New Jersey, to kill a man.

The three younger men—Cash, Feather, and Blackie—worked for a Chinese crime boss named Uncle Chen. Joe worked as a bouncer at a club that belonged to his childhood pal Gio Caprisi, who had grown up to run the business once headed by his father—a Mafia boss. Before becoming a bouncer, Joe had grown up to be a soldier, an elite black

4

ops "specialist"—his specialty was killing people—and he'd been very good at it, too, until a small opium problem he developed in Afghanistan led to a not-all-that-honorable exit from the military and the job working for Gio. It had been Gio's idea to make Joe the sheriff.

He wasn't a real sheriff, of course. But when a terrorist plot arose to unleash a virus lethal enough to wipe out a Yankee Stadium–size chunk of the population, Gio, Uncle Chen, and all the other New York bosses—the CEOs of the city's underworld—chafing under pressure from the government had decided to band together as patriots and New Yorkers and root out any terrorists lurking in their midst. They had not only recruited Joe for his unique skill set but had also invested him with unique authority to chase his quarry through all their territories with their cooperation and support. In the straight world, when you saw something you said something, supposedly, to the law. In the bent world, they called Joe.

Joe had done the job they gave him. The result was four dead terrorists and two dead criminals. But Uncle Chen's nephew Derek, a talented young car thief, had gotten killed along the way when he and Joe had crossed paths with some redneck gun nuts at an illegal weapons market. At first, Uncle Chen had blamed Joe. Then it became clear that the bullet that killed Derek was fired from a weapon found on one of the gun nuts, a white supremacist named Jonesy Grables. But due to the lack of witnesses and the general chaos that had reigned at the crime scene, his lawyer had gotten the charges reduced to involuntary manslaughter and bailed him out, at which point Jonesy promptly disappeared. Now one of Uncle Chen's sources had located him, and he'd sent his men down to tie up this loose end, with Joe very reluctantly along for the ride.

Meanwhile, with the terrorists eliminated, life back in New York had returned to normal for Gio, for the other bosses, for the law, and for the entire blissfully ignorant civilian population of the city. But not for Joe.

Not that he didn't try. He went home to his grandmother's apartment, where she'd raised him after his parents, both criminals, had died young. He went back to work at the club. But when Joe picked up a gun again, his nightmares, flashbacks, and panic attacks returned with it, along with the craving for booze and dope to control them. And once that evil genie was out of the bottle, she wasn't going back without trouble.

2

The trouble started as soon as he returned to work at the club. Being a bouncer takes strength, skill, and fast reflexes, but most of all it takes patience. Talking down drunks, extracting gropers, and defusing fights—all without scaring off the paying customers—has as much or more to do with a calm voice and easygoing demeanor as it does with fists. But now Joe was touchy, hungover at work from partying too late the night before or buzzed by the time the club opened from starting too early. He was quick to lose his temper with assholes or, even worse, to be a bit of an asshole himself, running his mouth and aggravating the situation instead of soothing it. That's how the beef with the gangster rap mogul happened. A week or so after Joe got back to work, the gangster's star moneymaker, a little white rapper, came into the club. Though really, it began even earlier that evening, at home, when Yelena unexpectedly showed up with Joe's money.

Yelena Noylaskya was an expert safecracker, cat burglar, ass kicker, and most likely, stone-cold killer, judging by the underworld tattoos that covered her body and that she had acquired back home in Russia. She and Joe had ended up together on the last job, working, fighting, and eventually sleeping side by side. The last time Joe saw Yelena, she'd been wounded. One of the terrorists' bullets had sliced her arm as she killed him to save Joe, while Joe raced straight toward a car, firing into the windshield. He was chasing his target—the terrorists' leader, Adrian Kaan—through the building and up to the roof, which was where Joe left him, with a single bullet through the forehead. Kaan's wife and partner, Heather, had escaped. And so had Yelena, disappearing with the bag of dough into the Russian parts of Brooklyn.

Joe didn't know Yelena's address. He wasn't even sure how she spelled her last name. But while it was hard to think of a law she hadn't broken at some point, she did live by a code, and ten days after that battle, Joe and his grandmother Gladys were settling down to watch *Jeopardy!* like she did five nights a week, when the doorbell rang.

"Who's that?" Gladys asked, checking her watch. Ten minutes to Alex.

"How do I know?" Joe was washing dishes in the long, narrow kitchen. "Probably one of your cronies."

With a sigh, Gladys lowered her recliner and went to the small foyer to peer through the peephole. "Looks more like one of yours," she called to him, and when Joe came out, Yelena was with her, looking sleek and healthy in expensive-looking dark-blue jeans and a peasant top that let the edges of her ink show. She'd chopped her bangs up a bit and looked well cared for, like she'd been getting enough sleep and water. Even the gauze wrapped around her bicep where the bullet

8

had cut through was fresh and white and somehow chic, like an armband.

"Hello Yelena." Joe smiled. "Have you met my grandmother, Gladys?"

"It's a pleasure," Yelena said in her light Russian accent, kissing Gladys on the cheek, "to meet the most important woman in Joe's life." She pulled a bottle of vodka and a tin of caviar from her bag and handed them to her. "These are for you."

"Ha! Thanks, hon," she said. "I'll get some ice."

"And this is for you, Joe." Yelena tossed him a fat envelope.

"Thanks," Joe said. "But actually this is for you, too," he told Gladys, handing her the envelope and taking the bottle. "I'll go get the ice." He walked toward the kitchen and Yelena followed.

"Get a Fresca, too, Joey, while you're in there," Gladys called and sat down to count the cash in the envelope.

Yelena spoke in low tones while Joe got out glasses and ice. "Most of the money was no good. Korean counterfeit. After expenses, it came up to fifteen thousand each, for you, me, and Juno."

Joe poured the vodka over the ice. "Za zdorovie," he said, and they clinked glasses and drank.

"So you are drinking still, Joe?" she asked.

Joe refilled their glasses. "I thought you wanted me to drink with you, like the Russian men you knew."

She shrugged. "Sure, but they are mostly all dead." She stroked his forearm, tracing a fat vein. "And this?" she asked.

"It's starting," Gladys yelled from the other room. "Where's that Fresca?"

9

Joe smiled, patting her hand. "You see? I already have a grandma." He grabbed the Fresca and another glass with ice and went back into the living room, while Yelena followed with the vodka.

"Just cover the ice, hon," Gladys instructed as Yelena poured. "I'll add the Fresca." The envelope was gone from sight. Gladys's eyes were glued to the screen, and the familiar theme song played.

"Come on, let's go in my room," Joe said, taking Yelena by the hand. "No talking allowed during *Jeopardy!*"

An hour later, lying naked beside each other with the A/C cranked high to dry their sweat, Joe checked his watch, then rolled up to a sitting position, feet on the floor.

"I have to get to work," he said.

"You have a job?" Yelena asked. "I will come with you."

Joe smiled. "Not that kind of job. But sure, come if you want."

They showered quickly and dressed. And then Joe took her to Club Rendezvous.

3

It was Yelena who got into the fight at the club—over Crystal, a half-black, half-Columbian stripper from Philly who was studying accounting during the day—but it was the little white rapper dude who started it. Joe was on duty, more or less, but he was alternating his usual black coffee with the occasional shot sent over by Yelena. Yelena was front and center, at one of the ringside VIP tables, tossing money onto the stage and buying lap dances and ordering rounds of drinks for the waitress and the bartender as well.

When a beautiful woman walks into a strip club, the staff's reaction is mixed. On the one hand, the dancers are intrigued, and if the woman is game, excited. It's fun to dance for someone you actually think is hot for a change, to rub against soft, sweet-scented skin instead of yet another stinky dude. At first the girls tend to flock around and play it up. It's fun for all concerned. On the other hand, the strippers aren't there to have fun. They're there to earn. To them, the hot female customer is like having birthday cake at work: everyone gathers in the conference room for a sugar fix, looking forward to a break from the routine, but that's not how anyone in the office actually pays the rent. For that you've got to get back to your desk and grind. Cake is cake, but a stripper's bread and butter is the horny but ultimately compliant, ordinary dude, the nerd or workingman who will sit all night buying dances, coughing up twenty after twenty for each three-minute song, then go home, broke and alone but with a smile. No hot girl is going to do that.

The other seemingly exciting customer who is more trouble than he's worth is the guy who thinks he's a player: the celebrity or athlete. He might wave a fat wad of cash around to show off, but since he expects women to fawn over him and is often himself being hosted by various big shots or fans—that is, *he* is the date—he tends either to be stingy, because he thinks he's doing the girl a favor by letting her rub her tits in his face, or get out of line, because he assumes the lucky girl can't wait to get it on with a star like him. He's also more likely to throw a tantrum and get mean about it when he gets rebuffed.

That's exactly what happened with Li'l Whitey. A pint-size white rapper from Long Island, who'd scored a hit recently with his song "Cookies and Cream," he rolled in to the club with his entourage, which included a pot dealer, a lesser-known rapper, an up-and-coming MMA fighter who called himself Flex, and his bodyguards, two walking sides of beef in tracksuits. After Crystal's turn on the stage, Li'l Whitey called her over and bought a lap dance. Now strip club protocol is well established: the customer sits still and lets the stripper work. She touches you, but you don't touch her unless she asks you to or places your hand on the spot of her choice herself. Whitey forgot—or didn't think the rules applied to him—and placed his hand in the spot Crystal liked least. She jumped up, and when he grabbed her and yanked her back, she slapped him one. Yelena, sitting nearby, saw this situation evolving, and when Whitey's hand went up to smack Crystal, she moved. In a flash, Whitey's hand was bent behind his back, wrist sprained, and shoulder on its way to being dislocated.

The bodyguards grabbed Yelena, who squirmed free, flipping one of them onto the table. Crystal screamed and hit the other one with a bottle. The pot dealer fled since he was holding, and the minor rapper tried to intervene but got accidentally elbowed in the nose by bodyguard number two as he turned to shove Crystal off. And then Joe went to work.

As a bouncer, Joe's job was to (1) protect the employees, (2) squash any trouble quickly without disturbing the customers, and, if necessary, (3) remove the troublemakers from the premises, all with a minimum of force. Pissed off at seeing Yelena and Crystal get hit and a few drinks over the line himself, Joe momentarily forgot that last clause about a minimum of force. Rushing into the center of the squabble, he slammed bodyguard one facedown into the ice bucket, kidney punched bodyguard two, and drove a fist into Whitey's solar plexus, knocking the wind out of him. By now, the bartender, a tall, handsome black guy who was studying acting but had played ball in college, had come over, along with the stocky young Mexican bar back, and with them wrestling one bodyguard and Yelena taking apart the other, Joe yanked Whitey up and steered him toward the exit door, which a waitress quickly opened. The whole bunch spilled outside. That's when Flex jumped in.

With a winning record and his first television appearance coming up, Flex considered himself to be a professional athlete not a street fighter. He wasn't interested in getting hurt or hurting anyone else for free. But getting into clubs and industry events as Whitey's best pal and having the famous rapper ringside at his matches was a professional matter, and when he saw his lucky charm getting rudely eighty-sixed from the club and tossed onto the sidewalk like trash ready for pickup, he stepped in. As a pro, he also understood right away that no one else there could handle Joe.

First, Flex swiftly took out the bartender, who was strong and fast but not a trained fighter, and had him on the ground, groaning. The bar back had guts and swung hard, but he was outmatched: Flex easily dodged his punch and knocked him dizzy with a forearm across the bridge of his nose. Then he went for Joe and took him low, lifting his legs from under him and flipping him, so he went over Flex's back. Caught off guard, Joe went right over headfirst, but as he came down, he tucked into a roll and grabbed Flex's ankle along the way, taking him down, too. Both men sprang up to face each other. Flex eyeballed Joe with the madman glare he used in the ring and pointed at the tattoos on his pectorals: YOLO on the right, FLEX on the left. "You know what this means, right?" he asked, popping them.

Joe thought about it. "You really like yogurt?"

Flex scowled. "That's froyo, motherfucker. This means I'm crazy as shit and don't give a fuck. You just made the worst mistake of your life."

Joe smiled. "I'm afraid this isn't even my worst of the day."

Enraged, Flex jumped him, and Joe began to parry his fists and feet. Yelena was fighting both bodyguards herself, kicking one in the nuts so hard he curled up into a ball but catching a fist from the other, right to her jaw. She staggered back, stumbling woozily, but came right back at him, grinning and licking blood from her lips. Then, before things really got out of hand, the authorities arrived, the authorities in this case being a large Range Rover filled with large black guys and a big, boxy Denali filled with big, boxy white guys.

In a world where no one calls the cops ever, people in crisis tend to call someone further up the chain of command. Whitey's pot dealer and sidekick, once he was safely outside, had called Ernest "Cold Daddy" Collins, who owned not only Li'l Whitey's record label but also the MMA fighters' gym where Flex trained and a show-biz management company. The manager of Club Rendezvous called Gio, who dispatched Nero and some guys before jumping in his own car and running over.

When Cold rolled up and saw Joe trading blows with Flex, who was bleeding profusely from his nose, and his boy Whitey on the floor groaning, he flew into a rage and, storming past his own muscle, grabbed Joe by the back of the neck. Joe, acting on instinct, swung around and punched Cold in the gut, folding him right in half. Both of Cold's men pulled guns and pointed them at Joe. Seeing this as they spilled from the Denali, Nero and his guys pulled their guns, too, and pointed them at Cold's guys. Yelena, looking up from the bodyguard she was pummeling, immediately drew the small revolver she had strapped to her ankle and pressed it to Whitey's head. He began whimpering, not a sound heard on any of his tracks.

"What the fuck is going on here?" Nero yelled. "Who are you?"

"Who am I?" Cold yelled back. "Who are you to ask me that, motherfucker?"

"Put the guns down and let's talk," Nero said.

"You put your fucking guns down and let's talk."

It was an impasse. Everyone looked at each other, and no one moved. Then Gio pulled up. He got out of his Audi and, unarmed, walked right into the center of the party.

"Nero. Joe." He nodded at the others. "Fellas. What are you guys up to? I know none of you is stupid enough to kill anybody at my club."

After Cold Daddy Collins left with his people, including Whitey and Flex, Nero took off, too, stationing one of his guys by the door as a substitute bouncer. The bartender and bar back recovered quickly with some ice for their wounds and some cash for their troubles and went back to work. Gio sat down in a back booth that always had a RESERVED sign, across from Joe and Yelena. Joe held a glass of ice against his swelling eye. Yelena pressed a cold beer to her bruised cheek and cut lip, between sips.

"Sorry Gio," Joe said. "It's my fault. I had an off night."

Gio shrugged. "You're lucky I was already on my way here to see you. But you know that Collins is going to come back at you. He pretty much has to. You smacked him in front of his people and made his tough-guy rapper cry."

"It was Yelena who did that actually. And he deserved it."

"Sorry, Gio," she said. "Next time I will take him out of the club."

"That's all right, kid. But maybe you've had enough fun for tonight? I need to talk to your playmate here."

Joe turned to her. "If you want, Eddie at the door there can call you a cab."

"It's okay." She kissed his cheek. "Crystal already offered me a ride home."

Joe smiled. "Tell her I said to take good care of you." She waved goodbye to Gio and went to where Crystal was waiting, changed into her street clothes, by the door. The two men watched them leave, arm in arm.

"Never mind the rest of those assholes," Gio observed. "That girl's the one who's going to get you into some serious trouble."

"She's gotten me out of some, too."

Gio sighed. "If you say so. Meantime, you better go wash up in the men's room and get your wits about you. Uncle Chen called. One of his gun suppliers got a location on that goddamn redneck who shot his nephew that he's been busting our balls about. He's holed up at some kind of white power sleepaway camp, way the fuck out in Jersey somewhere. He's sending his guys by now to pick you up."

"I don't know, Gio. I liked Derek. But revenge is not my thing."

"I know. I said you'd just go along to help ID the guy, in like an advisory capacity. He was their friend, so they pull the trigger. That will clear you with Chen. Then we can figure out what to do about your new enemies."

17

4

That's how, several hours later, Joe found himself, beaten up and hungover with three kids from Flushing in a diner parking lot in South Jersey, squinting at the rising sun. Blackie and Feather lit cigarettes, and Cash unwrapped a fresh piece of gum, offering one to Joe, who shook his head.

"You know," Cash said, regarding Joe thoughtfully from behind his mirrored shades, "Derek was my oldest friend. We grew up together. Started boosting together. He taught me to hotwire a ride. He was just about to get married."

"I know he was," Joe told him. "I'm sorry for your loss. I liked Derek."

"He liked you, too. Said you were a real pro. Old school."

Joe nodded. "He was a good kid."

"Then how come you didn't want to come along and settle things with his killer?" Cash asked, voice rising. He took his glasses off. "If he was your friend?"

Blackie and Feather stood still, waiting for Joe's reply. Joe's tone didn't change.

"I didn't say he was my friend. I said he was a good kid. We worked a job together. He got shot. That's how it goes.

He knew that as well as anybody." He looked Cash calmly in the eye. "I don't commit murder every time a good kid gets shot."

Blackie snorted at that. Feather shook his head.

"When do you commit it, Mr. Old School?" Cash asked him.

Joe shrugged. "When it's to my advantage."

Lip curled scornfully, Cash slid his shades back on. He blew a bubble, then turned his back on Joe to watch a truck pull into the lot. An oversized Ford Expedition rolled up beside them, its modified V8 rumbling. A sunburned white guy in a ball cap leaned out, peering at them carefully.

"You Chen's guys?" he asked, with a lot of Southern syrup in his voice.

Cash nodded. "Be a hell of a coincidence if we weren't, wouldn't it?"

"I suppose," he said, unsmiling, and climbed down. "I'm Clevon. Dermott sent me."

Dermott was one of Chen's suppliers. Headquartered in Florida, he had people acquiring guns all over the South where laws were loose and access was easy and then sending them north to Chen, for his own people or for resale on the black market. As a favor to his best client, Dermott had located Jonesy Grables, gone to ground at a survivalist training camp, and sent Clevon, one of his transporters, to point them in his direction. The camp was a way station for illegal weapons as well as meth and Oxy moving through the area. Now, while the others huddled with Clevon, Joe leaned back against the side of the truck, waiting. He found a broken pair of sunglasses in his pocket, bent them back into shape, and then slipped them on. Clevon had a map he'd printed off the internet.

"I wrote the GPS coordinates there," he was saying. "But I wanted to point out a couple things. See here, the camp is a couple miles out of town, up in these pine woods. The only way in is across this creek here. It's a wooden plank bridge just one vehicle wide. Then you take that road over the ridge there, and it leads you straight into camp."

"So when we get over the bridge," Cash said to the others, "I'll drop you two off to cut through the woods, then take the road in fast and distract them."

"That's how I figure it," Clevon agreed. "Any questions?"

"Sounds good," Blackie said.

"No problem," Feather said.

Cash shook his head and blew a bubble.

Joe sighed. "I have one," he said.

They all looked over.

"How do I get home from here after you all get yourselves killed?"

The three kids stared at him. Cash popped his bubble. Clevon frowned. "Sorry," he said. "But who are you? Some kind of mercenary?"

"No," Joe said. "I'm a bouncer."

"Bouncer?"

"In a strip club."

"Well, no offense but from the look of your face, I'd say you got your hands full just protecting the titties. Leave this to us." He spread his map back out and started to trace the road with a fingernail when Joe interrupted again.

20

"Look, these guys are survivalists, right? Gun freaks playing at war camp, sitting on a pile of guns and drugs?"

Clevon shrugged. "I suppose."

"Then there's no way those woods aren't booby-trapped. You'll blow your legs off getting through. If the bridge isn't wired, then they've got a man watching it or some kind of alarm rigged. You're walking right into a trap."

They all frowned at him now. Cash blew another bubble. "Good point," he said.

"You just gonna sit there and criticize?" Clevon asked. "Or you got a constructive suggestion?"

"I might," Joe said. "But we're going to need to borrow your truck."

"Like hell you are," he said. "This here is specially modified."

"I noticed," Joe said. "We're going to need whatever goodies you've got stashed in there, too."

"So I'm just supposed to trade this for your car?"

"No," Joe said. "We want the car, too."

"And then how do I get home?"

Joe shrugged. "Bus?"

"I don't know what your problem is, bouncer. But I think you'd better step down, unless you want that black eye to be part of a matching set."

Joe smiled. "Why don't you just call your boss?"

"And who should I say is asking?"

"Joe."

"Joe?" He laughed. "Joe who? The bouncer? You've got to be kidding."

Joe sighed. A little embarrassed, he lifted his shirt and showed him a star-shaped scar branded on his chest, on the left side over his ribs, under his heart. The other guys checked it discreetly as well. "Tell him this Joe."

Clevon shook his head. "If you say so. Y'all are too weird for me. But I'm gonna go make the call."

"Great. Thank you," Joe said. "We'll be inside." He turned to the others. "I think I'm going to need some eggs and coffee after all," he told them as they headed into the diner. "And then let's go talk to the local law."

"Law?" Blackie asked. "What the fuck is he talking about?" Feather shook his head.

"Why you so worried about us all of a sudden?" Cash asked. "Thought you were a conscientious objector here?"

"Yeah," Feather chimed in. "What do you care if some more good kids get shot?"

"Things changed. Now keeping you three alive is to my advantage." He smiled at Feather. "And I didn't say you were good kids."

5

Agent Donna Zamora walked across the bridge to New Jersey. When she got the tip about the location of one Jonesy Grables, the gun dealer and general dirtbag who jumped bail after being arrested in connection with the killing of Derek Chen, she contacted the US Marshal's office in Trenton and arranged this meeting. She had a personal interest in the matter. The shooting had occurred during an FBI/ATF operation in which she'd been involved, though she hadn't actually apprehended Mr. Grables. She'd been flat on her ass at the time, knocked down by a beanbag round fired by a masked man she came to believe was one Joseph Brody, aka Joe the Bouncer. It was their first date or maybe second if you counted her arresting him in a strip-club sweep as the first. Ordered by his accomplice to kill her, shooting her with the nonlethal load had been, all in all, a nice gesture—he'd even said sorry as he did it—and she'd found herself, to her annoyance, fascinated with Joe.

The marshal's service had put her in touch with a field agent, Deputy Marshal Blaze Logan, and they'd agreed to meet on the New Jersey side of the George Washington

Bridge. Donna lived in Washington Heights, had grown up in the shadow of the bridge, and had planned to hop in one of the two-dollar shuttles piloted by Spanish-speaking drivers that ran commuters back and forth all day. But when she woke up, it was such a clear and glorious day she decided to walk instead. It was early, still cool, and the rising sun was behind her, cresting the ridge of the skyline while she hiked toward the green-covered rock face of the Palisades. The Hudson dazzled beneath her. Less famous, less pretty, and less Gothically ornate than the Brooklyn Bridge, the GW still surprised her: that bare steel skeleton exposed, the soaring cables, that single leap over the river, 3,500 feet across and 604 breathtaking feet above the glittering, swirling depths. It was a beauty and it caught her off guard every time.

Deputy Logan was parked and waiting, her government-issued Impala in the line of cabs, the one woman, broad and blond, in a crowd of dark-complexioned men. She spotted Donna and nodded, leaning on her hood, the jacket of her pantsuit bulging slightly at the hip where she kept her gun. Donna had worn jeans and a sweatshirt, her hair up in a ponytail under a cap. She felt a bit underdressed, then laughed at herself for thinking of it like a date, then felt weird wondering if she had thought that because Logan was gay.

At least according to Andrew she was, and he would know. As an openly gay, married FBI agent, he considered himself an expert on all LBGTQIAPK law enforcement related matters (including updating her on what that constantly expanding acronym stood for). When she mentioned who she was liaising with on this case, he laughed.

"You mean lezzing with," he said. "Deputy Logan is the butchest marshal since Wyatt Earp's mustache turned gray."

"Andy!" She looked around the office to be sure no one had heard. "How come the only black, gay agent married to a Jew in the room is also the one saying the most offensive shit?"

He shrugged. "We're funnier."

"Which we? Blacks? Jews? Gays?"

"All three. That's why we dominate showbiz."

"But not the FBI, so watch it. These white people can't take a joke. Not even the liberals."

"Fine," he said, leaning in to whisper in her ear: "Let me know how the date goes."

"Agent Zamora?" Logan called now, standing as Donna approached. She held out her hand.

"Good morning," Donna said. "Thanks for meeting me like this." They shook.

"No problem," Logan said. "You need anything? Coffee? Bathroom break?"

"No. I'm good."

"All right then." She stepped around to the driver's side. "Hop in. It's a beautiful day for a manhunt."

6

Joe drove the truck up to the small municipal building, which housed the town hall as well as the police station. The fire station was next door. He parked, glanced back at the two rows of empty seats behind him, and locked the truck before heading in the door marked POLICE. There was a small, fluorescent-lit waiting area with plastic chairs soldered together in a row and, on the other side of a waist-high divider, a big blond man behind a desk. His blue uniform shirt and pants strained over his bulk and his hair was flattened down from sweat and the hat that sat on the other chair beside him. He was doing a jumble in pencil.

"Good morning," he said. "Can I help you?"

"I hope so," Joe said. "Is the chief around?"

"He's busy. I'm Deputy Cook. Why don't you tell me what this is about?"

"Happy to," Joe said. "You want me to yell it from here?"

The deputy pointed to the swinging door in the divider and reluctantly took his hat from the chair. Joe sat down and glanced at the jumble. "Saddens," he said.

"What?" Cook asked.

Joe pointed. "The word is 'saddens.' Not sad. You missed four points."

Cook frowned at it, then carefully erased his circle and corrected it. "So what can I do for you?" he asked, annoyed.

Joe put out his hand, and the deputy shook it reluctantly. "My name is John Mayoff. But people call me Jack."

"Okay, Jack."

"I'm here in pursuit of a fugitive from justice. A fellow by the name of Jonesy Grables who skipped out on bail. I have it on good authority that he is hiding out up in some hills nearby."

"That so?" Cook asked. "You a bounty hunter?"

"Yes, sir."

"Got some credentials?"

"Well deputy, that's the thing of it." Joe leaned in and smiled. "I'm kind of doing this unofficially. But I was hoping, if you could see your way to lending some unofficial assistance, I could give you, say, twenty-five percent of my finder's fee. That's a thousand bucks to you."

"You're getting four thousand?"

"Yes, sir. If I bring him back alive before his court date."

"Well, then I think if we're going to partner on this, unofficially, it should be fifty-fifty, don't you?"

"You're a tough man," Joe said, then he smiled. "But a fair one. It's a deal." He held his hand out again, and this time the deputy shook it with enthusiasm. He put on his hat.

"My car's out back."

"Actually," Joe said, standing, "we should really take my truck. It's built for that terrain. And once I get the fugitive

27

manacled in there, it's straight back with no stops. Better security."

"Suits me," Cook said. "I'll meet you out front. Just let me take a leak."

Joe and Deputy Cook drove out to the survivalist camp. They left the main road a few miles out of town and followed a winding single lane uphill through trees and weeds that topped the truck, driving in silence, the classic rock radio station playing low. They reached a deep creek, like a sharp fissure in the road, crossed by a rough bridge made of planks. Joe stopped.

"Easy now," Cook said. "She's wide enough, but there's no rails."

"Right." Joe hung his head out the window so he could keep his eye on the tires as they rolled slowly across the bridge, Cook watching out the right side, calling, "Good. Good. You got it." Joe saw the water below, swirling over sharp rocks. On the other side the trees were denser, and the road turned to dirt. Dust rose as they climbed the steep hill to the camp, which was set in a clearing, screened off by camo netting. There was a Quonset hut, a trailer up on cinder blocks, and a couple of plywood shacks, also painted camo green and brown, with propane tanks and a gas-powered generator. Pickups and cars were parked to one side and on the other was a homemade firing range and a human-shaped wooden target stuck with throwing knives.

"Follow my lead. They can be skittish," Cook said as they pulled in. Bearded men in fatigue pants and camo vests stepped out of the shelters, holding assault rifles. Two came forward, the others hanging behind.

"Right," Joe said, cutting the engine and killing the music, but leaving the keys in the ignition. He opened his door and climbed down as the deputy led the way.

"Good morning," Cook called out as he approached the men, Joe a step behind.

"Morning . . ." the men nodded and replied.

Cook continued: "This is Mayoff. A bounty hunter visiting from New York City." Cook pointed at a guy with a red goatee and a ball cap on along with his military gear. "That's Jonesy right there," Cook said as he drew his gun and pointed it at Joe. "And that," he added, nodding at another stocky blond with a dense beard, "is my cousin Randy."

Joe put his hands up. "I'm not here looking to interfere with you guys. But you do know that Mr. Grables is wanted to stand trial?"

Grables smiled, showing brown stubby teeth through his beard. "Good thing we ain't in Jew York, then, right?"

Cousin Randy nodded, staring Joe down, fingering his firearm. "This here is the Sovereign Territory of the United States of America."

"Sorry, Jack," Deputy Cook said. "Looks like you picked the wrong deputy."

"Don't be sorry," Joe said. "I picked just right." Then he ducked, shutting his eyes and covering his ears as he heard the first rocket scream by. The Quonset hut exploded. As everyone else ducked and scrambled, a volley of gunfire rattled against the propane tank beside the trailer, and that went, too, throwing up a rush of orange flame and dark smoke.

While Cook was still staring in wonder, Joe came up and grabbed his gun arm across the wrist with his right hand while his left seized the gun by the barrel and pushed it aside. Cook fired a shot into the dirt before Joe twisted the gun away, snapping his trigger finger. Cook grunted in pain and Joe, now wielding the gun, cracked him hard across the forehead with it. As Grables rushed him, he turned again, pointing the deputy's pistol at his forehead.

"Hold it," Joe said, and Grables froze. "Don't move," he told Randy, the cousin, who was still crouched down, hiding his head from the explosions. Joe got behind Grables, wrapping an arm around his neck, using him a shield, and pressed the gun to his temple. Still, Randy went for his weapon, gripping the assault rifle hanging from his shoulder and swinging it toward Joe, so Joe shot him through the heart.

Joe had talked the guys through his plan in the diner, using the map of the camp that Clevon had provided, then rehearsed them quickly in the lot, including a quick tutorial on firing the rocket-propelled grenade launcher that Clevon had stashed, along with a few AR-15s in the lockers that he had installed under the back two rows of seats. Then Feather and Blackie hopped in, taking a locker each. Joe shut the lids and lowered the seats, but left them unlocked, so they could hide with the weapons while he was with the deputy. They drove up to camp, Joe trying to keep the ride as smooth as he could, while Cash, the best driver among them, followed discreetly in his own car, also with an assault rifle. Joe told them when the engine cut off and the music stopped to count ten, then come out and start blowing shit up. Blackie had blasted the hut with an RPG while Feather fired on the tanks. Now they were both firing bursts of gunfire at the retreating survivalists while Joe hustled Grables to the truck.

"Get in," he ordered, stripping Grables of weapons and pushing him into the locker.

"Wait," Grables shouted. "This ain't legal. I got rights."

"I'll read them to you later," Joe said and cracked him across the jaw with the gun. He shut the locker, and this time he threw the bolts that secured it before lowering the cushioned seat. "Let's go!" he yelled.

Blackie got behind the wheel, Feather still firing at the survivalists from the passenger side, while Joe picked up the grenade launcher and reloaded it, sitting on the rear seat under which Grables was lying. "Seat belts," Joe called out as they began to move, while the survivalists scrambled to regroup and opened fire. Joe crouched low, aiming the grenade launcher out the open rear window. He fired, blowing up a pickup truck parked near the entrance to the camp to scare the survivalists back as they sped out.

They bounced and bucked down the steep dirt road, no longer worried about the comfort of the passenger in the locker, whom Joe could hear rolling and groaning beneath him. They were kicking up a lot of dust, but now Joe could see the survivalists in their trucks, a way back still, but gaining. There were two grenades left. Joe reloaded, then braced himself and waited.

They got to the wooden bridge and Blackie slowed. They could see Cash waiting on the paved road up the other bank.

He'd backed his car up for a quick retreat and was now stationed behind it, weapon poised, ready to give them cover.

"Okay, Blackie," Joe said. "Now take your time. Easy does it."

Blackie began driving the truck slowly over the bridge, careful to stay centered. The survivalists appeared over the hill behind them and Cash opened fire, holding them back. As the truck crossed, Joe aimed carefully, planning to blow the bridge after they cleared it. Then one of the survivalists popped up from the back of a pickup, aiming a shotgun over the roof, and blew out their rear left tire. The truck lurched sickeningly, and for a second Joe thought they were going into the creek. But Blackie floored it, wrestling the wheel as the powerful engine roared and getting the truck's front tires up onto the bank as the back end skidded sideways. The pickup started over the bridge behind them. Joe fired.

At that short range, firing just a few yards, the blast was tremendous. The bridge splintered, the front of the pickup was destroyed, and the truck dropped violently, ending up halfway up the bank with its rear end hanging over the collapsed bridge, now beginning to burn. Joe had ducked to the floor of the truck after firing, but he was rattled and had no idea where the launcher or the remaining grenade had gone. The back of the truck was crushed where it had hit the ground and broken the axle. Feather and Blackie, strapped into their seats at Joe's insistence, were shaken but fine. They began scrambling out of the truck's front windows and yelling for Joe.

Joe heard Grables banging softly but frantically under the seat. He lifted the seat cover and tried the lock. It was jammed. He rattled it, but the bolt had bent in the crash and wouldn't slide at all. Grables heard him and pounded louder. "Hey!" Joe heard a voice, muffled as through a pillow. "Hey!"

"Joe!" It was Feather. "Come on. This shit's going to go up any second."

He was right. Joe could see the flames rising as the bridge and the pickup both burned. Gunfire drilled through the back of the truck. It couldn't reach him through all the steel if he stayed low, but the bullets or the flames would reach the gas tank soon or find that loose grenade. Joe leaned back and kicked the jammed lock hard with the flat of his foot. Nothing. Again. It didn't budge.

Blackie and Feather were yelling. "Joe! What the fuck! Come on!"

The truck lurched again, as a burning plank gave way beneath it, and Joe saw flames rising in the back window. Automatic gunfire crackled and a howl came from the locker as Grables was hit, a bullet piercing the locker from that side.

"Sorry," Joe said, knowing he couldn't be heard. Then he went.

Joe climbed out of the truck's driver's side window, Blackie yanking him up while Feather and Cash both laid down covering fire, spraying the other bank. They scrambled up the slope to the BMW and Cash floored it, fishtailing as they raced away. They heard the blast.

The flames reached the grenade and it exploded, igniting the fumes in the gas tank almost immediately and sending up first an orange fireball and then a belch of black, gasoline-fueled smoke as parts of two trucks and, presumably, Grables, were scattered over the area. The bridge buckled, its remaining structure shattered in the blast, and the whole mess collapsed into the creek, hissing as it was extinguished.

As they careened down the narrow road, trees flashing beside them, Joe quickly removed the clip from the deputy's Glock and tossed it out the window. Then he racked the slide, ejecting the bullet in the chamber out the window, and removed that whole part of the assemblage from the frame. Inserting his apartment key into a small opening, he removed the backstop and took out the firing pin, disabling the pistol. He tossed all the parts out, one by one, as they drove.

"Guns out. Wipe them down and hand them to me."

"Are you sure?" Feather asked, beside him in the back seat. "What if they come after us?"

"Even if they cross the river, they'll be on foot. But if we get pulled over, we're fucked."

Feather nodded. He pulled out a bandanna and began wiping and dismantling his rifle while Blackie did the same to his gun up front and handed Cash's back to Joe. They tossed the pieces into the forest.

7

By the time Donna and Logan got to the police station, Donna was staring out the window in silence. At first she'd tried to make conversation, update Logan on the guy they were chasing, but Logan just cut her off with: "Yeah, I read the file." So Donna dropped it, and when her phone beeped with a message from the office, she used it as an excuse, first checking work emails, then, discreetly, Instagram. They parked in front of a small municipal building that had a courtroom and town hall up front and the police around the side.

"Here we go," Logan said, her first words in an hour. "Local PD."

"Right." Donna got out and let her take the lead. They followed the signs to an empty waiting room and waited, standing on the public side of a waist-high room divider. Donna could hear a voice murmuring from behind the far door.

"Hello?" she called out. "Anybody here?" She shrugged at Logan, opened the swinging door in the divider, and went through to the door in back. There was a hall with a number of doors off it. The voice was coming from an open one marked CHIEF. She stuck her head in. A large white man

35

with white hair and a big pustule-covered nose was talking into a radio.

"Excuse me, Chief?" He looked up. She held up her credentials. "Special Agent Donna Zamora. Sorry to barge in, but there was no one up front."

"There should be a deputy. Can't raise him on the radio either. Weird thing is his car's outside." He sighed. "Well, anyway, that's not your problem. What can I do you for?"

"Really just a courtesy stop. I'm with a US Marshal in pursuit of a federal fugitive." She told him the basics about Grables and the tip that he was at the camp.

"Well," the chief said, "I've been meaning to get up there myself. Maybe I'll tag along to observe." He went to a gun cabinet and took out his keys. "And bring my shotgun in case we see some quail."

He followed them out, locking doors behind him and hanging a BACK SOON sign on the door, then got into his patrol car. The two women got back in their Impala and pulled up behind him while he started his engine, still trying to raise his damned deputy on the radio. Then they heard the blast.

When Joe saw Donna, for a moment he felt like he was dreaming. After the explosion, Cash had raced down the hill from the camp, piloting the car expertly around the curves, then braking smoothly to a legal speed as they turned onto the main road and cruised back through town toward the highway. Joe was just starting to relax a little, to feel they were almost in the clear. He removed the damaged sunglasses from his pocket and unfolded them; an arm dropped off.

They were done for. A casualty of war. He could still hear it, that muffled thump coming from the jammed locker, Grables frantically, hopelessly fighting for his admittedly pretty worthless, mean, and stupid life. But still, a life. And life always fought against death. Even a rat, a bug, a germ. Not always though, Joe reminded himself. Some gave up or were defeated before their hearts ever stopped. Not Grables, his shitty little heart pounded like a fist till the end.

Then they heard the sirens, not coming after them but approaching from the center of town. A minute later, they saw the cop car. It was in the oncoming lane, lights flashing.

"Fuck," Blackie muttered up front.

"Easy," Joe said. "We're fine."

As the corner light turned red, the cop car rushed through.

"Don't worry," Cash said in an even tone, checking his rearview, chewing his gum slowly. "I got it." He stopped with the rest of the traffic to let the cop car pass. It was driven by an older white guy in a hat and uniform like the deputy's, with aviator sunglasses and a big, lumpy nose. Right behind him was a black Impala with government plates. And there, in the passenger seat, casually looking out her window and right into Joe's, was Donna. Her eyes widened as if she were seeing a ghost. She glanced back, doing a double take. Their gazes met and though he remained perfectly still, he realized that without meaning to he was smiling. Then in a couple of seconds, she was gone. A beat later, as if breaking the spell, the fire truck came, wailing, guys in rubber gear clinging to the sides and the red ambulance right behind. All four of the men in the car sat in tense silence as the convoy rushed past.

37

"Damn, that was close," Feather said, turning to look out the back. He patted Joe's arm. "Good thing we ditched the guns, dude."

"Yeah," Joe said. "Good thing."

When Donna saw Joe, for a moment she thought she was dreaming. The sudden sound of an explosion, booming like thunder from the hills outside town had thrown them into action. The chief had flipped on his siren and taken off, with Logan close on his tail, and the fire department joining a few minutes behind. The blast came from the direction of the camp, but what possible connection could there be between a routine follow-up on a report of a wanted fugitive and a sudden explosion in the same general area? Still, Donna did not believe in coincidences, and she had the feeling that another seemingly standard operation was about to slide into chaos. That's when, glancing out her window at the cars that had pulled over to let them pass, she saw him in the back seat of a white BMW, staring casually back out at her. Joe Brody. It was only a second or two, but their eyes clearly met, and he clearly recognized her. He looked like he'd seen a ghost. And then, just as they slid away, she thought she saw him smile.

"You really think this could have something to do with Grables?" Logan was asking, half to Donna, half to herself.

"Something is telling me it just might," Donna said.

The chief turned off the main road and led them up a steep hill, engines roaring as they climbed, and Logan was caught off guard when the chief screeched to a halt, pulling left, his rear end blocking the road. Logan went right, standing on the brake and kicking up a cloud as she stopped.

"What the fuck is—" Logan began, but then through the dust she saw why the chief had pulled up: they were perched over a creek, a deep narrow cut in the hill. The wrecks of what looked like two vehicles were dumped into the creek along with the smoldering remains of a bridge. And standing before them, heavily armed and looking both dangerous and confused, was a line of mostly bearded men in camo and military surplus gear.

Donna drew her weapon as she unbuckled her seat belt and was out the door in one fluid motion, while Logan did the same on her side.

"Hold it," they shouted, almost in unison, both taking two-handed stances while the chief sprang from his car, racking his rifle.

There was a second of hesitation, the survivalists looking back and forth like scared creatures choosing between fight and flight. Then on the far right, the one closest to Donna drew down, swinging his assault rifle toward them, and she fired, killing him instantly as her shot tore open his chest. In a flash, as though someone had dropped a match into a box of firecrackers, everyone was blazing away. Donna shot the next one in line, two through the belly, while Logan took down two more on her side, killing one outright as he fired and wounding the next as he turned away and her bullet passed through his side. The chief took out a large, heavyset guy in hunting clothes, knocking him right off his feet with the blast from the shotgun.

39

"Stop! Hold it!" A voice cried out from behind the rocks. "Chief, it's me!"

"Cease fire," the chief yelled, and Donna took cover behind the car, surveying the scene as the dust settled. Five men lay in the road, one still twitching and moaning. An arm waved a hat.

The chief shouted, "That you, Cook?"

"It's me!"

"How many still alive back there?"

"Three," the deputy called out. "Four if you count Ronny there."

"Okay. Drop your guns and come out with your hands up. All of you!" The men emerged, slowly. Donna and Logan trained their guns on them. "Now get down on the ground," the chief continued. He pointed his rifle at his deputy. "You too, Cook. Don't make me wish I'd shot you."

He lay down, and the three of them set about cuffing everyone, then checking the area before letting fire and ambulance come through. The state troopers arrived and provided backup and swept the rest of the camp, grabbing a few stragglers and locating a stash of drugs hidden down a dry well. After Donna called in, the FBI showed up in force to handle forensics and the ATF to look over the immense firepower stockpiled in the camp. Logan hung around, interviewing suspects and waiting to see if her fugitive was among the dead or not. Donna found her sitting in her car doing paperwork in the A/C and got in beside her.

"Well, the techs found the remains of a male in the wreckage whose one uncharred fingerprint matches Grables," Donna said. "Interesting part is cause of death. Looks like he was shot, probably by one of his own based on ballistics and trajectory. But that actually saved him from burning to death, which would have saved him from drowning."

"Not his lucky day, I guess," Logan said.

"Depends how you see it. He's dead, but it could have been worse."

Logan ruffled through her papers. "I've got a bunch of conflicting statements here, mostly saying that the camp was stormed by a well-armed team of anywhere from ten to twenty, quote, Asiatics, unquote. So make of that what you will. The kicker is Deputy Droopalong over there. He claims to have been hoodwinked by a bounty hunter named, get this, Jack Me Off." She grinned. "I ran it just for shits and giggles, but my keen deductive skills tell me that's a fake name."

"I'd concur," Donna said, thinking of Joe floating by in the car beside her. She wanted to both laugh and scream.

"It was a pleasure working with you, Agent Zamora," Logan said then, extending her hand. Donna shook it.

"Thanks, Marshal. I feel the same."

"I admit I checked you out, and when I heard you were the tip-line girl, I figured you'd be all talk and no guts."

Donna shrugged, thinking of what Andrew had told her. "No worries."

Logan smiled at her for the first time. "You probably heard I was a mean old bull dyke."

Donna blushed. "I wouldn't say that."

"You heard right. I am! But I was wrong about you. You know how to shoot and how to keep your mouth shut. Two of my favorite qualities in a woman. We should get a beer."

Donna laughed. "I'd love to. But I've got one more loose end to tie up back in the city. Some other time."

8

Joe woke up again in the same car but feeling even worse. Cash was shaking him.

"Hey, Joe. Get up. We're home."

"Home?" he mumbled. He wasn't sure what that meant. Sitting up, he saw that Feather and Blackie were gone.

"Back in Queens, man, safe and sound," Cash said. "I dropped the guys off, but I don't know where to take you."

Joe looked out the window. Flushing. Main Street surged with people, mostly Asian, though a tall black man in a dashiki was handing out fliers and a Mexican fruit vendor argued with an old Chinese woman or, to be accurate, he shrugged and smiled while she berated him. It was a world away from their last stop, and Joe wondered what the white power campers would think if they woke up here, in their version of hell.

"Joe?" Cash said, now facing him in the rearview mirror. "Can I ask you something?"

"Sure."

"Are you on something? Or off something?"

"A little of both maybe."

"I was wondering. Because you were thrashing around and moaning back there."

"Oh." Joe didn't remember his dreams, thankfully, but he knew what they contained. That was why he was on something. "Yeah, that. Sorry."

"Reason I was asking," Cash said, "it's none of my business but . . . there's this doctor I know around here. A friend of mine got strung out on dope, and she detoxed him with acupuncture and herbs and shit. I mean . . ." Cash looked away into traffic. "If you want."

Joe considered it. It was either that or back to his grandmother's and then what? Another fight at the club? More static with the rap guys? He felt exhausted, too tired to make a fist. His bones felt hollow, with that familiar ache that came with opiate withdrawal, and his joints were sore. His nerves twitched and creeped, sending little spasms and jerks through his limbs as he tried to sit still. That's why they call it kicking.

"Did it work?" he asked. "How's your friend doing now?"

"He's dead." Cash shrugged in the mirror. "But the detox worked great. Then he got high again a few months later and OD'd. His tolerance was too low."

Joe nodded. "Okay. We'll burn that bridge when we get to it. Let's go see the doc."

Donna found a parking spot on Roosevelt Avenue under the shadow of the elevated 7 train, which rattled back and forth overhead, carrying residents from the ever-richer, ever-whiter work world of Manhattan to the seething multi-ethnic cauldron of Queens, the most diverse spot on the planet, where millions lived, loved, ate, slept, played, fought, and died in what she'd heard were up to eight hundred different languages and dialects. Jackson Heights, the neighborhood through which she was walking now, had morphed in recent decades from Irish-Italian-Jewish-Dominican-Puerto Rican to Columbian to Indian. Now there was a Little Pakistan and a Little Bangladesh, Tibetan and Nepalese restaurants opening up, and a major Mexican influx. She was hungry just thinking about it and started deciding what kind of food to bring home to her daughter and her mom. Ecuadoran maybe? Suddenly she craved encebollado—fish stew with onion, tomato, and coriander. And some empanadas for Larissa. But first she had to pay the visit she'd come to make.

Her first call after returning to the city had been Club Rendezvous, the strip joint where Joe worked as a bouncer. She was told he was on a "leave of absence" for "personal reasons" and couldn't be reached. She decided to try his grandmother's next since, aside from the club, it was the only address Joe had on record anywhere.

She negotiated the steps and courtyard, busy with kids playing and a gossiping row of old biddies in folding chairs who she knew would be speculating about her as she passed. Gladys wasn't among them, so Donna stepped into the dim vestibule—the light bulb had died—and buzzed. A distorted if familiar voice squawked out.

"Hello? Who is it?"

"Hello Mrs. Brody. It's Donna Zamora."

"Who?"

"Special Agent Donna Zamora? We met before?"

"Who?"

Donna sighed. "The girl Fed."

There was a pause and then the door unlocked. The elevator was broken or anyway it didn't seem to come, so she walked the four flights and found Gladys peering from her door, which was on the chain. When she saw Donna, she smiled and opened up.

"Oh, it's you," she said. "Sorry, hon." She gave Donna a peck on the cheek and let her in. "You know how it is. Can't be too careful."

"You're right, Mrs. Brody," Donna said, though she wondered whether the intruders she feared were robbers or cops.

"Call me Gladys," she told her, sitting back in her chair next to the phone and across from the muted TV on which a soap was playing. She waved at the couch. "We're old friends now."

"Thanks, Gladys," Donna said, sitting. "I'm glad to hear that. I do like to think of us as friends." She looked around. "I was hoping that Joe might be here, too. Do you expect him soon?"

"Joe? No. He hasn't been around lately."

"Not at all?" Donna asked. She saw the half-full bottle of Russian vodka on the table along with a few empty glasses and the remains of what looked like a tin of caviar. A pair of men's slippers were on the carpet near her feet.

"Nope," Gladys said, looking her right in the eye and smiling. "Of course I do have other friends besides you who stop by." She was a good liar. No hesitation, no shame, no defensiveness. Her life as a grifter showed. That's why they called them con artists, after all: confidence. They won your

45

confidence with theirs. And for a real pro, that confidence—that conviction in her own lie—became so absolute that she in a sense believed it herself, adopted it as the truth. Challenging it, saying for instance: "Aren't those his T-shirts in that laundry basket over there?" would only invite greater defiance, even genuine outrage that you would have the nerve to doubt her, even when she was totally full of shit.

"I called the club," Donna said, switching tactics. "They said he took a leave of absence for personal reasons. I hope he's okay? That's why I came by."

"He's fine I'm sure."

"He didn't say where he was going?"

"Hon, he joined the army once without saying where he was going."

"He didn't even call? What if he's in trouble?"

"He never even called when he got arrested. He'd come by after to tell me he was out. Look"—she patted Donna's leg—"you've got to relax. Joe's like a cat. He comes and goes and if you try to put a collar on him, you get scratched. But if you let him alone, then he'll come home eventually, purring and sweet as can be."

"Or with a dead bird in his mouth."

"Ha!" Gladys laughed and reached for the vodka. "Now you get the idea. Do me a favor, hon? Get some ice and a Fresca from the fridge? And a glass for yourself, too." She picked up the remote. "My show is about to start."

The cute little Fed skipped the drink, as expected. Gladys would have been surprised—and impressed—if she'd just

46

fixed herself a vodka and Fresca and sat back to watch a soap. But she left, pressing another card in Gladys's hand and reiterating how important it was that she speak to Joe. Important to who? Not to Joe, that much was clear. Law of various types had been stopping by to ask about her grandson since he was ten. And before that his father. And her ex-husband. And her, too. Just like her parents before her. Most of the people she knew had the cops come calling sometime. But no one she knew had ever called them.

Being a professional criminal, of course, meant that by definition many of her activities were against the law. But she also belonged to a class of people who simply lived outside the law altogether, even though the majority never committed any crime. Not even the victim of a crime, in her world, would ever call the police: you called your friends or, if you could, you called on the local powers for help. It simply never occurred to you that the law would help. Many black men, for instance, felt that calling the cops might end with them in cuffs—or worse, full of bullets—no matter the situation. And they clocked a patrol car rolling by with the same wariness they would a known thug or a vicious dog—as something risky and unpredictable to avoid. Immigrants, legal or not, might worry that any involvement with the government at all, however innocuous, might land them in the clutches of the INS, endangering their visas or green cards. Some women, suffering harassment at work or on the streets or even abuse at home, had come to expect nothing—or less than nothing—from the authorities. And so on. If you had no insurance or steady health care, if you owned no property or portfolio, if you had no voice in

47

politics and didn't see your reality reflected in the media or on TV, if you realized, whether suddenly or as a given from birth, that the social safety net, the assurance of protection and support that society offered, was not spread to catch you, or was so full of holes that it was useless, then you might not feel obliged to hold up your end of the deal either. If you felt the law was not there for you, then you might not be all that inclined to obey it. The rules of the game become meaningless when you realize the game is rigged.

People like that were, in a sense, natural anarchists, whatever their political opinions or lifestyles. They made their own way, took their own chances, and suffered their own consequences. They were free. But if they fell, they fell—no one picked them up. If they got hurt, got sick, got old, got caught, if they ended up starving or cold or locked up, they were on their own—unless they had friends or family to turn to. So when Joe walked out the door, Gladys knew: he might come home with a bag of money to hand her, he might crawl home bleeding, he might call and ask her to grab that bag and send some of it somewhere for him, or he might never come back at all.

And that was why, no matter what, that Fed, Donna whoever, would never be more than an outsider in Gladys's world. They were outlaws, and she was the law. It was cats and dogs. The problem was, though, Gladys liked Donna. And Donna liked Joe, Gladys saw, maybe more than she even realized herself. And Gladys sensed instinctively that this could be just the woman Joe needed in his life. Someone real he could get real with. Someone who could make him happy. Anyway, she was better than that crazy Russian chick,

Yelena. Gladys could smell trouble on her from across the room like it was perfume. Even if she did bring vodka and caviar. And match Gladys drink for drink. And crack safes like an artist. And move like a cat, born and bred to outwit and outrun the dogs.

That was the funny part: Donna seemed like a great match for Joe, though the very thought was ridiculous, like mating a fish with a bird. And Yelena seemed like the last thing her grandson needed. But she was one of them, a natural member of the tribe. They belonged together, like always, against the law.

9

Goddamn you, Joe, Gio was thinking as he rode to the meeting with Alonzo and the rap mogul Cold Daddy Collins. He didn't mean it. Or rather he meant it in the way one might think such a thing about one's oldest and, he had to admit, closest friend. They'd been pals since Joe saved him from a couple of bullies in junior high—Gio had basically adopted him as a brother—and his family had arranged for Joe to win a scholarship to the exclusive Catholic school he attended. He'd been dismayed to see the condition that Joe was left in after his years in the Special Forces: strung out on drugs and PTSD'd as fuck. So he'd given him the bouncer job as a kind of retirement package, an easy gig that provided a steady income for him and his grandma Gladys, semiretired herself from life as a grifter. To have that suddenly blow up in Gio's face was a real pain in the ass. Gio Caprisi was a busy man, running a far-flung family empire, both the legitimate, top half of real estate, stocks, restaurants, trucking, paving, hauling, and construction companies, and the not-so-legit subterranean half of, thanks to him, highly organized crime, a man whom hundreds both feared and depended on, knowingly or not, as a kind of combination general and CEO. For him to be in a car with his guy Nero and a couple of other soldiers in the back, heading to meet Alonzo, who reigned over the black gangs of central Brooklyn, and quash some minor beef with a couple of nobodies over nothing, was not only a waste of precious time, it was an insult. That's why he was cursing Joe under his breath, while Nero stared straight ahead and drove, saying nothing.

On the other hand, there was no one else in Gio's life like Joe. He trusted him with his secrets, his money, his safety. He was, without doubt, the person he would call if he himself were in jeopardy. And if Gio had given him the bouncer job out of sympathy, he had also appealed to Joe's other talents out of respect: ten years at war had fucked his friend up in the head a little, but it had also hammered him into a lethal weapon, the sharp point of a spear. And when terrorists had infiltrated Gio's world and threatened his hometown, he had launched that spear. Now those terrorists were dead, their virus destroyed. That's why, despite the annoyance, despite the muttered curses and grumbles, he would drive across town to take care of Joe's problem, would look after him now and always. And Nero, keeping silent to avoid bugging his prickly boss, couldn't help grinning as they arrived for the meeting at a high-end chicken-and-waffles joint set up to cash in on the rapidly gentrifying scene in Crown Heights. It was Alonzo's place, though the paperwork was all in another name. The building, a converted warehouse, was owned, through another front of course—by another old pal—Menachem "Rebbe" Stone, who ran the Hasidic underworld. Alonzo and Gio were peers who had crossed paths repeatedly, clashed occasionally, and eventually formed an alliance on their way to the top. But Rebbe had been Gio's father's peer: he was already at the top when Gio got his driver's license and had remained enthroned ever since, leading his Orthodox army, who with their beards and suits and long coats looked more like an outlaw band than any of them, really: an old west gang that Gio thought of as the Black Hats.

But now the only hat in sight was a Nets cap on the head of the kitchen worker, who started over, annoyed and waving a clipboard, when Gio and his entourage pulled into the loading zone where produce was being delivered. Then he saw the faces in the car and stepped away deferentially, ignoring them as they got out. Barry, one of Alonzo's men, a huge dude in a tracksuit and a Kangol cap, nodded them through the kitchen door. Pete, one of Gio's guys, stayed behind, leaning back on the car's hood and lighting a smoke while the others went in. It looked like another warm summer day.

Inside, countertops and knives gleamed as workers in white bustled about, unloading supplies and chopping piles of vegetables for lunch while big pots simmered on the industrial stoves. In a corner, between the walk-in freezer and the pantry, one table was set off by itself, covered with an immaculate white cloth, and at it Alonzo sat alone, eating a big plate of chicken and waffles, sipping coffee, and reading the *Wall Street Journal*. He looked up and smiled.

"Gio!" He stood, removing the white napkin from his collar and revealing his three-piece navy-pinstripe suit, light-blue shirt, and electric-blue tie. Diamonds glittered on his rings and watch face and in his earlobes. Gio, too, was sharply dressed—they often talked fabrics and swapped tailors—but more sedately, in a linen summer suit, white shirt, and pale-blue tie. He wore no jewelry besides his wedding ring and his Rolex, a birthday gift from his wife and kids. They hugged.

"You hungry?" Alonzo asked as Gio and Nero sat down. Gio's other guy, Big Eddie, lingered by the door with Barry. Once they got done eyeballing each other, they'd spend the time happily, discussing protein shake recipes and workout routines. "Not to brag," Alonzo told them, "but the food here's like my grandma made, if she'd raised her own organic chickens and had a pure maple syrup connect from Vermont."

"It smells amazing," Gio said, which was true. "But I will just take a coffee for now and come back for dinner another night." It was ten in the morning, after all, and he had a lunch with some bankers in Midtown later.

"Alright then." Alonzo tossed his napkin on the table. "Let's settle this shit." He called to Barry: "Get Cold in here."

The bodyguard went to the door that led to the dining room and stuck his head through, while a young woman wearing kitchen whites and a scarf over her braids served the coffee, then returned to a nearby counter and began expertly chopping greens with a huge gleaming knife. Cold Daddy Collins entered, also in a suit but flashier than Alonzo and Gio, light green with wide lapels and a matching hat. He had a thug in a tight T-shirt and wraparound shades with him, incongruously holding a briefcase. For the past week, he and his friends had been making noise, and finally Collins had asked Alonzo to arrange a sit-down.

"Gio, this is my associate Cold Daddy Collins. Cold, this is my old friend Gio Caprisi."

"Nice to meet you," Gio said, half rising and shaking his hand.

"It's an honor, Mr. Caprisi," Cold replied, looking from Gio to Alonzo. Alonzo nodded and they sat. Cold cleared his throat.

"First of all, I want to say that if I'd known it was your place I never would have rolled up on it like that. And my boy, Li'l Whitey. He should never have disrespected the club."

Gio smiled. "He should know better than to put his hands on a woman like that anywhere. She's the one he disrespected."

"True. He shouldn't have grabbed that pussy. Look, I ain't gonna lie, his nickname around the office is Li'l Tighty, because he's such a puckered asshole, but that asshole shit out a million downloads last month, so . . ."

Gio glanced at Alonzo, who shrugged. Cold's music label was making a fortune off of Li'l Whitey, and Alonzo was raking it in, too, as his silent partner.

"I understand," Gio said, being reasonable. "Business is business. No reason to let a small misunderstanding get in the way. I suggest we just forget the whole thing. No hard feelings."

Alonzo smiled. "Thanks for being so understanding, Gio." He turned to Cold. "See, I told you. We're all businessmen here. No time for gangster nonsense. Let's just go forward as if this never happened."

54

"Excellent," Cold said. "Now, just one final thing." He held his hand out and his bodyguard pulled a folder from the briefcase and handed it to him. He opened it on the table, revealing a stack of legal documents. "I had my lawyers draw up these simple nondisclosure agreements. If you could just sign and get your people to do the same."

Gio stared at the papers for a long beat, while Alonzo and Nero stared at him carefully, bracing for his reaction. Then he burst into laughter. Relieved, Alonzo and Nero laughed, too. Furious, Cold jumped to his feet, pounding the table and spilling coffee all over the papers, which his sidekick tried to blot.

"You laughing at me? You know what it will do to sales if word gets out that Li'l Whitey got bitch slapped . . . by a bitch? That's my money you're fucking with right there. And your bouncer broke my fighter's arm! He had to cancel his next match." He pointed a thick, jewel-encrusted finger at Gio. "Way I see it, your people cost me a fortune. But I'm settling it like a gentleman on account of my boy Alonzo here. So I suggest you stop laughing, motherfucker."

Gio stopped laughing. His dark brown eyes seemed to go truly black as they focused on that thick finger. "Excuse me, miss," he called to the cook who was chopping greens nearby. "Can you come here for just one minute?"

The girl stopped, the staccato rhythm of her blade ceasing as she stepped over curiously.

"Alonzo," Gio said. "Do you like Japanese gangster movies as much as I do?"

Alonzo, who'd been holding his breath, was caught off guard. "Movies? Yeah, sure, Gio. They're pretty cool."

"They are, right? And you know how there's always that part where some yakuza disrespects one of his superiors? Remember what they make him do?"

Now Alonzo nodded, grimly. "Yeah, sure. They make him chop off a finger."

"That's right," Gio said. He nodded at the young cook. "Honey, let Mr. Cold here borrow your knife for a second."

Wide-eyed, she held it out. Cold looked back and forth from the knife to the stony faces around the table. None smiled or laughed now. Gio stared right at him and spoke in the same even tone. "Put your hand on the table."

"What the fuck?" Cold said. "I thought you said this was just business, man. Money."

"Don't worry. I'll let you keep the ring. I just want my finger."

Alonzo spoke up. "With all due respect, Gio, I do believe that in those movies it's a pinky they cut."

Gio's eyes were blank and soulless as a lizard's. "Then he should have pointed a pinky at me, shouldn't he?"

Alonzo leaned in and whispered to Gio. "Look, I'm going to ask you to let this go as a favor here, to me, and promise you, personally, that there will be no more trouble from him or any of his people. Or I will be cutting off some things my own self. And they won't be fingers. This kid doesn't know shit. If he did, he'd know that no one here needs to sign shit. Your handshake is enough." Alonzo held out a hand. After a beat, Gio shook it. Then he stood up.

"Thanks for the coffee," he said to Alonzo. Then to the cook: "And miss, whatever you're cooking, smells great."

"Thanks," she said softly. Then he walked out, trailed by Nero and Big Eddie. The door shut behind them.

Cold sat back, sighing. The girl silently returned to her chopping. Alonzo shook his head. "You dumbass mother-fucker. You lucky he didn't just chop your head off right here and drop it in my grits pot. I wouldn't blame him neither. Papers? Gangsters don't sign fucking papers. What kind of weak-ass limp-dick bougie shit is that?" Cold shrugged, gathering the wet papers and stuffing them back in the briefcase.

"That's what my lawyer told me," he huffed. "And like you said, we businessmen."

"Listen." Alonzo leaned in. "Let me make it clear to you. What we were saying before about us all being businessmen?"

Cold nodded.

"Well that was a bunch of bullshit. You a businessman in a gangster suit. That man there, in the business suit? That was a fucking gangster."

Gio and Nero and Big Eddie waited till they got outside and the door closed behind them, before they started laughing.

"Holy shit, G," Nero said, lighting a smoke. "For a second there you had me going, too. I thought you were really going to make that mutt chop his own finger off."

"I'm glad we ain't yakuza," Big Eddie said, regarding his own diamond pinkie ring. He could think of at least a hand's worth of screwups in his own career. Were there Japanese gangsters walking around missing five or six fingers? Did they use up one hand at a time or do both pinkies first?

57

Gio grinned. "I bet he shit that silk suit. Don't smoke in the car."

"No, I wasn't going to," Nero said, quickly, taking a long draw and stamping it out, although in point of fact, it was his car. Big Eddie opened the front passenger door and Gio got in. Eddie and Pete got in back. Nero drove. As he pulled into the road, a phone rang, and Pete answered.

"Yeah? Who's this? Hold on." He leaned forward to Gio, covering the phone. "It's Little Maria, Boss. For you."

Gio spoke over his shoulder. "Don't answer like that, Pete. Say: 'May I ask who's calling?' And then ask them to please hold for me, all right?"

"Sorry, Boss," Pete said, then spoke into the phone: "Please hold for Gio."

Gio sighed. "Thanks, Pete." He took the phone. "Good morning, Maria, how can I help you today?"

"Gio, mi papi chulo, we need to talk." She spoke in a lilting Dominican accent that somehow reminded him of his own grandmother. And like his nonna, Little Maria was very small and very tough. Her husband had controlled much of the heroin trade in Washington Heights and the Bronx. When he died she not only held on to his business, she expanded it.

"Sure Maria. What about?"

"Is about your friend Joe."

"Fuck!" Gio slammed the dashboard, and Nero glanced quickly in the rearview to see Eddie and Pete sitting still as statues. "What the hell did he do now?"

"Do? I don't understand. He didn't do nothing. Yet. But what he need to do, baby, you don't want me to say that on the phone."

58

10

Joe felt better. He'd been under Dr. Zhang's care for a week.

The whole thing could not be less like what the movies had led him to imagine: there were no statues of Buddha, no shave-headed monks chanting or sweeping up, no incense burning, just a crowded waiting room full of old Chinese people blabbing on cell phones, kids running around or playing on the floor, and a couple of harried young female receptionists in tight jeans, heels, and cute baby T's. His was the only white face. When he and Cash sat down, one of the girls came over with a clipboard of forms and asked him about insurance, but Cash had spoken harshly to her in Chinese and after that she left him alone. He was addressed only as Joe. He then called Gladys, his grandmother, and Cash drove to her place, where she handed him a thick envelope of hundreds drawn from the stash he had given her to hold, along with a shopping bag containing his toothbrush, clean T-shirts and underwear, and the book from his night table, a one-volume paperback of Beckett's novel trilogy. He was rereading *Molloy*. Cash handed it directly to Dr. Zhang.

That first day, she examined him, though not in a way any doctor had before: among other things, she inspected his tongue very closely and took his two pulses separately, tut-tutting to herself about how far out of balance he was. She asked him in embarrassing detail about his bathroom habits and his sleeping and eating and seemed deeply interested in a way no one had since he was a small child. Somehow he felt relaxed with her and answered frankly, detailing his drug use, his withdrawal symptoms, his nightmares. She was a small, sturdy woman with a round, open face and a bluntly cut black bob, dressed in a white lab coat, her penetrating gaze assessing him with sharp intelligence from behind round glasses. She spoke perfect clipped English with a soft accent and jokingly referred to herself as Shanghainese rather than Chinese—something that, as a New Yorker, he could understand. She wore a wedding ring and had pictures of herself skiing with children on her desk, but he would have guessed she was a mom anyway. She listened to him with a slight frown, scolded him for bad behavior, and handled him with gentle care, assuring him that his problem was well within her powers to solve, physically at least. Then she led him back through the waiting room, down a long hall with doors on both sides, and into a small exam room, where she had him strip to his underwear and lie down on a massage table. She got out her acupuncture needles and, when he flinched, gave him her mom look and said: "I know you're not afraid of needles." He laughed and lay still while she stuck him in the ears, the hands, between the toes, then hooked him up to electricity and sent a current through him. The weird feeling was unlike any he'd ever had, kind of like hitting your funny bone, but all over his body. "Relax," she told him, spreading a towel over him and dimming the light as she turned on a heat lamp. He wanted to tell her, "Are you nuts, how can I relax with electrified needles stuck all over me?" But she'd cowed him enough to keep him quiet, and a moment later, without even realizing it, he'd fallen asleep.

He slept like hadn't slept since childhood, deep and dreamless, and awoke refreshed and alert, unlike from the drugged stupors he doctored up for himself. An old lady he hadn't seen before, in Chinese pajama pants, house slippers, and an incongrous Hollister T-shirt, gave him a robe and, using hand gestures since she spoke no English, escorted him to a plain bedroom deeper in the building, more like a basic hotel room than a hospital. She came back with a bowl of white rice and a cup of weak sweet tea. He consumed it and went to sleep again.

The second day was more acupuncture and Dr. Z started the herbs, capsules that looked like vitamins and bags of homemade tea that she said would help him detox faster and with less suffering. She was right. It helped, but he still had the symptoms: the diarrhea, the chills and fevers, the runny nose and eyes. But the worst, always, was that horrible empty feeling in his bones, that puppet-like twitching in his joints as his body jerked compulsively, trying to find a position in which it was comfortable for more than a few seconds. He would describe it as a soul sickness, if in fact the soul were a material entity, a ghost that waxed and waned, a warm, vital substance that could turn to cold slime and clammy vapor in your marrow.

But as the days passed, under her care, he got better, sleeping through the night, waking without nightmares, eating full meals and drinking only water, juice, and herbal tea. After a week, he felt really good. Better than he had in a long time. And that scared him, for as every junkie knows, it is when you are feeling better that you are most in danger, most susceptible to the little voice, the demon in your ear, telling you that one won't hurt.

It was with this in mind that he went to the VA hospital. In the morning, Cash drove him over to the large facility on East Twenty-Third in Manhattan, and by the time he walked back out, six hours later, even a Mormon Olympic athlete would have been ready for a double shot of Jack with a Morphine chaser. First, he waited at the front desk, then followed the vague directions to various departments that sent him to other departments that sent him back to the first department, with long waits in between at the elevators, most of which were out of order. Finally he ended up back on the ground floor, in a large waiting room that was like a combination nursing home, emergency room, and psych ward, with a homeless shelter thrown in. A row of ancients sat moldering in wheelchairs, some hooked to IVs, some drooling, some staring into the distance. A bum slept across three seats, his ripe scent indicating a long tenure on the streets. A few guys mumbled to themselves as they paced or twitched.

Most people, however, were just sitting and reading or playing with their phones or spacing out with the tense yet hopeless gaze of those lost in transition, grounded in an airport or parked in the DMV, except that a larger proportion were coughing or sneezing or scratching or sweating or moaning, which definitely did not make Joe feel better. It might be wiser to just go home with his PTSD and blossoming drug habit than trade it in here for something even worse. But he stayed, sitting across from a Latina woman with one leg, holding her prosthetic foot under her arm like an umbrella on a sunny day. Hours passed. Joe tried to read, but somehow thinking about Molloy's broken figure dragging across a bleak and blasted landscape concentrated rather than relieved his present tension. Then the woman was called, and an obese white man with an oxygen tank and an unzipped fly took her place, hacking richly without covering his mouth. Finally, just as Joe was deciding that this in fact was going to trigger a PTSD episode itself, he was called into an office for intake.

Ten minutes later he was done: his sealed or excised and redacted records, combined with the fact that he was forbidden to name or even describe any of the highly classified traumatic events he had experienced, left him in a bureaucratic limbo: he could not get treatment because he could not prove that his condition existed, despite having all the symptoms. The social worker he saw was sympathetic. Genuinely distressed and stressed—with crumbs on her blouse from eating at her desk, files stacked to the ceiling and two pairs of glasses, one on her nose, one pushed up into her messy, gray hair—she had dedicated her life to serving those who served, so Joe just thanked her for trying and left. But as soon as he stepped outside he had something like a small panic attack, more from pent-up claustrophobia, frustration, and an almost toxic overdose of boredom than anything else.

He crossed the small island of greenery in front of the main entrance and sat down on the first bench he saw, shutting his eyes and trying to take deep breaths.

"I can't go on. I'll go on."

The voice was not Joe's and he felt reasonably sure it was not coming from inside his head. He opened his eyes. An old black man was sitting beside him. He wore a blue cotton work shirt, a checkered cap, tan carpenter's pants, and construction boots with paint splattered all over them. He had glasses on a string around his neck and held a cane.

"Sorry?" Joe asked.

"From here." He tapped the book in Joe's hand. "Though it's Godot I think of every time I walk through those doors." He stuck out his hand. "Frank Jones, USMC."

Joe shook it. "Joe Brody. Army. Nice to meet you." He was a big man in well-used work clothes, but his hand was smooth and graceful.

"Where'd you serve Joe?"

Joe shrugged. "I got around quite a bit."

Frank peered at him from under his cap. "Special Forces?"

"Apparently that's classified."

Frank nodded. "I hear you. I was sixteen when I went to Vietnam. Never even occurred to me anyplace could be worse than Harlem. When I came back I grew my hair out and stayed as high as I could for the next decade. My first wife didn't even know I'd served. She was a hippie chick, a Jewish girl from Long Island. It wouldn't have gone over too well, me being a baby killer. So I forgot it all even happened and joined the peace-and-love generation."

"Right," Joe said. "Smart."

"Except I didn't forget, did I? Not really. I mean, I put it out of my mind and time went by. But every so often I'd be sitting in a bar or at some rock show and I'd have one too many. Or ten too many. And I'd look around at all those normal fucking people laughing and talking and dancing and this voice in my head would say: *You've killed more people than anybody in here. You are the most lethal motherfucker in this place.*"

"So what did you do?"

"Drank more. Until that stopped working. Then I channeled it into my work."

"What do you do?"

"Paint mostly. You?"

"I'm on personal leave from my job as a strip-club bouncer."

Frank chuckled. "Sounds perfect. Nothing relieves the tension like knocking around a few drunken fools. I'd ask to hire on if it wasn't for this knee. Maybe after Uncle Sam gives me a new one." He leaned on his cane and slowly hoisted himself up with a sigh. Joe stood, too.

"None of my business," he asked, "but doesn't that knee make it hard to paint? Aren't you climbing ladders all day or on your knees?"

Frank laughed. "Nah. I'm not that kind of painter." He reached into his shirt pocket and took out a card. "Here. Come by the studio sometime and see." He pointed the cane at a black Lexus that had pulled up to the curb while they were talking. "I think your ride is here."

"Mine?" Joe was expecting Cash in his white Bimmer. Then Nero stepped out and nodded at Joe. He opened the rear door and waited. "I guess you're right," Joe said. "See you around, Frank."

Frank nodded. "Take it easy, Joe." He watched Joe cross the divide to where the black car idled, engine throbbing, the figure of another man dimly visible in the dark interior. He turned west and began walking, leaning on the cane.

"Hey, Joe," Nero said as he approached. "Cash said we could find you here." He pulled a paper parcel from his pocket. "He said to give you this and tell you Dr. Z says a cup with meals and before bed at night."

"Thanks, Nero." He took the packet and got in back, where Gio was waiting. Nero shut the door.

"You look good," Gio said. "Rested. Well fed."

"Yeah," he said. "I feel a lot better. Sorry again about all that."

Gio waved it off. "Forget it. It's handled." He smiled. "Or fingered . . . right Nero?" Nero laughed and nodded as he got in, shutting his door and putting on his belt. "But the question now is, how much better do you feel?" Gio asked, peering at him carefully. "Good enough to go back to work?"

"Tonight?" Joe shrugged. "Sure I guess. I've got to drink this tea, but I can get some hot water at the club."

"That's not the kind of work I had in mind." Gio said, as Nero piloted the car into the flow of traffic.

PART II

PART II

11

They drove to Long Island City, a onetime industrial waste-land, first transformed into an art colony and then recolo-nized by the new corporate towers that now populated the riverfront of this westernmost bit of Queens. They rode down a potholed road, to be repaved no doubt when the half-built skyscraper it led to was complete. It stood now exposed in its raw form, sheathed in glass from the waist down, the upper half a skeleton of steel. On the jagged top, a crane perched, like a gigantic beak or robotic claw. Standing in the barren construction site, it dominated the landscape like a fortress dropped here from space. The western sun lit the glass in a blaze of red and gold and orange. It glittered like a half-hatched dragon climbing from its shell. A guy in a yellow hard hat and orange vest opened the gate as they arrived, then chained it behind them. Gio's family owned the trucking and concrete companies working on the site and also controlled the union electricians and ironworkers and, through a shell corporation, held a sizable stake in the real estate on which it stood, which they'd bought up as pol-luted badlands. But work here had ceased for the day, and they drove quickly across the quiet site, past piled materials, stuffed dumpsters, sleeping cement mixers, and the trailer where a security guard sat reading the paper and minding his own business.

Nero drove through the open hole where the doors would go and entered the ground floor of the building, a raw, cavernous space with concrete floors and pylons rising to the rafters. Cables hung like vines, stacks of drywall sat on pallets and bright-yellow forklifts waited like abandoned toys. Big Eddie, incongruous in a spotless blue suit and brown dress shoes, like a tenant who had moved in too early, stood beside the freight elevator, a large cage in the central core of the structure, a tower of steel that would hold the elevators, bathrooms, garbage chutes and electronics rooms one day. Nero nosed the car into the elevator and stopped. Eddie pulled the door down from a strap and ran the elevator, which shuddered, hummed, and then began to rise.

Inside the car, Nero stared straight ahead, hands on the wheel as if he were driving. Gio and Joe stared out their windows at the passing empty floors. Without walls, each was a landscape or diorama, a dusty forest of pillars or cave of concrete stalactites, beyond which the glass walls framed a stunning view of the river and the Midtown Manhattan skyline. They didn't speak. The elevator rose beyond the last glassed-in floor and now they were floating through space it seemed, with light and air all around them, as though they were moving up the stages of a rocket on the launchpad or climbing a ladder to nothing. Gio's phone rang.

"Carol," he told Joe. Joe nodded, looking back out his window as Gio spoke into the phone. "Hi honey. You get my message?" He moved the phone away from his ear as a distorted voice blared out. "I know," he said. "I know, I'm sorry. Something came up at work. Just something. At work. An emergency. Well, tell them I had an emergency at work. Okay. I will call when I'm on my way. Yeah, just order it and I'll pick it up."

He turned off the phone. "Parent-teacher night," he told Joe. "Nora is doing poorly at trig and I'm supposed to discuss it with the teacher. I don't even know what the fuck trig is."

"Beats me," Joe said.

"Guess they didn't cover that at Harvard."

"I majored in literature and philosophy. Then they kicked me out, remember?"

Nero spoke up. "It's short for trigonometry, Boss."

"Thanks Nero, I knew that. I mean what the fuck is it?"

"It's the study of triangles, Boss. A branch of mathematics that deals with the sides of triangles and with the functions of angles. I got a B plus in it."

"Triangles? That's it? A whole course? So why isn't there like a class for square-ometry? Circle-ometry?"

"I think that's just regular geometry, Boss."

"Whatever. I'm talking to Joe here."

"Sorry, Boss."

"Point is," Gio continued, "there's going to be drama and Carol's pissed I'll miss it. I'm picking up Chinese food for after, though. That always cheers everyone up."

"Nice," Joe said as the elevator lurched to a stop. Eddie raised the door and Nero eased out slowly and joined a row of parked cars—Benzes, Caddies, Lexi—all expensive and new. The drivers stood together, smoking and talking. The rest of the floor was empty and unwalled, a huge platform with a constant wind blowing in off the river.

"Upstairs," Eddie said and gestured toward a metal flight of steps. Joe and Gio went up while Nero lit a smoke and went to join the others, who were already greeting him by name. The top floor was roofless and open on all four sides. Steel girders stuck up and the giant crane loomed over them, its arm hanging over the edge of the roof. Although the platform was solid and the edge of the building many yards away on all sides, the sudden exposure to light and wind, the feeling of openness all around, the limitless sky above and the nearly limitless city spread in every direction below all gave one a rush of vertigo, a desire to crouch lower, to touch the floor. Instead, Gio led Joe to a temporary prefab shed that had been installed as an office for the people supervising the job, a windowless, plastic-walled room up on cinder blocks with rough wooden steps and a couple of porta-potties sitting beside it like old-time outhouses. Gio opened the door and they went in.

Five people sat around a few folding tables that had been pushed together, the surface clear except for a couple of unused ashtrays and a case of unopened waters. The desks and shelves on the other side of the room were heaped with papers, files, and blueprints, suggesting this area had been hastily cleared. At the head of the table sat Little Maria in stretch jeans, a red blouse, red heels and lips and nails, gold hoop earrings, her eyes and hair shining black. Uncle Chen, the Chinese boss of Flushing sat beside Menachem "Rebbe" Stone, the Hasidic crime boss, both very old and dressed in black, though only Menachem was in a skullcap. Alonzo was there, in the same suit as this morning, looking just as fresh.

Pat White, the last of the Irish Westies who once ruled Hell's Kitchen but were still deep into politics, loan-sharking, and gambling as well as contract hits, was dressed like a retiree in a Knicks cap, a short-sleeved plaid shirt, and gold pants. Anton, the Russian from Brighton Beach, was in a black shirt unbuttoned halfway down to reveal gold chains and tattoos. He was the only one smoking—Russian cigarettes with cardboard filters that surrounded him with acrid fumes.

"Hello everybody and thanks for making the trip," Gio said. "Sorry about the climb." The group chuckled. "I needed to find a safe place on short notice, and unless anybody spotted a helicopter, I don't think we need to worry about being heard or seen together here." Gio and Joe sat down side by side at the end of the table. "Maria asked for this meeting, so I'm going to let her explain things."

"Thank you, Gio. Thank you all. And thank you, Joe, for coming. I know you just get back from vacation. I hope you had a nice time." Joe nodded and smiled. "Then I will get right to it. A couple weeks ago I got an offer. Forty kilos of *puro*, Persian White coming in from Afghanistan. But I never heard of this seller, so I make some calls. Turns out, one of my regular connections got hit and now they trying to sell the dope. So I say no, I won't touch it. But *anda el Diablo*, this little bitch who works for me, name Carlo, he goes behind my back and sets it up. Wants to be his own boss now, the *matatan*."

Uncle Chen shrugged. "We all have traitors to deal with sometimes, Maria. But this sounds like a private problem."

Maria smiled big. "Don't misunderstand. I will be very happy to chop this *mama guevo* into pieces with my machete

73

and feed him to my dog. But Carlo, when like you say, I have a private talk with him last night, he tell me the Persian is already here in New York. So somebody is going to buy it. I can't chop up everyone."

Chuckles ripped around the table. Gio spoke: "But what's this got to do with Joe? When we gave him authority to operate across all our territories, we made it clear. He doesn't do hits. Or turf wars. Or take out rival drug gangs. This isn't his kind of thing."

"This is a horse of a different color, Gio." It was Pat. "I passed Maria's info along to my pals in the military. There's no question. They belong to an Al-Qaeda splinter group whose MO is to raid the opium pipelines then use the money to fund terrorism. They blew up a US base in Africa last year. Six months ago they took out a UN convoy. Three months ago they blew up a marketplace in Syria and killed a dozen civilians. Now it looks like they're here."

"Let's all put the word out to our people to find who's moving the shipment," Alonzo said. "Then just take their shit. Junkies drool for that Persian dope. And I guarantee not a penny to fucking Al-Qaeda."

Anton cleared his throat, coughing loudly, and blew smoke across the room. Gio's nose twitched. Who would smoke in a room with no windows? "We set the deal up," he said. "Have this Carlo call. Then like Alonzo says, we take their dope and bury them on Staten Island."

"He's got a point," Gio admitted. "Don't tell me no one else here can jack a drug dealer besides Joe. And it's still not his kind of thing."

74

Now Menachem raised his hand, and the chatter and chuckling ceased. "There's more. They are insisting on a special form of payment. They want diamonds."

"Diamonds?" Alonzo asked. "These are some flash terrorists. Thought they were generally into dressing plain."

Maria shook her head. "They can't deal the way we usually do. Who would trust them? And who can they trust? Nobody." Maria's business, like most enterprises based on trade, generally came down to relationships. Her connections were men she'd known for decades. A shipment was arranged, and when Maria got word it had landed safely, she transferred funds from her numbered overseas account to someone else's. She never touched the money or the drugs. Everything ran on trust and friendship, and the special bond between those who, everyone knew, would kill whoever betrayed that trust and friendship. Unlike plenty of straight business people, heavy drug dealers, at least the live ones, mostly kept their word among themselves. But these people were outsiders. No one would take their word for anything, nor could they count on anybody's goodwill. They were pariahs, even among the outlaws.

"They need something that can't be traced," Menachem said. "And they need it liquid. But this much cash isn't practical. How do they get it out of the country? Check it in their luggage? Four million in diamonds you put in your pocket. And you sell them wherever, Antwerp, Tokyo, Tel Aviv. Or New York. You want a safe, durable, portable asset? Diamonds are the hardest stuff on earth."

"What about fugazis?" Gio asked. "Get some glass."

"They're not fools," Maria said. "Carlo said they will have an expert to check."

Alonzo whistled. "Four mil? Sorry folks. Not even the flyest gangsters got that much ice on hand."

"Who does?" Menachem shrugged. "Only the dealers. And I don't think they will be interested in donating to the cause."

Finally, Joe, who'd been sitting back, his chair pushed away from the table, just listening, spoke up: "So what you need then, is for somebody to steal these diamonds, then trade them for the dope, then steal the diamonds back again before they can get them out of the country."

"You understand, amigo." Maria nodded at Joe.

"Three separate moves," Alonzo said.

Anton put his smoke out on the floor, though the ashtray was right there. "And if any of them go sour, those bastards win."

Menachem nodded. "It's tricky. But it's the only way."

"And we have only one friend tricky enough do it," Uncle Chen said. He winked at Joe.

Gio shrugged and turned to Joe. "Sorry, but I got to admit. This is starting to sound like your kind of thing after all."

12

By the time the meeting broke up, Joe had begun sorting out his crew and making plans. Maria would extract all the information Joe needed to impersonate Carlo online and make the connection; his only contact with the seller was email. "And that's our only lead," he reminded her. "So I hope he's still breathing enough to talk."

"Don't you worry," she said and smiled, showing her teeth against the red lips, the wolf inside the grandma. "I always cut the tongue off last."

Rebbe and Pat would provide information, too, and muscle, committing a man each to Joe's team. Joe told Alonzo he'd be wanting Juno, since he lived in his domain and Alonzo knew the family. "And I'm sorry you had to clean up that other mess about the fight at the club," he added.

Alonzo slapped him on the back. "Don't fret. Your man Gio came and scared the dude so bad that now he thinks he owes me his life, and we own even more of his company. Everybody's friends again."

Joe smiled. "You're welcome, then."

They shook hands. "Just holler if you need any concert tickets," Alonzo told him.

Joe wanted Cash, too, as a driver, and Uncle Chen was glad to volunteer him. He was pleased with the way the trip to Jersey had turned out and had heard good reports about Joe from Dr. Z. She treated Uncle Chen himself for sciatica and back pain among other things, and he channeled money to her clinic through the Triad's public face, as a community association, to pay for elders in need or FOBs, newcomers fresh off the boat from China.

He also wanted Yelena. That didn't go over as smoothly.

"That Russian who tore up my joint?" Gio asked him, frowning at the memory.

Joe said, "She's the best sneak thief I know. And that's what this job needs."

Gio turned to Anton. "You know this girl?"

"Yelena the cat?" Anton shrugged. "She is not with us, but she is friends with our friends back in Russia. I hear she is very good to work with. And very bad to work against."

"What Gio means, I think," Rebbe put in, "with everyone else involved, one of us here can vouch for them. So this Russian girl. Can she be trusted?"

"I've trusted her with my life already, and I'm still here," Joe said. "With your money?" He shrugged. "We'll find out."

Rebbe nodded. "That's good enough for us, right?" The others nodded, with varying degrees of enthusiasm. "And speaking of money," he added, "we are not asking you to do this for free. We're not the government." Everyone laughed.

"Or socialists," Anton added. As always, Gio felt he was milking the joke a bit, but he forced a chuckle.

"What you steal you keep," Gio told him. "That's only fair. Split it up with your crew."

"And if the dope is what they say," Maria added, "I will buy it from you at market rates. Four million."

"Is that COD?" Joe asked her.

"Of course," she purred, returning his smile.

He turned toward the group, who were watching him intently.

"Looks like my vacation is over."

In the car, as Nero steered them back onto the elevator, Gio chuckled and shook his head. "I have to hand it to Maria," he told Joe. "She knows how to play an angle. She gets the dope, crushes her competition, and instead of pissing off her overseas suppliers, she can say she helped wipe out the people who robbed them."

Joe nodded. "And we're playing right along."

Gio shrugged. "The heroin trade doesn't affect me. I steer clear of the hard stuff when I can." He frowned at Joe. "You might try that, too, for a change."

"That was my plan," Joe said. "Until you volunteered me to steal forty kilos of pure dope."

Gio laughed. "Yeah, you're right. Sorry about that."

Joe smiled. "That's how it goes. Just because you decide to keep away from the hard stuff, doesn't mean it will keep away from you."

The car pulled out of the elevator. Nero addressed them in the rearview.

"Where to, Boss?"

"Want me to drop you somewhere?" Gio asked Joe.

"Just at the corner," he said. "I want to walk and think."

"What's your first move?"

Joe picked up the paper bag from Dr. Z that he'd left on the seat. "First I'm going home to watch *Jeopardy!* with Gladys and drink this tea. Then tomorrow I start shopping for diamonds."

13

"Heavy" Harry Harrigan had spent his life in Hell's Kitchen. He was born in Roosevelt Hospital and grew up living in the tenement walk-ups in the West Fifties. His mother worked sewing and steaming in the Garment District and his father had been a union set builder on Broadway shows, theoretically, when he wasn't drinking or gambling. He never cared much for classrooms. He lived and learned on the streets: from the bums begging in Port Authority, the dancers rehearsing in studios, the actors drinking with gangsters in bars, the limos outside the fancy restaurants, and from the hookers, dealers, and peep shows lining the old Forty-Second Street.

It was as a teenager that he fell in with Pat White, a rising star in the underworld and one of the most dangerous guys in Hell's Kitchen, notorious for his work as a ruthless and reliable hit man. In the late eighties, Harry joined Pat's crew for a string of bank robberies that made their name and fortune. Pat expanded into extortion, gambling, loan sharking, running a protection racket for the local joints, brothels, clubs, and dives, and acting as an enforcer over the unions and businesses in the garment business, theater, and construction. But as Pat's star rose, Harry's didn't exactly rise with him. A couple of unlucky moves got him time Upstate in the pen and huge legal debts. Back and knee problems, which led to serious weight gains, ended his days of leaping over bank counters and running from cops. He was no longer young and mean enough to be muscle and he'd never been smart enough to handle the high-level shit, like political influence peddling, contract fixing, and so forth that Pat spent his time on now that he was a boss.

And so Harry was reduced to running a small sports book, struggling to keep up with his alimonies, child support, and legal bills, and sitting on one of his few remaining treasures: the rent-controlled apartment his mother had lived in. The fifth-floor walk-up was hell on his knees, but the next step down for him was the gutter. Or prison, if he didn't keep on the right side of his new bosses: the Feds, who had finally caught up with him for good when his last lame attempt at a one-man bank heist in New Rochelle went sour. The cabbie he'd hired to drive him there and back turned out to be an undercover cop. Like a true Manhattanite, Harry had never learned to drive. So there he was—same apartment, same neighborhood, same guys—except now he wore a wire taped to his chest along with his gold cross. Harry was back where he started, if he ever really left.

Tonight however, he was in a good mood. Tonight Harry was getting paid. One of his regular clients, having lost a bundle on the games, had tipped Harry off to a truckload of high-end electronics gear being brought in for some fancy condos going up in the neighborhood—the gizmos that ran smoke sensors, elevators, and, in the sweetest irony of all, building surveillance and alarms. Harry told Pat, who sent some young guys, those Irish punk "nephews" he'd brought over, the Madigan brothers, to hijack it. The swag was sold off, the local cops and the Italian crew that controlled the trucking and construction union—Gio Caprisi's people—were duly paid their cuts, and now, tonight, they were splitting the take. Harry expected upward of fifty grand. So when he got dressed and ready to head out at 2:00 a.m. on a weeknight—the streets quiet but still humming with garbage trucks rumbling by and taxis hunting for drunks—he put on a clean shirt and a sharp jacket, but he left his wire at home. No reason to let the fucking feebs know about this. Bastards would probably want a cut, too.

His good mood took a hit, however, when he showed up at the back door of Old Shenanigan's House to find Liam, the youngest and to Harry most irritating of the Madigan brothers, waiting in the alley. Thin and pale, with long hair and light eyes, he was just the kind of little twerp Harry would have sneered at and bullied in school back when he was swaggering around the neighborhood.

"Good evening, Harry," Liam said in that Lucky Charms lilt that everyone found so fucking delightful. "Or should I say good morning?"

"Liam," Harry managed a nod and started to move past him to the basement stairs, where he could see lights aglow. The metal doors were propped open, and a roller conveyer lay propped on the narrow, steep steps that led down into the kitchen. His knees hurt just looking at them.

"Sorry, Harry," Liam said, putting a hand out, like a damn traffic cop. "I have to frisk you."

Anger flared in Harry's eyes. "You? Frisk me? Do you know who I am?"

Liam's mild grin didn't budge. "I should, Harry. You remind me often enough."

"I was robbing banks with Pat thirty years ago when you were sucking on your mother's tit."

"I'm twenty-five, Harry," Liam noted. "That must be me brother you're thinking of."

"This is bullshit," Harry muttered, though inside he was flush with relief that he hadn't worn the wire tonight.

"Since you know Pat so well," Liam was saying, "I'm sure he won't mind you telling him his orders are bullshit when you get down there. Or you can just go home, and we will mail your cut."

With a dramatic sigh, Harry put his arms up and Liam patted him down, chest, back, under the arms, up and down the legs, even a quick swipe between them. Then he stepped back.

"Anything else?" Harry asked as he crossed the alley. He was just angling his big body to take the first awkward step down into the basement when the kid called out.

"Oh, Harry, wait, I just remembered. There is one more thing."

"What the fuck?" he muttered, turning back to see Liam pointing a gun down at him, an automatic with a silencer. His eyes went wide.

"Pat said to give you this, too," Liam said, still smiling, and fired.

* * *

84

Liam used a Walther P22 with a Finnish SAK suppressor to muffle the shots. He emptied the magazine directly into the chest, and when Harry dropped to his knees and slumped over the top step, Liam could see clearly that he was dead. He used his foot to push the big body back and called out "delivery," as Harry's corpse rattled down the conveyer and landed with a thump. Then he went down the steps, quickly and lightly on his young legs, and pulled the doors shut behind him.

In the kitchen basement, Sean, Liam's middle brother—Jack was the oldest—stood over Harry, who was now sprawled like a shipment of potato sacks on the plastic tarp they'd spread out below. Sam was dressed in the same kind of disposable work coveralls, booties, and hairnet that real cleaning crews would wear when they came to disinfect this place or pump out the oil they'd use to fry all those potatoes.

"Come on, let's get started," Liam said as he pulled on a matching outfit. "The kitchen workers get here by six. I'll call Jack and tell him to meet us up at the farm."

"Will they really use him for fertilizer, Liam?" Sam asked, removing Harry's watch and rings, going through his pockets, and then dumping the items in a plastic baggie to be disposed of later. He yanked off the gold cross.

"Why not?" Liam zipped up his coveralls. "He's organic. Anyway, what's fertilizer but shite in a bag?" Liam slipped his booties on and pulled down the cap. "Here's one extralarge bag of pure shite on the way."

Sam picked up the meat cleavers and handed one to Liam. "More like four bags, I reckon," he said as he got to work.

14

Joe had lunch with Rebbe. They met at Ben's Kosher Deli on Thirty-Eighth. Joe got hot pastrami on rye and a Dr. Brown's Cream Soda and Rebbe got tongue, which they cured on the premises, and a Cel-Ray to drink. They split a knish. Afterward, Rebbe ordered coffee and pulled a face as Joe ordered hot water and dunked the custom-made herbal tea bag from Dr. Z.

"What's that? Some *fakakte* health fad?"

"Kind of," Joe admitted. Then he nodded at the nondairy creamer Rebbe was stirring into his coffee. "Look who's talking. You take your coffee gray?"

Rebbe chuckled. "It's true. God does not make it easy for those who follow him." Joe could think of some jihadists who'd agree but said nothing. He sipped his tea, Rebbe sipped his coffee, they both made unhappy faces, and then Rebbe taught him about the diamond trade.

The United States is the world's largest market for diamonds, and over 90 percent of the diamonds that enter the country come through New York. The vast majority of those pass through the Diamond District on Forty-Seventh Street between Fifth Avenue and the Avenue of the Americas. Over twenty-six hundred separate businesses populate that block, nearly all related to diamonds, gems, or fine jewelry. In the windows and the counters, in the tiny booths that crowd the indoor retail markets, in the warrens of offices filling floor upon floor of the buildings, housing wholesalers and craftsmen, importers and traders, stones gleam and glow, jewelry glitters, and money flows like a buzzing hive honeycombed with riches. That one narrow street runs between hulking stone buildings like a canyon, and that canyon is a mine, more packed with diamonds that any prospector could hope for. It was the dragon's lair. Ali Baba's cave. A dream for any thief.

It was also a thief's nightmare. There were armed guards patrolling everywhere. There were cops always hanging around. There were alarms and cameras, safes and locks, deeper and deeper holds inside the fortress. Plus many of the diamond merchants were armed. A large proportion of the Hasidim shuffling by in black coats or the suave dealers in sharp suits with glittering goods on their hands and throats or even the hunched, schlumpy artisans with magnifying glasses screwed into their eye sockets had concealed carry permits—and that was just the legal guns. Who knew how many Uzis slept in desk drawers or behind counters?

Even with a safecracker as good as Yelena and someone like Joe to get her and her tools in there and out again—and enough time to work unnoticed by cameras and watching eyes, without a suspicious getaway car parked on the block or a drilling noise or a flashlight in a dark hall—they would still need to know who had that kind of stash on hand before they went in.

Joe had spent the morning wandering the district with a hoodie and a messenger bag over his usual jeans and Converse high-tops, invisible as only a messenger in Manhattan can be, sipping a deli coffee, pretending to talk on his phone, drifting with the crowds of shoppers—and he had come to a conclusion: it couldn't be done without inside knowledge, and even then there was only one somewhat plausible way. Fortunately, Rebbe had access to that knowledge and had come to the same conclusion: "You have to take them on the move, boychik. It's the only smart way."

"Exactly," Joe said. "Even if I figured a way to muscle in and get back out alive, you could never be sure of smashing and grabbing enough. It's not like we can go back for seconds."

"And to sneak in?"

"I'd have to know who had enough in their vault that night and then get plans, alarms, and so forth. It's possible but again very risky, especially getting out. With a bank job, let's say, you can try to go in the roof or from next door. But here, next door is another bank. That whole block is like a wall of safe-deposit boxes." He finished his tea with a grimace. "The only smart play is to hit them when they're moving. That's always the weakest point in the chain. But of course they know that, too."

"That's why a smart dealer moves a little at a time, puts it in his pocket and takes a cab, along with a hundred other schmoes in black suits. Except"—Rebbe sipped his coffee thoughtfully—"sometimes they need to move a lot for a show, let's say, or to ship merchandise from one branch to another. But of course, they keep this very secret. No one knows who or when."

Joe smiled. "Except you."

Joe talked to Juno next. Juno was a tech wizard. A kid from the block like Joe had been, he also moved effortlessly through realms that to Joe were as remote as Neptune, and his expertise had been invaluable on their last joint caper. He visited him in his mom's basement, which he was slowly trying to convert into a studio but remained mostly his teenage bedroom and nerd headquarters for now. The first time Joe had been in this house, he and Yelena had been looking for Juno after their last job went sour and Juno's older brother, Eric, had been pointing a gun at Joe's head. In the end, not only did Joe help save Juno's life, but he also insisted on giving him his cut from the job. This earned Juno's loyalty and respect and also paid for the sound and digital recording equipment heaped on the desk. So, when Joe called and said he was coming by to discuss a job, Juno served Joe a grape Snapple, moved some laundry from the busted couch, and, as soon as they got settled, just asked him: "What are we stealing? And when?"

Joe smiled. He put his Snapple on the coffee table made of a wooden crate covered in a sheet—ten grand in gadgets and no table—and said: "Four million in diamonds. In two days. For starters. Then it gets complicated."

Juno looked at him. Every one of these statements was its own question: Four million? In diamonds? In two days?

For starters? Then he grinned and just said: "Cool. What do you need?"

Next Joe had to track down Yelena. Although they had shared a number of beds, none had belonged to her and he didn't know where she lived or even if she had a steady place, only that she generally hung out in the Russian parts of Brooklyn out by Brighton Beach. In fact, considering how intense their time together had been, an average person might be surprised at how little he really knew about her: they'd committed crimes together and fled from the law; they'd killed people together and saved each other's lives. But of course Joe had fought beside men many times, training together, depending on each other for survival, and then never seen them again. The fact that he and Yelena also had such combustible sexual chemistry, and that they genuinely seemed to like and understand each other, intensified their connection but did not inherently alter it: They worked well together. They fit. It made them good partners. It did not mean they sent each other birthday cards. He actually had no idea when her birthday was or even her exact age. He did have a phone number, though, so he called and left her a message: "Hey, it's Joe. We should meet." And since she in her own way knew Joe quite well, knew how little use he had for phones and that she was one of only a handful of people who even had his number—Gio, Gladys, the manager from the club—she texted back right away: *When?*

ASAP, he answered. And she sent an address.

The address, however, was not in Brighton Beach. It was in Chinatown, the Chinatown in Downtown Manhattan, which was smaller and more tourist filled than the gigantic one out in Flushing but also much older and with layers running deep in the history of New York, both culturally—as the original community of mainly Cantonese immigrants—and literally, as this old part of town was riddled with tunnels, basements, narrow streets, alleys, and tenements that had been in use going back to the days of the Five Points gangs that once ran underworld New York.

Joe had no idea what to expect when he got out of the train on Canal and wandered down Mott Street till he found the building—a quaint dump that seemed to lean slightly left, with a shop selling souvenirs, fans, jade plants, and bootleg Hong Kong DVDs on the first floor—and buzzed before climbing two flights of narrow stairs, also slanted left, to knock on the door. It was opened by Crystal from the club. She wore a Chinese robe that she might have bought in the downstairs shop. Her hair was down and she looked younger and, to Joe, much prettier without the expertly applied makeup she always had on at work.

"Hi Joe," she said. "Come on in."

He smiled. "Hey Crystal. Good to see you." A small calico kitten meowed and fled as he entered and she closed the door behind him. It was a studio, small but very well arranged, with a linen-colored IKEA couch and white cube coffee table in front of a large flat screen, a neat little kitchen area, and in back, under the sheer-curtained windows, a low bed full of big white pillows on which Yelena was propped, dressed in a sleeveless, ribbed white undershirt and cutoff jean shorts, drinking coffee.

"Hey Joe," she said and smiled. "Want some coffee?"

"Sure," he said. "That sounds fine."

Crystal got him a cup and then the three of them chitchatted—or Crystal did since neither Yelena nor Joe were much for chitchat—while Crystal got changed, disrobing and then pulling on clothes while she talked with the total lack of self-consciousness about her body that all dancers have—from ballerinas to strippers. Then she announced that she was running out for cigarettes before tactfully leaving them to talk about the things she was not meant to hear and knew she did not want to know. When she got back, her place was empty, except for the mewling kitten, and she was neither surprised nor insulted to find that neither of them had left a note.

15

Joe took Yelena to get the supplies they needed for the plan he'd proposed, then they met with Juno and got dressed up: Joe in a thick brown wig that Yelena trimmed and fitted to look real, or at least like a guy who hoped no one noticed his expensive rug, a matching bushy mustache that curled down along the grooves of his mouth, and heavy-framed, expensive-looking glasses in the corners of which Juno had installed tiny pin cameras that took wide-angle shots when Joe clicked the button in his pocket. He wore summer-weight dress slacks, an Italian silk shirt similar to the ones many of these diamond guys wore, and brand-new sneakers so trendy that Joe himself had never even heard of them. Juno and Yelena chose them and laughed out loud when Joe put them on. He didn't see what was so funny.

Yelena dressed like the hot Russian babe she would never for a second deign to be in a push-up bra and frilled Oscar de la Renta blouse, gaspingly tight leggings, and Louboutin heels that even stolen from the showroom still cost enough to confound Joe. She had a camera in the Apple Watch on her wrist and one in the clip that she wore in the back of her hair: generally it was pulled in a tight ponytail or hanging more or less straight. Now she had curled and primped and sprayed it into a confection of golden curls that rose and fell over her shoulders and drifted down her back. Her nails were dipped and beaded like ceremonial daggers.

The trickiest bit had been the bling. They were trying to con their way past the biggest gem dealers in town, eyes trained to rate and weigh stones all day, and the idea of hustling by with a bunch of paste on Yelena's fingers or a Canal Street knockoff watch on Joe's wrist was laughable. Fake moustache fine. Fake Rolex, forget it. Gio had lent Joe both his Submariner and his wedding ring without hesitation. His only comment: "If you have to lose one, make it the Rolex, for both our sakes." But for Yelena they took up a collection: a ring and a bracelet from Maria, a necklace from Alonzo's wife, and another ring and anklet from Rebbe's mistress, a young Jamaican girl he kept on the Upper East Side. Each of them handed the goods over with great reluctance, many warnings and promises, and the general sense that if Yelena were to disappear or come to harm, a bloody gang war would ensue like nothing the city had seen in generations.

As a gesture, in the way of an insurance company goon trailing a gem-studded starlet at the Oscars, Joe and Yelena arrived in a black Escalade driven by Alonzo's bodyguard, Barry. Juno hid in back behind the tinted glass, ready to pluck Joe and Yelena's photos from the air.

Yelena was a natural. Though Joe had never seen her wear any jewelry at all, she entered the market like she owned it and began promenading down the aisles, deliberately

94

drawing attention to herself rather than attempting to fade out or blend in like you were supposed to casing a job. But of course parading like a princess toying with baubles fit in perfectly here.

"Oh my God, honey, look at this," she yelled to Joe, who dutifully hustled over. A grinning saleslady—her own hair an ash-blond meringue and her ears, throat, wrists, and fingers bedazzled—was sliding a square-cut stone on to Yelena's ring finger. Another saleswoman, with long black hair and emerald earrings, came over to help coo.

"Isn't it cute?" she asked Joe, hand modeling for him. He kissed her finger.

"Your finger's adorable, baby," he declared. "But that ring looks a little small."

"Actually it is a bit loose on her," the blond saleswoman corrected. "But we can have it sized."

"I meant the rock," Joe said. "I want something special for my special girl!"

He strode off.

"Isn't he the sweetest?" Yelena asked the crestfallen saleswomen as she held her finger out to be unringed.

In this way they covered the whole place before ending up at Shatzenberg and Sons, the outfit Rebbe had fingered to Joe in the first place. Yelena sashayed up and down their counter of blinding treasure, then sighed.

"I don't know honey, it's all the same old stuff," she told Joe loudly while one of the Shatzenberg sons hovered. "Maybe we should just wait till we get to Hong Kong."

"Whatever you say, baby. You know how bored I get with shopping," Joe said, winking at Shatzenberg.

"You know," he said, leaning in unctuously—Joe could smell his cologne—"if you like, why not come up to the private showroom? You can sit and relax while we show your lovely wife some of our wholesale stock."

"How do you mean, wholesale? I just want one perfect ring for my lady."

"Yes, yes. I understand very well. I mean loose stones. You pay by the carat and then we can set it however she likes. It will be truly unique." He put a hand out, pinky finger gleaming. "I'm Morty Shatzenberg."

"Well, that's very big of you, Morty," Joe said, pumping him. "This is Ivana and I'm Dixon. We're the Syders." He squeezed Yelena's shoulder. "How's about that, babe? A one-of-a-kind piece for my one-of-a-kind piece of ass?"

She slapped his arm and rolled her eyes at Shatzenberg. "Excuse him, please. He has no class. I'd love to see your loosies."

Nodding and scraping, Shatzenberg led them to the rear of the market, where an armed guard held the door for them. They went down a bare, concrete hall to an elevator and rode up ten flights, where a key turned a lock in the panel that opened the elevator doors. Across that hall, through another locked door, they entered a small, windowless room. The walls, floors, and ceiling were all covered in thick, brown carpet, and recessed lights threw spots along the walls and shined down on the center, where the only furniture was an antique desk with two chairs on one side and a single one on the other. Shatzenberg invited them to sit and then spoke into a small intercom that looked out of place on the elaborately carved and inlaid French desk. A moment later, a door opened in the carpeted wall: there was no handle on their side, and in the second it was ajar Yelena glimpsed a steel-lined room with a vault. A young woman stepped through holding a case and shut the door behind her. She strode over, her heels sinking soundlessly into the deep pile, and set the case down. Shatzenberg opened it. A scatter of stars shined out from the midnight-black velvet lining. Round diamonds, in sizes up to ten carats.

"My God," Yelena murmured, and for the first time, Joe didn't think she was pretending.

Twenty minutes later, Yelena and Joe left, smiling and chatting excitedly about sizes and settings and cuts, and Shatzenberg, playing the long game, hid his disappointment, assuring them he'd be here when they were ready, though he did try warning them that this particular stock would soon be gone, off to their Antwerp office. On the street outside, rush hour was in full force, the sidewalk like a river of bodies trying to wash you right down the drain of the subway on the corner, and as they fought the current to cross to where the car was waiting, a couple of Hasids blocked Joe's path.

"You Jewish?" they demanded. "You Jewish?"

Joe shrugged them off, his mind on the problem at hand. "Not today," he said and took Yelena's hand. They hurried across the street and climbed into the door that Barry held open. In back, Juno was already scanning through the photos they'd been continuously sending, arranging them into mapped and scaled layouts of the market, the hall, the elevator, and the inner sanctum.

As soon as the door was shut, Joe pulled the wig off and scratched his scalp, which had been driving him crazy.

"You get all that?" he asked Juno, handing him the glasses.

"Yeah, and I got all up and down the block while we were waiting, but I'm not sure how much good it will do. It's tighter than a preacher's ass in there."

"I know. And twice as hairy. What do you think?" he asked Yelena, who was pulling off her shoes and slipping on her sneakers.

She shrugged. "Maybe with an army we storm it, and I break the safe while the police make a siege. But then what? Where do we go? The roof? Maybe you will have a helicopter waiting?"

"No. It's got to be when they move it. But how? Look at this." He gestured toward the front seat. "We haven't even gone one block."

"Sorry," Barry called back. "It's the traffic. By the time I go a few feet the light changes again."

"Sorry, Barry, I wasn't blaming you. Just griping."

"What about just smash and grab?" Juno said. "Like snatching chains back in the hood? I could bring in a couple guys I know make bank just grabbing iPhones from dumb tourists and college kids. They call it apple picking. They can grab the stones and run down into the train and then hand the shit off to you two, a nice harmless white couple. Even if the cops grab up my boys after that, they'll have to let them go."

Joe smiled. "That's assuming they remember to run in our direction and not home to Brooklyn by mistake."

Juno shrugged. "It's possible their sense of direction might get fuzzy outside the hood."

"This won't be a sprint anyhow. Rebbe says they wheel a steel strongbox right onto the armored truck. Only the brother here and the one in Antwerp know the combination. They don't even trust their own security guards with this." He stared thoughtfully out the window as they finally crept across the avenue to a chorus of frustrated honking. The Hasids were busy harassing other passersby. It was a clogged mess. "No," he said, thinking out loud as he peeled off his fake moustache. "This is going to require something a bit weirder."

16

Joe sent Alonzo and Rebbe's property home to Brooklyn with Juno and the driver, and he and Yelena took the subway uptown to return Maria's jewelry.

"All the way to Washington Heights on the subway?" Yelena teased. "I guess the rich husband act is over. At least you could steal me a car, Joe. It's faster."

"Not during rush hour," he told her. "We can steal one for the ride home if you like."

In fact neither of them would do any such thing. They wouldn't even jump a turnstile. A professional doesn't commit misdemeanors on the way to committing a felony. They took the 1 train.

"Take that, you little slut! You know it's what you deserve!" Paul brought the whip down smartly across Gianna's pale, white rump, already crossed with red. The leather snapped, and she twitched, gasping.

"Thank you, sir, may I have another," she breathed. She was bent over the hotel bed, dressed in a black lace bra and panties, thigh-high stockings, red heels. Her blond head was facedown in a pillow to muffle her cries. Her panties were yanked down.

Paul gave her another stroke. He was working up a sweat actually, and he pulled off his shirt, tossing it onto the chair where his tie and jacket already lay, neatly folded. In the closet, another suit and shirt hung, to prevent creasing—the clothes Gianna would change into later when she turned back into Gio.

Paul Rogers was Gio's accountant and an expert money launderer. Thanks to Paul, Gio had millions stashed safely around the world, insuring his family's future and also, thanks to the fronts and shells Paul had set up, a way to funnel the laundered money clean as freshly pressed dress shirts back into the many legitimate businesses he owned or controlled, providing a fat legal income to show the tax man.

But Paul had also taken on another, even more secret and precious role in Gio's life. For as long as he could remember, Gio had nurtured fantasies of being dominated, abused really, by a handsome young man, especially a man of Paul's type: blond, blue eyed, Waspy, Princeton educated. After they connected by chance in a gay S&M bar Gio controlled, they began meeting privately, providing Gio with purely sexual fulfillment and relief. But over time, real feelings had grown between them, and now Gio wasn't sure what they were: Lovers? Friends? Boyfriends? Gio didn't even think of himself as gay. He was happy with his wife, they had a good sex life, and he had no desires for men outside of this particular role-play scenario, which had become an obsession. Yet he did feel tenderly toward Paul.

"Thank you, sir, may I have another!"

The whip came down again, hard, and Gianna moaned. Her ass was throbbing. Paul stopped, catching his breath.

"Are you ready, Gianna? Ready to show me what a good little slut you can be?"

"Yes, sir. Please," Gianna said and kneeled before her master. She undid his belt with shaky hands and unzipped him. A phone rang.

Gio froze. "Which one is that?"

"Who cares," Paul said urgently. "Ignore it. We can't stop now."

The ring continued. "It's the work phone," Gio said. "I have to take this."

He stood, still tottering uncertainly in his heels, after all this time never having gotten the hang of them, and grabbed the phone.

"Yeah," he said into it, in his normal voice.

Paul sighed elaborately and went into the bathroom to splash cold water on his face.

"It's me. Can we talk?" It was Fusco, an NYPD detective, corrupt cop, and compulsive gambler who owed Gio more than he could ever pay.

"Yeah, it's a burner," Gio said. "It's safe." He'd texted Fusco this number and would ditch it as soon as they spoke.

"So I've been asking around like you said," Fusco told him. "Even on the task force, and nobody knows for sure where this talk is coming from, but it's not NYPD. FBI maybe? Who knows?"

Fusco had been telling Gio that there was chatter about a big dope deal going down and that the Caprisi family name had been linked to it. This was especially disconcerting to Gio, since he had only become associated with the situation a day ago. Nor was this the first time. A German smuggler who moved stolen electronics and cars worldwide had been arrested by Interpol shortly after Gio had closed a deal with him. The implication was clear: Somebody was talking to the law. And it looked like the leak was in Gio's ship.

Gio took a deep breath and counted to ten. He felt his rage rising but also knew that taking it out on Fusco or Paul or the furniture in the hotel room, while it might feel good for a second, was not going to help.

"Okay," he said calmly. "Keep digging. And thanks."

He hung up the phone. Almost immediately a text came through on his other, personal phone. It was Carol. He glanced at his wrist, then realized Joe had his watch.

Paul came out of the bathroom, naked and beautiful.

"Now then," he said with a smile. "Let's finish what we started."

"Sorry," Gio said, removing his wig, his face now odd in the mirror, with his eye shadow and lipstick smudged by the pillow. "I have to get in the shower and meet my wife." He kissed Paul quickly as he went by into the bathroom. "She'll kill me if I'm late. It's date night."

Maria's apartment seemed humble from the outside. She had a big house in the Bronx near Riverdale but kept this place for business and also to be at home, among friends and family in the old neighborhood. She got bored sitting in her big house alone. The apartment was in a nondescript brick building with the smell of cooking in the halls and kids and telenovelas blaring behind the doors, but the teenager hanging on the front steps worked for Maria, and the janitor sweeping the lobby got his job because his wife knew her. Both nodded to Joe and Yelena as they passed and got on the elevator. She lived in a rear corner apartment on the top floor, where most of the apartments were occupied by her relatives or people she'd known for decades: an old blind man who never left the neighborhood, a retired maid who spoke no English and used to clean Maria's house. Joe knew that eyes were watching through the peepholes as soon as they stepped off the elevator, and the door opened the second his knuckles tapped the door.

It was Little Maria herself, barely reaching Joe's shoulder even in her spike heels, a flower-patterned apron over her black sweater and blue slacks. She held a wooden spoon in her hand and something that smelled great was cooking somewhere behind her. She kissed his cheek.

"*Hola mijo*," she said. "I hope you're hungry."

"I am now that I smell your pernil cooking," Joe said. "Here's your stuff back." He handed her pieces over.

"And this is your *novia*? *Guapísima*."

"This is Yelena. She's the one who's going to steal the diamonds."

"A pleasure to meet you," Yelena said and held out her hand.

"*Buena*. Pretty and smart, too." She rose on her toes to kiss Yelena's cheek.

"We need Carlo," Joe said. "It's time to email. I hope he's still alive."

She sneered. "*Me tienes la creta hirviendo*. But *sí*. That *cuero* is alive." She led them into the living room, where another woman—older, plumper, and even smaller—was watching Spanish TV. Barking could be heard faintly, too, coming from behind a door. The room was large and ornately furnished: a red-velvet couch, a huge flat screen, dark wooden tables, tasseled lamps, paintings of Jesus and of a tropical scene on the flocked walls. The windows commanded a view of the bridge and of the Jersey Palisades, aglow with the sinking sun.

"*Tía*," Maria called. "*Mira los frijoles*." The old lady rocked to get momentum, then stood and waddled efficiently by, taking the spoon from Maria as she passed into the kitchen. Maria knocked on the door where the barking was coming from. "Paco! *Abre la puerta*!"

The door opened and a goateed young man in jeans, a white tank top, gold cross, and Yankees cap let them in. It was an office, furnished as opulently as the living room, with a thick carpet, wide dark desk, and leather chairs. But the velvet drapes were drawn, and the center of the room was taken up by a large dog cage in which a naked man cowered. He was covered in cuts and bruises. A choke chain hung around his neck. A large pit bull in a much nicer, studded collar stood outside the cage barking and drooling, either because he wanted to kill the man inside it or because he wanted his cage back.

"Ay! Duque! Be quiet!" Maria yelled, and the kid grabbed the dog by the collar, yanked him back, then petted him till he sat down calmly and licked his hand, tail wagging. Maria approached the cage. The man inside it watched and whimpered.

"You. *Lambe bolsa*! This man has some questions."

He blinked up at them in abject terror.

"Can you let him out?" Joe asked. "I need him to email."

Maria took a small key from her apron pocket and opened the padlock. The kid stepped up with a leash in his hand and opened the door of the cage.

"Crawl, bitch," Maria said, and the man crawled out, trembling as the dog went crazy.

"Duque!" Maria yelled, and the dog sat, tag wagging happily again. The kid attached the leash to the choke collar and offered it to Joe.

"Just bring him to the desk," Joe said. The boy walked him over, dragging him along. Maria kicked him in the ass with her pointy shoe. Yelena stood to the side, watching curiously. The man eased himself carefully up into the chair, and Joe pushed over the open laptop. He spoke calmly, looking the man in the eye.

"Hi Carlo. I know you're scared and in pain. But I need you to focus. If you take care of this, then maybe Maria will turn you over to me, and I can see about getting you out of here. We'll send you into exile."

The man looked up at Joe and then over to Maria. There was mostly fear in his eyes and confusion at being addressed like a person again, politely even. But Joe also saw a tiny flicker of hope. Deep down of course, Carlo knew he was doomed, but the human mind being what it is, he would not be able to resist the temptation of hope.

"Right, Maria?" Joe asked.

She shrugged disdainfully. "Sure, what do I care? Take this piece of trash when I'm done with him. Dead or alive is the same to me."

"See?" Joe said. "Now, I need you to email the seller and tell him you want the dope. Tell him you have a plan to get the diamonds and will have them day after tomorrow. That's important. And ask if the stuff is here yet."

Carlo went online and opened the email account. Joe read through the emails already there, just a few exchanges, setting the terms. While Joe coaxed him, Carlo typed:

I am ready to do this. I found a way to get the payment Friday. Is the product in NY?

"That's good, Carlo," Joe said. "Now send."

Carlo sent the email. Joe got a sheet of paper and had Carlo write down the email addresses and password, then folded it and put it in his pocket. He patted Carlo on the shoulder.

"Good job, Carlo. Thanks," he said. Carlo nodded, eyes still floating wildly around the room. Joe turned to the others. "I'll check later to see if he answers," he said, though what he meant was that he'd have Juno check. He didn't even have a computer.

There was a soft knock on the door and the kid stuck his head out to see what it was. "Dinner's ready," he announced.

Maria clapped her hands twice. "Let's eat. Come on everybody." To the kid she said: "Put this *pendejo* in his cage."

The kid grabbed the leash roughly and, in a panic, Carlo got to his knees and began to crawl quickly back to the cage. Joe and Yelena watched awkwardly as Maria locked it. Just then, the computer dinged as an email came in. Joe checked. It was a reply:

The product will be ready when you are.

Joe looked at his watch. "It's 4:00 a.m. in Afghanistan."

Yelena nodded. "You are thinking they are here."

"Yeah," Joe said as they started in to dinner, the kid holding the door. "I think they are somewhere in the city and I think they already have the dope."

Felix loved New York. Of course, he knew, who didn't? The whole world loved New York. Even people who deplored the United States, who despised Americans, if you mentioned New York would say, "I love it!" But Felix loved it in a special way. As the kind of man who at least in his youth thought of himself as an international playboy (and had actually spent many prepubescent nights feverishly poring over that very magazine in many of its international editions), Felix saw New York as the big league, a prize to win, a trophy to conquer.

He was the bastard son of a wealthy Jordanian and his French mistress, which was actually not a bad thing to be. While the legitimate sons got the property and prestige, they also lived under the rule of a deeply authoritarian and religiously conservative (if, it goes without saying, totally hypocritical) patriarch. Felix was brought up by his mother in a lovely apartment in Paris. True, once his father dropped her, his mother declined rapidly, first into alcoholism and obesity—inhaling chocolate and pâté like it was crack—then into her own brand of extreme Catholicism. But that was just another kind of freedom to Felix: he flunked out of the best Swiss boarding schools, was sent down from an excellent college at Oxford, failed upward through several very brief and silly careers in marketing and music promotions, all without consequences. His parents were indifferent, and the allowance checks kept coming.

Then a young prostitute turned up dead: drugged and strangled. She was not the first, but this one was not an undocumented sex worker; she was the wild child of a French politician. Suddenly, Felix was on the run with no money and no passport. And the checks stopped. In fact his accounts were frozen. And his father, or rather his father's staff, stopped answering his calls.

Those were desperate times for Felix, but he was a resourceful fellow: charming, clever, ruthless, and, after some frightening experiences, he found that the world of fake documents and shady border crossings suited him quite nicely. Along with international playboy, the other thing he turned out to be was a born middleman, specifically a smuggler. Not that he strapped drugs to his stomach or shoved them up his ass and got on a plane—that was for suckers. He made the deal, charmed the principals, made the connections, and when need be, cut out the competition. The big-time heroin trade was, he found, a remarkably steady business. The problems were generally geopolitical or climatological, matters of corrupt officials or delayed shipments, not far from what he imagined an oil executive dealt with. Pretty soon he was shepherding product from Afghanistan up into Italy and beyond, living the life of luxury he enjoyed so much and with plenty of opportunity to develop and indulge his more extreme tastes as well. After all, smuggled flesh was as cheap as smuggled dope, maybe cheaper.

Then one night in Kandahar, sitting on a hotel terrace drinking tea, he was approached by two bearded men around his age. They wore local clothes—the long tunic-like *khet* over the loose, pleated *partug*, and turbans—but spoke to him in French to avoid eavesdroppers. They knew who he was. That is, they knew who he really was, his true name and the crime for which he was still wanted in France, as well as most of what he'd done since. For a moment of stark terror, Felix thought they were undercover cops or some kind of spies there to arrest him. Then, to his relief, he understood: they were terrorists.

Of course they didn't put it that way, exactly. They asked him if he knew who Zahir was. He did. Zahir al Zilli, Zahir the Shadow, was known to everyone in the trade, if only as a rumor. Felix had never seen him and didn't believe those who claimed they had. Zahir—no one knew his true family names or, for that matter, if his first was really Zahir—was a bandit, a mujahedeen who had been preying on the opium warlords, using high-tech weapons and trained fighters to seize their shipments of heroin and then, he'd heard, using the money to fund attacks by jihadi. That's why they called him the Shadow: he was dark, obscure, no one knew his face, and yet he was right behind you.

Now he wanted Felix to help him expand his operation and use his sales connections to move their product. Felix was happy to oblige. The threat of exposure got his attention, but he was easily persuaded by the very generous rate Zahir offered, the volume of his traffic, his global ambitions, and his power, power that was now at Felix's disposal: money, cars, apartments, passports, and credit cards. He sent him a driver and assistant, Armond, a loyal true believer, who obeyed without question. He also sent him a bodyguard and enforcer, Vlad, who was like his one-man army, his Goliath, or maybe his Godzilla. And Vlad, as it happened, liked doing to boys what Felix liked doing to girls; they got on well.

In fact, Felix was self-aware and, despite getting kicked out of such fine schools, educated enough to realize Zahir was a substitute for his own father: powerful, remote, absent, severe, and in his own strange way, godly. Except Zahir was far more powerful—and far more remote and severe. He was not just godly. He was God. This was blasphemy, of course, and Zahir himself would never permit it. He'd cut out the tongues of idolaters and blasphemers. But while Felix understood that Zahir and his men were on a holy mission to restore the true caliphate, fighting in the name of Allah, for Felix, Zahir himself was a more believable god, one he could not see but could nevertheless reach: prayers to him were answered and services rendered in his name were rewarded here on earth, not in heaven.

After his success in Europe, for which he'd been abundantly blessed, Felix had been dispatched to the belly of the beast: America. It was the next phase, the natural outcome of Zahir's ambitions: a bigger market for their goods and a bigger target for their attacks. There were three main sources for the world's opium trade. Product from Southeast Asia's Golden Triangle was called China White, and that was what had traditionally dominated the big cities of the northeastern United States. The sticky, dark stuff that came up from Mexico into California and the Southwest was called black tar, and, increasingly, white heroin from Latin America was flooding the United States as well. Heroin from Felix's part of the world was called Persian, and it accounted for merely

4 percent of the US market. It was considered a rare treat and would fetch a high price. Of course, the actual difference was in the mind of the consumer: a lover of fine wine or cigars might covet a certain bottle or band, but the need for alcohol or nicotine will be fed just as well by rotgut booze and hand-rolled shag. And nothing beats addiction to insure a stable market. Synthetic opiates like Oxy arrive on the scene, trendier drugs like MDMA come and go, but opium had been beguiling, bedeviling, and enriching humanity for millennia. Dope was forever. And Persian was king.

Felix's mission was to work with Zahir's New York contact, who had been studying the lay of the land and finding likely buyers and possible threats from the law and from the underworld. He would also be shepherding through this first shipment, sent via a new connection to New York. If this first test shipment went well, if the goods arrived safely and the money flowed back securely, then they would open the pipeline—larger loads of stolen heroin, regular shipments, reliable distribution, and more money all around. And if they eventually sent something else through that same pipeline, like a dirty bomb or a suitcase nuke, then so be it. True, Felix loved New York, but he'd get over it. He'd heard that Los Angeles was even better these days.

17

Later, as they were leaving Maria's building, Yelena said, "I do not think I like that woman."

"No," Joe said. "But I like how she cooks pork."

Yelena shrugged. Fair enough. She'd had seconds herself. "And you thought of a way to get the diamonds for her dope?"

Joe nodded as they walked down the block. "I think so. I'm going to need you to go shopping tomorrow. And I have to talk to Juno." He glanced at Gio's Rolex. "But right now I'm late to meet Gio and give him back his wedding ring and watch." At the corner of Broadway he hailed a cab.

Gio arranged to meet Joe at Old Shenanigan's, one of the huge Irish pubs that dominated the area north of Penn Station, the onetime stomping ground of the Westies. Just as the Deuce, once a gauntlet of old-fashioned vice—sex, drugs, booze, horror, and kung fu movies—had become the new Times Square's giant tourist trap, each version a different man's vision of hell, so Hell's Kitchen itself now housed these theme-park versions of the old-time buckets of blood:

vast pubs full of Irish flags, waitresses in green aprons, and Guinness on tap, but without the soul or the menace. Except for Pat—he was the soul and the menace, and like the ghost of the Westies, he was still hanging around.

Not that he ever hung out in this place. He merely owned it, in the sense that he controlled it and pocketed much of the proceeds; his name appeared on no document. Earlier, Gio had texted a number that he knew one of Pat's underlings checked, and the response had invited him here for a beer. Now, entering the pub, the roar of happy hour blasted him as hard as the air-conditioning, and he weaved through the crowd, mostly office workers in ties and shirtsleeves, skirts and blouses, or tourists in cargo shorts and jeans. He bought a Harp Lager and made his way upstairs where there was table service, families eating burgers or fish and chips, and flat screens showing silent sports. He continued through another door marked EMPLOYEES ONLY and up another flight of stairs, clean but minus the polished wood banister and green wallpaper. The din was now a faint throb in the air. He pushed through a door into a crowded storeroom with cleaning products and toilet paper everywhere and cases of liquor stacked high, then up one more flight of stairs. These were dirty and dusty, with cracked concrete and discarded newspapers underfoot. At the top, he reached a door marked DO NOT ENTER—ALARM WILL SOUND. He entered. No alarm sounded. This was raw space, lit with bare bulbs and the street glow from uncovered windows. The floor was concrete, the walls exposed studs and unpainted drywall. Wiring and ducts ran under the ceiling. In the back two doors were marked LADIES and GENTS. He opened the GENTS. It was a large restroom, even larger without the appliances: just a tiled box, clean but cold, with a mirror across one wall, pipes where the sinks and urinals would go, and a row of toilets without stalls. On a corner toilet, under a bare bulb, sat Patty White, holding a pint glass of Guinness stout.

"Gio, my friend, how can I help you?"

Gio put out his hand and they shook. "Thanks for meeting me on such short notice."

Pat smiled. "It's always a pleasure to drink with an old friend. I'm just sorry it has to be in such ignoble surroundings."

"Seems nice and cool in here. And private."

"Indeed. And hard to hide a bug in. Have a seat. No need to drop your trousers." He waved his drink. "Though at my age drinking my stout like this might actually be more convenient."

Gio considered the toilet. It was unused, not even installed yet, so it was clean, but still there was no lid, just the institutional-style seat over the rim, and he was wearing a light gray summer-weight suit that would stain easily. He draped his hanky over it and sat, holding up his beer. "To healthy plumbing, at any age." They clinked glasses and drank.

"I wanted to ask you about Uder." Uder was the smuggler who had recently been busted. Gio and Patty had arranged for a truckload of expensive electronics gear to be hijacked, an inside job through the union he controlled, then shipped to his associates in Naples. Patty had provided the muscle for the job and connected Gio's Naples people to the buyer, Uder, a German from the old East Berlin whom he knew from IRA days. The deal had gone through, and the money had come home, but shortly thereafter, Interpol had grabbed up Uder. Too bad for Uder. Gio hadn't given it much thought till now. It had never occurred to him that the information leading to his arrest might be from Gio's side.

"Ah, poor Uder," Patty said. "Last I heard he is awaiting trial. Sitting in a room much like this only smaller and with bars on it."

"I'm wondering if you know how he got pinched. If someone talked. And if so, who?"

Patty shook his head. "I'm afraid I haven't the foggiest. After all, Europe's an ocean away, even in our global age. No American law enforcement was involved. Nor does he know anything that could hurt you or me." He patted Gio's leg. "Of that I assure you."

"That's good to know. But I've been hearing talk about myself from my sources in law enforcement. Just chatter but it seems to be from out of town. And now with this Maria thing. I know you have a lot of friends in the government, especially Feds." He shrugged. "You might ask around."

"I will make some discreet inquiries."

"I'd appreciate it," Gio said. "It may be nothing. Just being cautious."

"By all means. We all know pigs and rats are a hazard to your health." He held up his glass, as though for attention: "But so is paranoia, my friend."

Gio clinked glasses again: "Says the wise man sitting on the toilet."

Pat laughed, and they finished their beers.

When Gio got back downstairs, after stopping by a real men's room to check that his pants were clean (they were),

Joe was waiting at the bar with a barely touched club soda and lime.

"Thanks for coming," Gio told him as they shook hands. "And waiting." He put his empty on the bar. Joe handed him his watch and ring and he slipped them both on. "Great. I felt naked without these." He glanced around at the crowd, which was at maximum. It was hard to imagine anyone eavesdropping in this din but still: "I also want to talk to you about something outside. But I can wait till you finish your drink."

Joe took another sip of his club soda. "Finished," he said. They went out and started walking across town. It was night now and the mood of the crowd on the street was looser, less stressed, the energy still high but with more expectation, people going out somewhere, not people coming from work. The air was warm and full of promise, good or bad.

"I suspect there's a rat in my house," Gio said. Joe said nothing. He just waited for his old friend to continue. Gio went on, explaining everything that Fusco had said, the business with Uder and the conversation with Pat.

"Do you trust Pat?" Joe asked.

"I trust you," Gio said.

"What do you want me to do?"

Gio shrugged. "Do some spy shit."

Joe laughed. They stood at the avenue, waiting for the light. Traffic rolled by. "If we don't know who's talking or who they're talking to, it's hard to get started. I can't just put on a tuxedo like James Bond and show up at the bad guy's roulette game."

"I was picturing you in more like a SEAL diving outfit, but yeah I know what you mean."

"I think you need an outside audit of all your people's electronic communication since before the Uder deal."

"How outside?"

"Someone who can't be involved or compromised because they're not associated with your business. And who can't betray you because they don't know what they're looking for. Just preparing a report. Who talked to who, when and what about."

"You have someone in mind?"

"Maybe. Let me get back to you tomorrow."

"Good. Thanks," Gio said. "And I have another thought," he added as they crossed the street. "Since it looks like this is federal, we could at least put a feeler out to someone in the FBI."

"You know someone?"

"We both do. Agent Donna."

"Nah," Joe shook his head. "No way is she bent."

"Agreed. She's as straight as they come. But she is in the information business herself. She might want to help keep us free and useful to her, in the name of homeland security."

Joe considered it. "I don't know, Gio. I just don't see her going out of her way to keep you out of jail."

Gio smiled. "Not me, no. But you, maybe."

"Me? Why me?"

"Come on, she's got a thing for you. Anyone can see that."

"Fuck off."

"And it's mutual." They were across the street from Penn Station and the round façade of Madison Square Garden.

Yelena was waiting in front of the station entrance as arranged. She saw them and waved. "But you better watch out," Gio went on, waving back. "If Yelena finds out, she might kill her."

Joe laughed. "Somehow I don't make her as the jealous type."

Gio looked at his watch, back where it belonged. "I've got to go. I'm meeting Carol at the Garden."

"Oh yeah?" Joe tried to remember what team was in town. "Who's playing tonight?"

"Billy Joel!" Gio shouted as he dashed across to make the light. "Alonzo got me great seats!"

Joe laughed. "Have fun," he shouted, then crossed to meet Yelena. Despite what Gio thought, all Joe had in mind was a quick dinner while they discussed Joe's plan for the diamonds. Tomorrow was a big day, after all.

18

Billy Joel was fantastic. "So what if he is like . . . a hundred years old," Carol thought. He is still amazing, and being older, if not quite a hundred herself, she admitted she liked being able to sit and listen to the music and understand the words, without a bunch of people standing and blocking her view or howling drunkenly. And the concert brought back happy memories, too, about her and Gio before they were even married. Not that they were unhappy now. Family, home, health—they were incredibly lucky, so lucky that sometimes it scared her, thinking of them versus the clients she saw as a therapist. She worked with kids, but of course their problems were themselves a symptom of the family's dysfunction. It was amazing how well theirs functioned. But things were complicated in any marriage, and with a man like Gio it was a bit more complicated than most. When her friends talked about their families or spouses having skeletons in the closet or knowing where the bodies were buried at work, they didn't mean actual dead people. Their husbands had dark sides, but Gio's was literally blacked out, completely opaque to her. It was, she sometimes thought, what being married to a spy must be like, having a husband who disappeared on secret missions he could never reveal. Except, where their men went off overseas for a week or a month, Gio crossed over into his other world every morning in a suit and tie, then came back into the light at night for family dinner.

No doubt it was that duality that led her to become insecure and suspicious. To follow him to a cheap hotel only to find that he was just meeting his accountant, that handsome young guy Paul. And that it was Paul who was actually having an affair with a much older, married, and rather homely blond woman. She felt silly now thinking about it and grateful Gio never knew. But it was part of the reason she had instituted this date-night policy. And when Gio whispered to her between songs and told her that he had secretly booked them a suite at the Pierre, she felt herself melt not just into love and desire for her husband but also peace and security, that feeling of protection, of being completely joined with one other person in the world. She snuggled into him as he put his arm around her and tucked her face against his chest, even closing her eyes as the next song began. That was when she felt something tickling her nose, so that she had to pull away and sneeze, kind of ruining the romantic mood.

"Allergies?" Gio asked her. "Did you bring Zyrtec?"

"Just some dust or something." She shook her head. "I'm fine." Rubbing the itch, she found it, a long hair that had been on his jacket. And as she flicked it away, in the glare of the stage lights, she saw: it was long and blond and definitely not hers.

* * *

Joe couldn't sleep. Naked, he crept out of bed and left Yelena snoring softly, then went to the window where he could see the river glinting blackly below. He had not had a nightmare since he'd begun drinking Dr. Z's tea, but he'd forgotten to have some tonight, and the new job had his mind racing. Back in the service, they'd trained him to sleep whenever and wherever he could, even on the eve of battle. Then again they also handed out Ambien like it was Chiclets. He got his book out and dug in his wallet for the tea bag he had stashed there. He came across the card that Frank, that painter from the bench outside the VA had given him and stuck it in his book like a bookmark. Then he brewed the tea with the little electric kettle the hotel had provided and settled down in a corner armchair to read under a standing lamp.

But he couldn't focus. So he got up, carrying his tea and book, and went to the desk where a laptop sat open. Yelena had brought it to track down items they needed for the job. He opened Google and typed in Frank's full name from the card: Frank Jones. A million hits. The name was too common. He tried to narrow it: "Frank Jones painter" and then, a little reluctantly: "African American." His screen burst into color.

Apparently Frank Jones was a well-known contemporary artist, represented by a big gallery in Chelsea with lots of work in museums and rich people's collections as well. Not that Joe would know. He liked visiting museums, but he always went alone and never discussed what he saw with anyone; it wouldn't even occur to him to talk about it. What

122

was there to say? As for contemporary art and the gallery scene, that was a different world, though it was centered just a short walk from where he sat now. That was New York, many cities superimposed on each other and yet just as far apart, just as alien, as if they were in another country, speaking another language. He could hardly imagine traveling to theirs, knowing what to do or say. But then how many of those people could survive in his?

He scrolled through images of Frank's paintings: Big brushy close-ups of body parts, male or female or both entangled but like just an ass crack that must have covered a wall. Then there were outside scenes, he hesitated to call them "landscapes," that looked like a vacant lot with just a few bums in the corner around a fire but also every brick and broken bottle scrupulously rendered, or a busy street scene full of moving people and cars but all from odd perspectives, like high up or very low and angled so that things bent off and didn't look real, though Joe could easily tell that this was Harlem. Then there were the war ones. Joe assumed they were Vietnam, with the black chopper and the palm tree lit up like an orange fireball, the stacked skulls and yellow-tinged limbs. But there was one in particular that sucked him in. It looked like a long tunnel with wooden supports, but the painting was nearly black, with just muddy browns and grays to give a sense of things, all of it dim, except for a lighter haze coming at you from deep in the vanishing point, a flashlight, blurred and yellow, and behind, holding the flashlight, silhouetted black on black stood a black man with a black gun, a Colt .45 it looked like, a service piece in his hand, aiming at you. Joe blinked hard, opening and closing his eyes as if trying to reset or focus. He knew this scene, this picture. It was from his nightmare.

Then he felt a hand on his shoulder and he jumped, twisting hard as if to punch whoever it was right in the kidney, but another part of him knew it was Yelena, and he didn't raise his fist.

"Can't sleep?" she asked.

"Jesus, you startled me," he said.

"Sorry." She ran her hand down his back. "You're sweating."

"Yeah. I was hot under the blankets," Joe said. He stood and shut the laptop as he turned to face her.

"Come back to bed," she said, taking his hand. "I promise to tire you out."

He smiled. "Good idea." As he followed her he grabbed the cup and gulped down the rest of Dr. Z's anti-nightmare tea.

19

They met at the club. Some of the crew bitched mildly about the trip out to Queens, but it was a safe, secure spot to speak freely, and few places were more low profile than a strip club at ten in the morning. The janitor let Joe and Yelena in and started the coffee brewing before he split, happy to get off early. The others showed up on time, Cash in the white BMW, Juno with Rebbe's guy, who was named Joshua, carpooling together from Brooklyn, and Liam, Pat White's man, from Woodside, where he roomed with his two brothers, Sean and Tim Madigan, in a heavily Irish neighborhood. They helped themselves to coffee, Joe fetched Juno a soda from behind the bar, and then they all gathered in the manager's office. Liam and Joshua pulled chairs up to the low coffee table in the center. Juno sat with Cash and Yelena on the couch. Joe wheeled the manager's desk chair around and spread out a map showing the diamond market and surrounding Midtown blocks. The map was very detailed, with the names of stores noted as well as parking signs and the directions of one-way streets.

"The armored car pickup is for four thirty p.m. tomorrow," Joe said. "But we all know what Midtown traffic is like, so we will have to set up in a way that lets us wait without looking suspicious. Yelena and I will move along slowly this way, east to west, pretending to window-shop and you two"—he gestured to Cash and Joshua—"can come up out of the subway. Liam, you and Juno can park around the corner. Get there early and hold your spot. You'll have a good head start when it's time to move, so you can park anywhere close by, but make sure it's legal till five at least. We don't want any cops chasing you away."

Liam ran his finger along the map. "Aye, so along these streets here is good or around that corner."

Hearing the faint brogue, Joe asked him: "That is if you think you know the city well enough to drive? Or Josh can take that job."

"I've been here three feckin' years," Liam said. "I just sound like a leprechaun to you. And besides, this fella just got out of the Israeli army six months ago. I'll bet he's still getting lost on the subway."

Everyone laughed. Joshua grinned. "I'll ride with Cash. I am used to armored combat."

"Yeah, give me Josh," Cash said, high-fiving him. "Be cool having an Israeli commando ride shotgun."

Josh shook his head. "Shotgun is too big for this job. I will bring something easier to hide."

"No man, it's just a phrase, like," Cash explained.

Juno laughed. "Okay, Cash you take him. At least the Irishman sort of speaks English."

Joe laughed and tapped his finger on the map, focusing their attention. "The armored car will pull in here by this pump, right in front of the building. Two guards up front, one driving. And one in back. When they park, the driver will stay put, watching his mirrors. The second guard will get out and check the sidewalk. When he radios that it's clear, the guard inside the car will open the doors and lower the ramp. Meanwhile, a guard inside the building will open the service door, here, and another will wheel out the strongbox.

"Up it goes onto the truck. The inside man locks the doors while the others keep watch. Then the second guard gets back in next to the driver and the guard who wheeled the box out holds traffic, so they can pull out."

"Nice and simple," Liam said. "Except for us, ruining their day."

"How long does it take them to do this?" Josh asked. "Two minutes? Maybe less?"

"About that, yeah," Joe said.

"So then what about this strongbox?"

"That's Yelena's department." Joe turned to her.

She nodded. "Yes, I have talked to the Rebbe and he showed me the specs. No problem."

Liam frowned. "No offense, I've heard you're dead brilliant," he said to Yelena. "But even Houdini couldn't crack this thing in a minute."

"She won't have to," Joe said. "We're going to buy her all the time she needs."

After the meeting, everyone scattered to complete their tasks: Liam, Josh, and Cash to get weapons and vehicles; Yelena to the shops she'd researched online the night before for the more obscure items on the list. Juno had to go home with the extra blueprints Joe had given him and get to work preparing the electronics, but as the others walked out to the parking lot, Joe pulled him aside and asked him to wait.

"But my ride's leaving," he complained as Josh left. "Getting from Queens to Bed-Stuy on public transportation is a bummer, dude."

"I've got it covered," Joe said.

"Oh yeah? You finally get Uber, Joe?"

"I've got another job for you," he told him. "If you're interested."

"Sure. Why not? You know me. I'm entrepreneurial as fuck."

"It's like a digital security thing. Checking out a company's employees, all their email accounts, phones, whatever, then reporting back to the boss, like who calls who, who talks to who on text or email. Can you do that?"

"Hell, yeah. No biggie. It's like a corporate security gig. Hackers get hired for that shit all the time, invading their company system first to stop anyone else from trying. Just set me up with the boss and let me work my magic. Who's the CEO?"

"Gio Caprisi," Joe said, as he opened the door to the daylight. "He's waiting outside to give you a ride home."

"Gio? Gio Caprisi? El Chapo?"

"I think you mean Capo. El Chapo was Mexican."

"Whatever. The dude of dudes. I knew you were in with him but . . . Fuck. I've never even seen the man."

"Don't worry, I'll introduce you. He's very nice. And he pays well." Joe put a hand on his shoulder, guiding him out. "But I wouldn't keep him waiting."

20

Joe went to visit Donna. He didn't think there was any chance she would go along with Gio's plan; he didn't even think he'd mention it, but she had been on his mind ever since that strange sighting in New Jersey. He'd half expected her to track him down after that, with or without cuffs. But in fact she had let him slide by as if she hadn't seen him, though they had made eye contact for sure. It was as if he had been to her what she was to him: a waking dream, a visitation of sorts, a sign. And so here he was, obeying the sign, using Gio's bad idea as an excuse to follow his own, maybe much worse, impulse.

But if his own motives were suspect, what about hers? He'd been a criminal fleeing a crime scene. He wasn't going to stop and chat with the law no matter how cute she was. And he'd been out of his mind, dope sick. What was her excuse for just watching him drift by like a cloud?

Joe planted himself on a bench outside the Federal Building downtown and waited for the lunch crowd to pour out. He figured if she didn't show or if she was with people, then that was that. Noon came and went, and the suits started to appear but no Donna. Then 12:30. Finally by 1:00 he decided to just wait fifteen more minutes before he cut out. He'd leave it to chance. Though some people, like every professional he knew, would say that hanging with a Fed just before a job was already pushing your luck.

Then she appeared. Looking distracted, hustling along, face in her phone, clearly in a rush but also looking good in the black drapey suit that somehow fit her better than the other federal workers in their suits, and with her hair down and sort of riding in the slight breeze, which was probably just exhaust pouring from the buses and out of the grates. And she was walking right toward him.

Joe stood up and smiled, ready for her to cruise right by again, like he was invisible. But she stopped, abruptly, and then when she saw him, she smiled, too.

"Hi," he said.

"Hi Joe."

"In a rush?"

"Yes," she said. "To get pizza."

"Mind if I walk with you?"

"Join me. I know a good place."

He fell in beside her. "You know," he said. "I could have sworn I saw you in a car the other day. I can't remember where. Or it could have been a beautiful dream."

"I think I had the same dream," she said, glancing at him as they turned a corner. "Except in my dream you looked like crap. You look much better now."

"Thanks. I've been trying to get healthy. I even did acupuncture."

"Really? I always wanted to try that."

"Why don't you? I can recommend a great doctor."

"I'm waiting for something to go wrong so I have a reason."

"Ah. Well, I'm fortunate. Lots going wrong with me all the time."

She laughed. "Lucky you. Oh, there's the place. Come on. Let's catch the light." She took his hand as if it were the most natural thing in the world, and they jogged across the street to beat the traffic. As soon as they hit the sidewalk, she dropped it, suddenly feeling awkward, and then didn't look at him again until they had bought their slices and drinks at the counter.

"Here," he said, when they came out, pointing to a nearby stoop, and they sat on the top step, balancing their paper plates on their knees, drinks on the step between them. He took a bite.

"This is good."

"Told you. Argh, but I burnt my mouth." She sipped her drink. "Now I have that little flap of skin hanging down, you know? That bugs me like crazy."

He laughed. "If you want I can get that for you."

She rolled her eyes. "So . . ." she said. "Changing the subject . . . let's see. Commit any interesting crimes recently?"

He shrugged. "I just jaywalked. With you."

She shook her head. "Sorry. That's not federal. We at the FBI couldn't care less."

"Okay then," Joe said. "How about you? Solved any good ones lately?"

"Well, let's see. I did locate the remains of one Jonesy Grables, white-supremacist gun nut and all-around shit bag. Remains being the polite term for the mess that was left after he was shot to death, burned to a crisp, and then drowned just for good measure."

"He was shot to death?" Joe asked, then shrugged to hide his relief. "I guess that can happen to gun nuts. Any leads on who remaindered him?"

"Nope. And I don't think anyone cares too much. Except for one local deputy who is in serious shit with his chief and keeps claiming some bounty hunter named Jack Me Off was masterminding the whole thing."

He laughed. "Well, I wouldn't give that much credence. Seems a bit far-fetched. And it sounds like justice was served."

"Was it?" she asked.

There was a silence between them. He shrugged. "What do I know? I'm just a bouncer. We live by a simple code. If you bother the customers or put your hands on the employees, out you go."

"I wish my code was that simple," Donna said. She glanced down at her watch, then up into his eyes. "I should get back soon. Were you just stopping by to say hi? Or did you have something else you wanted to tell me?"

He held her look for a few long seconds, then finally said, "No. Not right at this moment." But still he hesitated, staring at her. "Did you?" he asked, realizing as he said it that he was moving, almost imperceptibly and against his own will, closer to her, close enough to kiss.

"Did I what?" she asked, not moving away, not moving closer, not moving at all.

"Have anything you wanted to tell me?"

"About what?" she asked.

"About anything?"

She stared back at him a beat and he could almost feel her breath on his lips. And for a second he really felt like, *Shit, this is going to happen.* And is it the best thing possible or the worst? And then she smiled, and the moment passed.

"Not right at this moment," she said.

"Okay," he said smiling, too, now, both in disappointment and relief. "I'll let you go then."

She stood and put her shades on, then said: "If you do think of anything, you know where to find me."

"Right. And if you think of anything to tell me . . ."

"I won't know where to find you!" she said, laughing as she turned away. He laughed as he watched her go.

Donna was preoccupied. The whole walk back to work she was in dreamland, barely saying hi when she stopped at the coffee cart outside the office where Sameer, a young Yemeni man, expertly made her postlunch extrapowered latte, then almost forgetting to display her ID until she got to the front of the security line. But when she got back to her basement room, where she sorted, picked, and mostly discarded the endless stream of tips that flowed in, reality woke her up with a firm slap.

Harry Harrigan, one of the bureau's most useful informants, had been MIA for several days. Harry was a small-timer with a bank robbery beef hanging over his head, but as a lifer in the Irish mob and a fixture on the scene for decades, he provided a constant flow of useful information. And then just like that he was gone, in a puff of smoke. Finally, after failing to raise him by phone or finding him at any of his usual haunts, agents disguised as Con Ed workers had gained access to his apartment: they found rotten food in the fridge, dust on the uncollected mail, and most ominous of all, Harry's wire, which he should have been wearing, in a night table drawer. It was possible he'd fled, but Donna knew in her gut that wasn't it. Harry was lost outside Hell's Kitchen, totally broke, and barely able to get down the stairs to the subway on his prison-issue knees. Where was he going to run away to? No, Heavy Harry had been shown across to the other homeland, the one no one ever came back from. Which was enough to put a damper on Donna's whole afternoon.

Agent Mike Powell was having a good day. They didn't come often, but when they did he tried to savor them. He wasn't even sure when the last one was. He'd been on a losing streak for a while, maybe since his wife had left him, and she had ended up with primary custody of their daughter, in part because Powell had been accused of emotional cruelty and harassment, even borderline stalking behavior, spying on his ex-wife. The fact that he actually was a spy, a CIA operative, and his ex was FBI, Agent Donna Zamora, didn't help his career either. He was privately rebuked and stuck stateside while his peers got to stir shit up overseas. The only thing that saved him from demotion or worse was that the CIA could not, in any form, be seen as operating on US soil. So it all got buried.

Then, when terrorists stole a lethal virus from a secret CIA lab, he ended up cooperating with Donna, though in fact he strongly suspected her of cooperating with one of the thieves: Joe Brody, who seemed to be nothing but a part-time bouncer and small-time crook, except for a record of military ops so black they had been erased from the system altogether. Once again it ended up with Donna looking like a winner and Powell having to eat shit.

But this time it was Powell who had the inside track. CIA officers stationed in Europe overseas had an asset, code-named Early Bird, who for years had been feeding them information about the international black market in arms and technology, terror, drugs, money laundering, even the group who'd been after the virus, in exchange for certain favors—a blind eye to his own activities and even a heads-up now and then when another law enforcement agency sniffed around—a devil's bargain that spooks were known to make. Then, a couple of weeks ago, Early Bird tipped his handlers off to a shipment of high-end surveillance technology, stolen in the United States, moving through southern Europe and bound, they suspected, for China. They gave the bust to Interpol but used their leverage—and Early Bird's information—to pressure more players. The trail led back to New York, and so it was passed to the company's local office and fell right into the lap of Agent Powell.

Imagine his delight when, as he began interrogating his new asset and unraveling the various entangled enterprises, he seemed to find some threads—thin at first but tight nonetheless—connecting the informer to the Caprisi crime family, among whose known associates was one Joe Brady, aka Joe the Bouncer.

That was a week ago, but ever since he'd been showing up early for work in the morning whistling a tune and picking up coffee for his coworkers. They operated out of an office on Wall Street that fronted as a boutique firm of financial quants, so the huge electric bill and broadband usage wouldn't raise an eyebrow. Nor would the young receptionist who sat out front behind a polished cherrywood counter in a waiting room where no one ever waited, routing the routine phone calls and visits that came through like food deliveries or copy-paper salesmen and buzzing in the staff who passed through the door behind her. However, unlike the girls and boys minding the other offices in the building, this cute young receptionist would also shoot you dead with the 9 mm she kept under her desk, most likely with the first shot, if you tried to get by her.

Her name was Karen and today Powell brought her a chai latte when he showed up in his spotless white shirt, straight red tie, and perfectly creased navy suit.

"Thanks, Mike," she said, buzzing him through. "There's a message for you from Nightcrawler. Came in over the secure line late last night."

"Great." Nightcrawler was his snitch, the worm Early Bird had caught for him, one he hoped would eventually give him a way to hook the Caprisi family and along with it Joe. And if that gave him some power over his ex-wife or even won her back, great. If not, he would just use it to ruin her career like she nearly ruined his and take back full custody of his daughter.

He got to his office with its view of the new World Trade Center looming above his already-high floor—no one but tourists ever called it Freedom Tower—and shut the sound-proof door. Then, sipping his own black coffee, he got on a secure line and called.

"Hello?"

"Good morning. Got any good news for me?"

"Maybe." He always sounded terrified. At first Powell thought that meant he was lying or in danger, but now he took it in stride. It was merely the voice of a man who knew Agent Powell had him by the balls. "I heard there is a big heroin shipment coming in."

"To the Caprisis?"

"No. They're not really in that market."

"So what then? You understand who I am right? The CIA. We don't do local drug busts." He almost said to call the FBI, but of course there was a good chance that if he did, Donna would get the tip.

"Yeah, I know, but this is different. They're saying the product comes directly from Afghanistan, with no middlemen. And that it's being sold by some kind of terrorists."

"Oh yeah? That's interesting. Tell me more."

"I don't know much more," Nightcrawler said, but he sounded hopeful, like maybe he'd found something to actually trade for his own freedom. "Just that it's not going through normal channels. I mean the payment would usually just be transferred overseas from one numbered account to another. But, maybe because of who it is, they want to make a direct trade, here in New York. For diamonds."

21

Driving the armored vehicle wasn't a bad job overall. Mark had driven a bread truck before, and this paid way better and had better hours, though sometimes the hauls were longer. Yes he had a gun strapped to his hip and he wore a bullet-proof vest, but once you got over the weirdness of it, you stopped thinking about what was in the truck and just drove. Jon, his partner, had been in security first, guarding banks and stores, and he was better with guns or at least liked talking about them a lot more, but he could also drive. Another John, with an *h*, so they called him H as a joke since he was the new guy, was sitting in the back of the truck, locked in with an automatic rifle and the day's pickups: several crates of documents, two canvas bags of cash, and some kind of patented corkscrew that couldn't be FedExed because it was a unique prototype and they wouldn't insure it.

The diamond dealer was the last pickup of the day. As they turned west onto Forty-Seventh, Mark's mind was on the traffic they would fight getting out of here and on beating the rush hour out to the airport, where they would sign this shipment over to be placed on various flights. Jon radioed ahead, letting the client know that they were approaching, and as they crossed Fifth Avenue and headed down the block, swarming as always with dealers, shoppers, tourists, messengers, and business folks, the uniformed security guard from Shatzenberg and Sons appeared on the sidewalk outside the building's service entrance. Spotting the truck, he stepped out in front of the hydrant and waved them in, stepping back onto the sidewalk as Mark pulled up, same as he did every single other time. As soon as Mark came to a full stop, Jon radioed to H in back, letting him know they'd arrived, and H unlocked the rear doors from inside, then got down and lowered the ramp for the strongbox.

That's when all hell broke loose.

Stan was senior security officer for Shatzenberg and Sons. He'd been an MP ages ago, but his military and law enforcement background got him hired and his ten years with the firm got him promoted and now he was at the top of this admittedly pretty short totem pole. Basically he made the schedule, gave the junior guys their orders, and dealt with the bosses, the Shatzenberg brothers, Hyman and Morty, who were real brothers, as well as Shlomo and Saul, a brother-in-law and a cousin who also worked at the firm but who were in other cities at other branches most of the time. Tonight, a big shipment was going over to Antwerp, where Saul would meet it, and the office had been busy weighing, recording, packing, and securing the load, which was locked in a strongbox. But all Stan had to worry about was getting the box on the truck when it arrived downstairs. The damn thing weighed a ton, far more than the incredibly valuable stones inside it, so valuable they were weighed in carats, of which there were almost 142 in one ounce. The strongbox was basically a transportable safe made of special steel alloys that it would take forever to cut through, locked with a combination that only Morty upstairs and Saul, who was flying separately, would know.

The box was state-of-the-art, but the loading procedure was old-school and simple, and Stan believed simple was best. When word came that the truck was approaching, he had Jimmy, his strongest guy, push the box onto a dolly, and they rode down together in the service elevator. Jimmy lifted, his biceps bulging the sleeves of his uniform to the bursting point.

Then Jimmy waited behind the locked street door while Stan went out. He checked the sidewalk—just the usual chaos—and then stood in the street in front of the hydrant. Because the fire hydrant was in front of their building, the space was almost always clear. If anyone else was there, Stan would have the truck wait, but usually it was nothing but a cab dropping off or a town car picking up.

Today it was clear, and he waved when he saw the truck coming. They pulled in, and he nodded hello at the guard on the passenger side, then went back to the service door. The truck's rear doors opened and the guy in there hopped out and lowered the ramp. Then Stan used his key to open the service door and told Jimmy okay, holding the door open while he rolled the strongbox across the sidewalk to where the other guard would help him push it onto the truck. It all went nice and simple, the way Stan liked it.

Liam and Juno were parked on Fifth in the ambulance. It was a real ambulance that Liam had borrowed from a garage that serviced emergency vehicles; the manager was cooperative and owed Liam's friends money. They'd changed the emblem on the side, but it was legit enough to pass muster as they idled, eating gyros and pretending to be EMTs on a break eating gyros, a traffic cop even nodding hey in passing. This freaked Juno out a bit, but any interactions with any kind of law freaked him out a bit and Liam was having a ball. Juno did like the uniforms—the crisp white shirt and navy pants with a crease. The stethoscope he wore around his neck was a nice touch, and the little radios on their shoulder were convenient: they were connected to the others' earpieces and mics.

Juno had to admit the setup was perfect for him. He'd been able to rig all his gear in the back, including the satellite antenna, without worrying about concealment, since ambulances were full of tech shit anyway, and he had his laptop mounted on the console up front. Then, just a few minutes after four, Joe's voice came over the box:

"Okay guys, time to roll."

Liam shoved the last of his gyro in his mouth and Juno frowned as he wiped his fingers on his freshly pressed pants before putting the ambo in drive. Juno brought his screen to life. They were rolling.

As Jimmy and the guard from the truck pushed the strong-box up the ramp, Stan stood in front of the building and watched the crowd. He focused on the people who flowed along the sidewalk from his left, knowing the guard from the truck was covering the other side. That was when the two Hasids came by—one older, one younger and shorter, both heavily bearded and in the usual black clothes and hats. An everyday sight on this block. At first Stan paid them no mind. Then the old one came right up and started talking in one of those thick accents: "Excuse me, sir, are you Jewish?"

"Me?" Stan asked, taken aback. "No."

"You're not Jewish?" the man pressed him. "You look Jewish."

"I do?"

The Hasid turned to his young sidekick. "Doesn't he look Jewish?"

The little one joined in. He sounded Russian, with a higher teenage voice. "You do! Your mother, maybe she is Jewish?" They were up close now, Stan realized, blocking his view of Jimmy and the strongbox. Then the ambulance that had pulled up flipped on its siren, no doubt getting a call.

"Step aside," he told the Hasids. "I'm working here." Stan was thinking about how they'd let the ambo go first before the truck pulled out.

"And so are we," the Hasid said, refusing to budge. "Doing God's work."

Annoyed, Stan tried to push through, when a jolt of lightning shot up his side. The absurd thought, "Did that little Hasid just taser me?" ran through his mind, right before he blacked out.

*　*　*

When Stan opened the service door, Jimmy had pushed the strongbox out like always, the dolly's rubber tires jittering over the sidewalk. The guard from inside the truck, who had hopped out to lower the ramp, helped him hump it over the curb, then climbed back up into the truck and pulled while Jimmy pushed it up the ramp. Neither of them looked at the ambulance that pulled up alongside them blocking them from view.

Meanwhile, Jon had stepped down from the passenger side of the truck and was keeping an eye on the sidewalk, watching his left while Stan kept watch on the right. Normal foot traffic passed by, a random assortment of the human circus that filled Midtown Manhattan on a weekday afternoon, and barely anyone paid much attention to the armored truck or the guards. Nor did anyone, including Jon, take any notice when the ambulance suddenly flipped on its sirens. This was New York after all. Every day was an emergency. But then something unusual did happen. All of a sudden, Stan, who was the old-fashioned drill sergeant type, seemed to be in an argument. With a couple of Hasids! Jon had to smile at that. And then, the next second, Stan was on the ground and the Hasids were yelling for help.

"Help, somebody! He's having a heart attack!" the bigger one yelled. The little one rushed up to Jon.

"Officer, hurry. This man—he just collapsed!"

Jon couldn't believe it. Stan was having some kind of heart attack or something and this Hasid thought he was a cop. He took a couple of steps forward, hesitating, trying to think what to do as other people, concerned or just curious, gathered around Stan. Maybe those ambulance guys could help?

Just then a bike messenger in a hooded sweatshirt, speeding along the sidewalk where he shouldn't have even been, zoomed by and, while the eyes of the passersby were on Stan, swung his helmet and slammed Jon hard across the back of the head, knocking him off his feet and into the crowd around Stan. Stunned, Jon rolled on the sidewalk, trying to get his bearings.

Meanwhile, a young Asian delivery guy in track pants, a white kitchen shirt, a wool cap and the kind of thin rubber gloves kitchen workers used when preparing food, had been walking down the block. While Jon, distracted by the Hasid, stepped away from the truck toward Stan and got clobbered himself, the delivery guy came up, pulling his cap down into a ski mask. Drawing a 9 mm Beretta from his paper delivery bag, he hopped into the truck's open and now-unguarded passenger door, sitting next to Mark. Mark, unfortunately, had been distracted by the loud siren that suddenly blared from the ambulance beside him and was looking out the window to his left, wondering why the ambulance didn't move. Before he even noticed anything, the delivery guy had grabbed his right hand, preventing him from reaching for his gun or the truck's ignition keys, and shoved a gun in his face.

"Don't move or I'll kill you. Understand?"

Petrified, Mark nodded. The gunman removed Mark's weapon from the holster and then grabbed his radio. "Now get out," he ordered.

John (the guys called him H, because he was the new guard on the team; he didn't mind) helped Jimmy, the buffed-up guard from the client, push the strongbox up the ramp and into the back of the truck. Well, really Jimmy pushed, H just kind of yanked from the top and made sure it didn't tip over or slide off the dolly. Still, when Jimmy, with a grunt, muscled it off the ramp and onto the truck, H had his rifle slung around back so he could help, which, he would realize later, made it pretty tough to reach if he needed it. So he really had no time to do anything when the Hasidic teenager jumped onto the truck and pointed a gun at them.

He seemed young, the Hasid—he and Jimmy would agree about that later—with a thick black beard, black frame glasses, and the usual hat and coat. They all dress like old men, but this one was littler, and his voice was still a bit high, though with one of those very thick accents, Russian or Yiddish or whatever. Also—and this struck both witnesses—the unfortunate young man seemed to have a hump, like a hunchback from the movies, though it didn't seem to slow him down any.

"Don't move or I will kill you both," the kid yelled, and they both froze as another bigger and older Hasid in a gray beard and the same black outfit appeared. He pushed the ramp up, climbed onboard, and pulled the doors shut. Then he pointed another gun at them, a Sig 9 mm, before saying "go," seemingly into his coat. Instantly, the truck lurched forward and was moving.

"On your knees," the old one barked, and they kneeled, the truck careening around a corner, and the younger one quickly removed their weapons and radios. "Facedown," he ordered in his higher voice. He guarded them, gun pointed at their heads, while the older one, after pulling on doctor's gloves, bound their wrists behind their backs with plastic ties, then their ankles. He took two small canvas bags from his pocket and fitted them over their heads, pulling the drawstrings snug. Now H saw nothing, but he was not choked and could breathe easily through the fabric. As the truck bounced along, jostling him, he realized there was still a siren blaring nearby. He wondered if it was the cops, coming to rescue him. It was not.

After Cash pushed the driver out of the armored truck, he slid into his seat, shut the door, and put on his seat belt, while Josh got in the passenger seat beside him and shut his door, likewise buckling up and sliding on a pair of gloves. Cash put the truck in drive and checked the side mirror, where the ambo, driven he knew by Liam, was blocking traffic and leaving them room to pull out, while also keeping up a distracting racket with its siren. A few seconds later, Joe, talkative as ever, came over the radio: "Go." Cash went, stomping the accelerator and, as the big truck engine roared, the truck shot down the block and made a screeching right onto Sixth Avenue, just as the light went yellow.

In the ambulance, Liam was set to follow, but the driver from the armored truck, seeming badly shaken by the holdup, was just standing in front of the ambulance, despite the deafening siren.

"We got to move," Juno told him, fingers flying over his keyboard.

"I know," Liam said. "Just give us a few seconds, if you can."

"Can do," Juno said as Liam turned on the loudspeaker: "Clear the way," his voice boomed out in a pretty good copy of a loudmouth New York accent. "This is an emergency."

The guard jumped, looked over as if just noticing the ambulance, and hurried to the sidewalk, where he began frantically trying to explain to passersby what had happened. Liam hit the gas and the ambo flew forward, making the same wild turn uptown onto Sixth, but he did not even bother to check the light. He knew it was still yellow, because Juno had held it for him. And now, as they cleared the intersection, Juno turned it red, letting the Uptown traffic surge in behind them.

22

As soon as the two guards inside the truck were bound and hooded, Yelena took off her beard. It was insanely itchy, and she was already imagining the breakout she would have to treat later. She put it in her hat and handed that, along with her gun, to Joe, who sat on the jump seat, where he could keep watch over the prisoners at his feet. Next Yelena pulled on some thin surgeon's gloves and removed a stethoscope from her pocket, sliding it in her ears. She then cleared her mind of other concerns and got to work on the strongbox.

As Cash crossed Forty-Eighth Street heading north, a cop car emerged from the west, siren on, and began pursuing the truck. In the ambulance, Liam cut his siren to make them less conspicuous and hung back, staying a few car lengths behind the cop.

"One on your tail," Liam told Cash over the radio.

"Got it," Cash said. "Hold the greens."

"Will do," Juno said and had the light stay green as the armored truck, the cop, the ambulance, and a few cabs and private cars who were riding in their wake sped through. Then he turned it red and crosstown traffic resumed. Meanwhile he opened a flood of green lights running up the avenue before them, creating an open road. While the traffic ahead rolled forward, clearing the way, the side streets were held, and the reds Juno turned on behind them made it hard for other cops to join the chase.

It also let Cash build up some real speed. And as they raced toward Fifty-First Street, passing Radio City Music Hall, he carefully checked both ways and in both of his side mirrors. The air was full of the angry honks of the drivers being held, which threatened to drown out the cop's siren.

"Ready?" he asked Juno over the radio.

"Say when," Juno responded.

"Now," Cash said and yanked the wheel.

Juno unleashed the traffic, turning all lights green.

Careening left, Cash drove the truck up onto the sidewalk, plowing through a garbage can and a food cart and scattering frantic pedestrians, then bumped back over the curb onto the street, which was now clear running west. Meanwhile, the angry bottled-up traffic pushed forward into the intersection, and the cop, frantic at finding the way blocked and with more cars coming up behind him, slammed on his breaks and yanked his wheel left. But it was too late to make the turn Cash had made and he skidded, sideswiping a passing car. Liam, meanwhile, turned his siren back on and followed more slowly in the path Cash had cleared, drawing shocked stares but no interference as the ambulance lumbered over the curb and back onto Fifty-First, trailing the armored truck, about a half block behind.

* * *

In back, Yelena was kneeling in front of the strongbox, slowly turning the dial as she listened to the tumblers. By listening carefully through the stethoscope and finding the dial's parked position, she had been able to count the number of times the lock clicked as it passed that certain spot on the dial. She paused, pulled a small notebook with graph paper from her pocket, and wrote the number 3. That was how many numbers there were in the combination. Now she set up a graph, with an x-axis running down the left margin and a y-axis across the bottom. She drew two lines, both reaching from the lowest to the highest number on the dial. Then she reset the dial at zero and went to work, concentrating intensely on the slow and methodical task of finding each number in the combination.

Meanwhile Joe watched her work, hair hanging over her weird hump, while he kept an eye on the guards, holding his gun loosely, barrel pointed down at the floor. It wasn't just Yelena's knowledge or skill he admired; that could be learned, if you had enough patience and the right teacher. It was also her ability to focus on such a meticulous task and stay calm under these conditions. That's why she was a pro and why he'd insisted on using her for this job. The truck bounced over a pothole and one of the guards, the big one, moaned; Yelena didn't flinch. She heard two clicks close together and wrote down a number. That was the first one. Two more to go.

"My back hurts," the guard groaned. "And my wrists are sore." Joe kicked him.

"Shut up," he said. "Or I will shut you up with a bullet."

He shut up.

Both vehicles turned south on Seventh now, and as they recrossed Fiftieth, going back downtown, two more cop cars joined the party. Juno kept the lights green while Liam hung back with the rest of the pack behind the cops, it being standard driving procedure in New York to follow any emergency vehicle in the hopes of riding their tail through traffic, like a biker drafting behind the leader in a race. They moved through Forty-Ninth and Forty-Eighth at a good clip, but as they crossed Forty-Seventh Street, completing their circle, Cash was forced to brake; they were headed toward the crossing where Seventh Avenue met Broadway. That was Times Square: tourist insanity and a black hole of traffic. There would be nothing Juno or even God could do. By the time they crossed Forty-Sixth, they had slowed to the normal Manhattan crawl, and now they could see it looming before them at Forty-Fifth, total gridlock that would block them in whatever the lights said. The cops knew it, too, and they closed in, ready to stop their cars and jump out for the arrest.

"How's it going back there?" Josh asked his radio and in the back Joe leaned toward Yelena.

"How's it going?" he asked softly. She held up a hand for silence. Joe waited, muting his radio. She wrote down another number. That was two.

"A few minutes more," she said.

"A few more minutes," Joe told Josh.

"Ready?" Josh asked Cash, who nodded, then blew a bubble, while cruising straight ahead, toward the wall of traffic with the two cop cars crawling right up his ass. Josh spoke into his mic: "Okay back there, we're ready to make the drop-off."

Cash made a left onto Forty-Sixth Street, nice and slow. He even signaled, almost as if he were pulling over for the cops, the way you would for a ticket. He waved an arm out the window. Both cop cars followed, just inches behind, one right in back of the other. They knew they had them. Then the rear doors of the armored car opened and two guards with hoods over their heads came rolling out, landing right on the front cop's hood. Panicked, he braked, and the other cop, with nowhere to go, banged into him from behind. As the armored car made off, a bearded Hasidic man in black pulled the rear doors shut.

Yelena scribbled down the third number and took a deep breath as she removed the stethoscope from her ears. Now she had the three numbers; all that remained was to try each possible combination. Behind her, Joe secured the doors and then got undressed. He removed his beard and hat and then took a few items from the long coat's deep pockets before removing that, too. He pulled the black pants off over his black sneakers. Underneath he was in cargo shorts and a polo shirt. He fitted a golf cap onto his head. Then he unfolded his knife and reached for one of the cash bags. He had an idea that might buy a few extra seconds.

Cash turned right on Forty-Third Street, then right again up Sixth Avenue, driving in circles like someone looking for a parking space, which in essence he was. As he crossed Forty-Fourth heading north he glimpsed cop cars making their way through the traffic toward him.

"We're running out of street here," he told Josh.

"What's up?" Josh asked his radio.

In the back, Yelena had tried three of the six possible combinations. She methodically crossed it off her list and then carefully turned the dial again. *Click*. Finally she smiled as the door opened.

"Open," she told Joe without even looking back.

"We're in," Joe told Josh.

"Thank God," Josh said over the radio.

Yelena moved quickly, removing the case of diamonds and handing it to Joe. Then she pulled a pair of sandals from her pockets and took off her black clothes and shoes while Joe opened the case, which was lined in cushioned velvet, and transferred the diamonds to a felt bag. There was no time to even think about the value or beauty of what he was holding, but for a moment it was like a broken star glittered in his hand. He pulled the bag shut and got a roll of duct tape from the pocket of his cargo shorts.

Underneath her long black jacket, Yelena had a light cotton dress tucked into the pants. The hump strapped to her back was a foam lump made to look like a pregnant belly. Joe duct-taped the bag of diamonds to the inside of the belly and then, while she fitted it properly under the dress, he dumped all their other stuff into the strongbox, forcing in as much as he could. Then he squirted a small can of lighter fluid on it and tossed the can it too, before lighting it up. The insides of the strongbox burst into flame like it was a barbeque grill. He let it get going good, then shut and locked the door. Meanwhile, Yelena wiped the guns down and then put on her sandals.

"Ready?" Joe asked, handing her one of the cash bags he had sliced open.

She nodded.

"We're ready," he told Josh, who replied, "Hold on."

They held on.

Cash headed uptown on Sixth Avenue, picking up speed as he moved toward the Rockefeller subway station on the corner of Forty-Seventh, a large, busy station where the B, D, F, and M trains all stopped. He could see cops in the rearview now, lights flashing, and there were others pulling out from Forty-Seventh Street to cut him off. There was no way out.

"Time to park this heap," he told Josh and then spit his gum out the window as he veered right.

"Hold on," Josh said over the radio to Joe and Yelena and then did the same, tucking his head down and bracing his arms against the dashboard as Cash drove up onto the sidewalk, leaning on the horn and chasing pedestrians out of the way, and then rammed the truck down the stairs and into the entrance to the station, while a cloud of money burst from the rear door.

23

First there was terror. The truck hit the steps at a good speed, smashing the fender, crumpling the hood, and rupturing the radiator in the process. Folks on the sidewalk, as well as those in the station, ran for their lives, but the truck had lost momentum and they got away with no problem. Like a wounded beast, it hobbled down the stairs, scraping along the handrail, before coming to rest, nose down at the bottom.

After the terror came the greed. When the truck bounced onto the sidewalk and began lumbering toward the subway, Joe had kicked a back door open and shaken out a bag of cash, sending it flying in their updraft. As a result, the same crowd that had scattered in blind panic immediately surged back the moment the truck halted, scrambling and fighting for the money, chasing flapping bills in the air like butterflies or crawling around on the ground. Inside the station was a similar scene. The truck had landed with a crash, tilted forward on the steps, and everyone had fled as if escaping a monster. Cash and Josh bailed immediately, leaving their guns in the truck. They ran into the station and jumped the turnstiles, ditching ski mask, bandanna, and white jacket in a trash can along the way, so that they were only in track pants and T-shirts. Josh had grabbed his backpack, and he pulled an MP player from it, as they met the curious crowd that was now pushing toward not away from the crash.

Meanwhile, as soon as the truck crashed, Joe and Yelena had hopped out of the back door, Joe waving the second cash bag and scattering money like it was chicken feed as they ran away. He tossed the empty bag and, as they entered the station, they both removed their gloves and began yelling for help and for someone to call the police. But as soon as people saw cash they broke into a run, surging around Joe and Yelena like a flood from a burst dam, ignoring them completely and scrambling to snatch up money, while the people who were following the money trail from the street came down the stairs, and the two crowds met. It was pandemonium.

Joe took Yelena by the hand and they made their way through the long station as people around them ran wildly either to or from the crash or else simply tried to reach their trains, oblivious to what had happened as only New Yorkers intent on minding their own business can be. As though taking a stroll in a hurricane, they walked calmly through the chaos they had created, untouched by the storm that whirled around them. Now the law had arrived in force, and cops were coming in the other entrances. Some ran past Joe and Yelena, yelling for them to step aside as they raced to the crime scene, others took up posts by the exits. No doubt the station was locked down, and even if it were not, trying to flee upstairs and out onto the street would be hopeless, as police and emergency personnel swarmed all over. The other option was to try to get on a train. But the trains in the station were being held. Nothing was moving, and anyone who tried to get off, from frustration or curiosity, was being accosted by police.

But Joe and Yelena didn't try either of those options. They took a third choice. They hurried right up to a cop, a big, heavyset white guy with a red, sweaty face, who was standing guard in front of an exit staircase. People milled all around, waiting, pacing, talking on their cell phones or bothering the cop about what was happening and when they could leave.

"Officer! Officer!" Joe yelled in his most panicked voice, pressing forward with Yelena by the hand. "Please, you have to help us. My wife is about to have a baby!"

"It's showtime, folks!"

Cash shouted happily as he strode onto the subway car. Josh jumped around beside him, holding up his player. A few people idly looked over. Most did not.

"I know ya'll are stuck here and prolly feeling grumpy," Cash chattered on, undaunted. "But have no fear! The Jam-It-Up Twins is here to lighten your load, brighten your day, and show you the way, by providing some free entertainment while you wait for the popo to do they thing. And by free, I do mean that donations will be gratefully accepted. God bless you, respect to all, and have a safe journey."

"Bless!" Josh yelled, kissing the first two fingers of his left hand, holding it out like a benediction, and then tapping his chest with his right fist and yelling, "'Spect!" He reached for the box and hit Play. He was letting Cash do the talking because of his noticeable and possibly memorable accent, but as the music came thumping and ringing, he began to move with the rhythm, shaking his hips and waving his arms in snaky patterns.

"Take it, baby," Cash told him. "Show them how we do it in New York City!"

Then Josh began to dance. He did the robot, then started popping and locking, sending waves up and down his arms and legs while his head jerked around on his neck. He moon-walked down the car backward and then did a split. A few blond children, French tourists, burst into applause and an older couple from Korea took a picture. He shook like a rag doll, letting his head loll while his arms flew crazily and his legs flopped in and out at the knee like he was double-jointed and greased. He jumped up, right over a French kid's head, and grabbed the bar, then swung his legs over and landed back on his feet. More people clapped and a black man who'd been playing a game on his phone shouted: "You got it! You got it!"

Now people were clapping along to the beat as Josh skipped up and down the car, turning a cartwheel and then, for his big finish, ran straight at the closed rear door and summersaulted himself over backward, landing in a crouch with his crossed arms showing two peace signs.

"Peace!" he and Cash shouted in unison and the crowd went wild. People shook Josh's hand while Cash walked up and down collecting the money. They got twelve dollars in singles and a handful of coins.

Then a cop stepped on.

"Hey!" he called to them. "What the hell's going on here?"

"Just working officer," Cash said, looking innocent. Josh smiled sheepishly.

"You can't be doing this here," he told them. "It's illegal."

The crowd stuck up for them. Several people booed the cop and others started telling him how the dancing had cheered them up, relieving the tedium, bringing everyone together.

"Okay, okay, whatever," the cop said, not wanting to deal with this. A real criminal investigation was happening, a big-time case, and here he was stuck dealing with kids. "I'll let you off with a warning this time. Let's go."

He led Cash and Josh off the train and over to the nearest exit. "Hey," he told the officer standing guard. "Let these two by. I cleared them. They're just hassling passengers."

The second cop nodded absently, not really listening, and let them by.

"Thanks officer," Cash said. "Have a blessed day."

"Yeah, yeah," the cop said. "Just don't let me see you here again."

"Having a baby?" the cop asked, incredulously. "You mean like right now?"

"Yes, sir. I guess it was all the noise and people yelling. But she thinks she's going into labor."

"My contractions are three minutes apart," Yelena said, holding her belly in both hands. "Oh, my God, here comes

159

one." She started to moan loudly, grabbing Joe's hand hard with one hand and clutching the cop's hand with the other.

"Holy jeeze," he shouted and instinctively pulled his hand away.

"Don't you know how to deliver a baby?" Joe asked him, making his voice high and panicky. Yelena moaned louder.

"Sort of," the cop said. "They showed us a video. But it was hard to watch."

"It's coming . . ." Yelena groaned.

The cop grabbed his radio. "Let me call an ambulance," he said.

"We did already," Joe said. "It's upstairs. But no one will let us out."

"Come on," he said and made his way through the crowd, with Joe behind him and Yelena waddling along, holding Joe's hand. "Step aside folks. Let us through."

They made it upstairs to the sidewalk, where cops had a barricade across the entrance and more barricades closing off the sidewalk and street. Across the avenue, Joe could see the ambulance waiting. He waved to Liam, who waved back.

"There it is," he told the cop.

"Right," he said, with the tone of a man eager to unload a problem. "Let them through," he told the cops minding the barricade. "This lady's having a baby."

The cops quickly moved the sawhorses back, letting them hurry by, Joe holding Yelena and helping her along. Juno came running around the side of the ambulance, cap on and stethoscope dangling, and opened its back doors. He helped Yelena up, and then, after Joe climbed on, he pulled the doors shut behind them. Liam hit the siren and slowly pulled out, as the cops lifted the barricades and waved them through.

Liam drove east, killing the siren as soon as they were a couple of blocks away, and when they reached the quieter stretches east of Lexington, he turned into the empty loading dock of a gigantic building and stopped. Meanwhile, Yelena had peeled off her dress and removed the belly. Down to her bra and panties, she grabbed her cutoff jean shorts, which were waiting in the ambulance, and pulled on a white tank top through which the red straps of her bra could be discerned. She kept the sandals. Joe changed, too, back into his jeans and black T-shirt, and he changed the sneakers he had on for his usual Chucks. Yelena picked up a small purse she'd brought along, and Joe gave her the sack with the diamonds to stash in there. When Liam knocked on the interior wall of the ambulance, signaling all clear, they climbed out and walked off together, headed east. Juno, now in a long white T-shirt over the blue uniform pants and a Brooklyn Nets cap, climbed out, too, a backpack full of computer gear slung over his shoulder. Looking like a college kid on his way from class at Hunter, he walked west toward the train.

Liam waited for them to go, then pulled out and went to return the ambulance. With the decals removed and the interior cleaned up, the real owner would never know a thing.

Joe and Yelena walked toward the river. On First Avenue, they had a car parked and waiting, a nondescript Toyota Corolla. Joe got behind the wheel and Yelena got in beside him. As he started the engine, she rolled her window down and lit a smoke.

"Put your belt on," Joe said. "And do you have to smoke that in here?"

She blew it at him. "Relax," she said. "I'm not really pregnant." But she did put on her belt. Joe got on the FDR Drive and was immediately stuck in rush hour traffic. It took them over an hour to get home.

PART III

PART III

24

As soon as Donna got the call, she knew she was in for a long night.

"Armored car heist in Midtown. All hands on deck."

She grabbed her gun and her bag and her FBI windbreaker and texted her mom as she ran, asking her to feed Larissa and stay with her until she got back. There were some downsides to living across the hall from your mom, but this was one of the perks. She rode uptown in a Chevy stuffed with agents, but the scene was pretty much covered by the time she arrived, and the carnival was in full swing. News crews with their satellite-equipped vans jockeyed for camera space, so all the reporters could look like they were right there first on the scene while really they were lined up beside one another. Crowds of gawkers buzzed around, especially since this was a tourist hot zone, making it one more stop on the ride. In fact, actual tour buses were trying to drive by and get as close as possible to the action. The traffic was apocalyptic. A crime scene that meandered over a dozen city blocks with various bits of evidence scattered about and a shut-down subway station, in Midtown, during rush hour: it was the perfect shit storm. While FBI agents and NYPD detectives were mainly puttering about looking puzzled or bemused, the uniforms—regular NYPD, traffic, transit—looked about one honk away from total freak-out.

In the subway station, they'd set up lights, and the wrecked truck, sprawled facedown on a staircase, had the unreal feeling of a movie set. It would be towed away to a lab eventually, but for now gloved and bootied agents climbed all over it, taking pictures and scrapings. Evidence was being laid out on a tarp to be measured, photographed, and packed for transport to forensics. Donna squatted down next to Janet Kim, a forensic pathologist whose lab was down the hall from her own basement den.

"Finally get out of the office and we're back underground," she told Janet.

"I know," she said, pausing to take a photo. "Then I take the PATH home to Jersey City."

"What's that?" Donna pointed at a nasty-looking item, some kind of gas-pressured sharp metal spring. "Some new kind of weapon?"

"We think it might be a corkscrew."

"Oh." Four handguns were lined up. "They left these behind?"

"Yup. Two in front, two in back. All wiped clean and untraceable. All fully loaded, too. Not a shot fired."

"Pros then."

"Total pros. The people who did this, they'd never be dumb enough to get caught walking around with an illegal weapon. You can always get a gun when you need one. Unfortunately."

"Witness statements?"

"Nothing or less than nothing. The guards on the street were knocked out from behind. The driver . . ." She looked around, then called to a short, Latino man with a thick black mustache: "Hey Ernesto, show Donna that sketch of the suspect."

Frowning, he held up a sketchbook. It showed a head covered in a black ski mask, with just holes for the eyes and mouth. "You're looking for a man with brown eyes," he announced.

"Roger that," Donna told him.

"Now the guys in back," Janet said, checking in both directions and then hitting her slender vape pipe, "that's a different story."

"Good descriptions?"

"Oh yeah. And they mostly agree. It was Hasids."

"Hasids?"

"Right. Two Hasidic males in the black coats, hats, the whole deal. Both heavily bearded. A big one who seemed older and a littler one who they both thought sounded like a teenage boy."

"Like a father and son team of Hasidic bandits?"

"Exactly. But that's not even the weird part."

"It's not?"

"Wait for it. The son . . ."

"Yeah?"

"Is a hunchback."

"Get the fuck out of here."

"I shit you not."

Donna shook her head. "That's pretty nuts."

"The whole caper is nuts. What about the chase? They just drove around the neighborhood in circles, at speeds up to maybe thirty miles per hour at most. Then crashed. What kind of getaway plan is that?"

"Maybe the only one possible in Midtown traffic?"

Janet nodded. "Maybe so. That would fit with the inside-job theory. Look at this."

She led her to the next tarp, where a strongbox sat open. The inside was scorched but the outside looked undamaged.

"It looks like they opened it with the combination, took the diamonds, then used it as a burner to destroy evidence."

"Clever. And it was intact?"

"Oh yeah. They relocked it. We had to contact one of the owners to get the combo. No way they could cut it open anyway, under those conditions. A box like this would take a welding torch, acetylene tank, a special saw, masks, safety gloves. You'd never get that all onto the truck fast enough. You'd have to steal the whole thing and do it later."

"So you're thinking they knew the combination."

"Right. That's the theory. Someone tipped them off. Although the Shatzenbergs claim only two people know the combo."

Donna peered at the mess of burned items that had been removed from the safe.

"What about all this?"

"We're just getting started, and I'm going to have to get it all back to my lab, but some of that looks like black fabric."

"So maybe disguises after all? To blend in maybe? But I mean, then why dress as a hunchback? Unless that part's real?"

Janet shrugged. "Beats me."

"What's that?" Donna pointed at a short piece of curved metal with a metal disc in the center. It was covered in black soot with charred matter at the tips.

Janet moved it closer with tweezers, then took a photo. "I don't know. A tool? A weapon?"

Donna leaned in and peered at the mysterious object. "Maybe it's another corkscrew."

As they headed upstairs, Donna and Janet noted some new arrivals: two men in dark suits, one taking photos, and a woman in a skirt and jacket taking notes on an iPad, while the older man spoke in hushed tones to the bureau's agent in charge, though unlike everyone else on the scene, they wore no credentials of any kind.

"Son of a bitch," Donna muttered.

Janet nodded and took out her vape pen. "Spooks. I wonder why. There's nothing here to suggest anything but a straight-up, old-school heist. It's refreshing actually." She drew on her pen. "Guess they're just sniffing around."

"Not him. If he's here, something stinks."

Janet raised an eyebrow. "You've crossed paths before?"

"Yeah," Donna said. "In divorce court."

"Agent Powell," she said. He turned from his colleagues and smiled.

"Agent Zamora," he answered, smiling at his ex-wife. "What a pleasant surprise."

"Wish I could say the same," she said, as his companions wandered discreetly away. "Why is the CIA here? Last I checked, New York City was still in the United States. I know it doesn't feel that way sometimes."

He chuckled. "Don't worry. We're not interfering. The investigation is local PD and FBI. But we are looking at a possible overseas connection."

"Like what?"

"Like organized crime cooperating with Middle Eastern terror groups."

Donna frowned. "How does that figure? It's cheaper and easier for them to rob someone over there than here."

Powell shrugged, showing his empty palms. "Maybe you're right. Like I said, we're just following up on a lead." He smiled again. "Believe me. If it pans out, you'll be the first to know. Or one of them anyway."

25

They had the celebration at a Korean restaurant, a fancy barbeque place located in the penthouse of a tall building in the Korean section of Flushing. The possible attention—and curiosity—that such a mixed bag of villains all partying together might draw made a secret, neutral location desirable. So Gio, after checking in with Uncle Chen out of respect, got in touch with Mr. Kim, the Korean crime boss whose domain they were in, and arranged for this private dining room and a personal assurance of absolute discretion among the staff.

After scattering to handle their final tasks, the crew arrived separately, Cash and Juno each wandering in through the downstairs shops—a sporting goods store, a couple of clothing places, nail and hair spas—Liam and Josh in separate taxis that pulled right into the building's parking entrance. Joe and Yelena had stashed the diamonds, then driven their clean car here, parked it inside, and rode the elevator to the top.

Mr. Kim had gone all out. The private dining room commanded a grand city view, and a team of robed waitresses moved constantly, preparing the open grills, laying out what seemed to be a hundred different metal bowls full of delicacies, and keeping glasses full of soju or scotch. Joe had a Coke. Mr. Kim, a handsome man in a black suit with his steel-gray hair combed back, appeared to make a toast and thank Gio for the honor of choosing his place, and Gio made a toast thanking him. Kim also announced that they were all comped at the spa a few floors below, which offered everything from massages and body scrubs to elaborate wraps and straight-razor shaves in the barber shop. Then he politely faded away to let them party in peace without the bosses present, as did Gio, though he pulled Joe onto the balcony first.

"About that other thing," he said.

Joe nodded. The others had all dressed for the occasion, Liam and Josh in suits, Cash in a new leather jacket and three-hundred-dollar jeans held up with a Gucci belt buckle; even Juno was in head-to-toe Bathing Ape. Yelena wore a simple but slinky black dress that showed off her shoulders, with a slit up the side revealing her stocking top and her hair down for once. Joe was in the same black T-shirt and jeans he'd been in that afternoon.

"I heard from my guy on the police force," Gio told him. "There's already word out about the heist."

"Like what?"

"An OC connection. My name mentioned or my family anyway." Gio gritted his teeth. He had an overwhelming urge to kill something, so he strangled the straw from his gin and tonic, twisting it into contortions. "We're leaking like a fucking sieve."

"Yeah. Though it occurs to me . . ."

"What?"

"For the moment, maybe that's not so bad. We had Carlo tell the seller he was getting the stones, right? So a high-profile diamond heist from a legit dealer, lots of talk on the street about it, and the law talking about a crime family's involvement. It all just helps lure the seller out into the open, right? If he's al Qaeda or another terror group, then his main fear is Homeland Security or some other kind of sting. From his point of view, it's far less likely to be a setup if the law's own snitches are putting it on gangsters."

Having tied the straw into torturous knots, Gio dropped it in his empty drink. "You're saying it's like a disinformation campaign."

"Right. Being leaked by us through back channels."

"Somehow this isn't making me feel better," Gio said. He gazed through the glass door at the party. "And why is that kid Juno eating shrimp instead of busy setting my rat traps?"

"Just take some deep breaths," Joe said. He slid the door open and waved Juno over, then shut it behind him as he trotted out. "Mr. Caprisi is waiting for an update on that project."

"Right," he said, standing with his brightly colored sneakers together as if at attention. He seemed to be resisting the urge to salute. "Ready to report, sir."

"Easy. It's not the army, kid," Gio said. "Just tell me what's what."

"Yes, sir. I mean Gio. I mean Mr. Caprisi." He cleared his throat. "This afternoon I took all the IP addresses and phone numbers and passcodes you gave me and hacked into your systems. I did it from the backdoor so no one would tip."

"English," Gio said.

"Right. Even though you gave me all the info, I still snuck in so no one would know I was there. Then I created a program that would search through all the records, looking for patterns, who calls or texts who, who emails who, and when. Then I can generate a report." He paused. "Soon. Sir."

Gio considered this. "That's smart. Thank you." He held out his hand.

Juno grinned and shook it. "Thank you!"

"Okay, thanks, Juno," Joe said. "I'll see you back inside."

Juno glanced back at the party. "Damn, the porterhouse is coming." He scampered off. Pete, who'd been waiting by the door, stepped out, holding a phone.

"Phone for you, Boss."

"Who's calling?"

Pete cleared his throat and spoke into the phone: "Whom, might I ask, is calling?"

He looked up. "It's Paul."

"You don't have to say 'whom,' Pete."

"I thought it sounded classier, Boss."

"In grammar, correct is classy. Whom is the object case, understand? Who is the subject case. So you can just say, 'Who is calling.'"

Confused, Pete held out the phone. "Paul."

Gio sighed, taking the phone. "Okay, thanks. Good work, Pete." Pete turned to go. "Don't pass up the spa," Gio said, hugging Joe. "It's terrific. I might stop off myself and get a massage. Try to get rid of this tension."

"Have fun," Joe said. "And be careful."

Gio hesitated a moment, as if about to speak, then thought better of it, talking into the phone as he walked away. Paul had booked a room in the hotel under a fake name and was waiting for him there.

The party progressed from dinner to karaoke. Cash sang Tom Petty's "Refugee," Juno sang "Purple Rain," Liam did the obligatory "My Way." Yelena wanted Joe to do the "Summer Nights" duet from *Grease*, but when Joe claimed not to know it, Josh stepped in and belted it out, along with some impressively Travolta-esque moves. Everyone cheered and drank. Then, as Cash was launching into his impression of Elvis singing "Suspicious Minds," Juno pulled Joe aside and showed him his tablet.

"Look what we got," he said. He'd pulled up the Carlo email account. Right after the job, Joe had told him to write to the seller, saying they had the goods. He'd responded: *I heard the news. Thought that was you. Ready to show samples to experts, both sides. Tomorrow.*

He went on to suggest a meeting at Sherm's early the next afternoon. Each party would bring a sample of their goods and one man for backup.

"Good," Joe said, patting Juno on the back. "Tell him we're on. And ask for a name to call him."

Almost immediately, the answer came back: *Felix. Though I won't say if that is my real name.*

Joe and Juno answered: *Who says my real name is Carlo? See you there.*

"Juno! You're up!" Cash shouted, waving the karaoke mic. Juno's song, David Bowie's "Changes," was about to start. He dashed to the front. As he began singing, Joe leaned over and whispered to Yelena: "What do you say, comrade? Ready for a shvitz?"

With a smile, she took his hand. They went downstairs to the spa.

Across town, Felix, too, needed to unwind. In general, when he wasn't working, he preferred luxury hotels for their room service, among other things. But on this business trip to New York, he saw the wisdom in using Airbnb to book a private apartment under an assumed name and pay with a card linked to a dummy shell corporation. The apartment itself was most likely owned by another shell: high-end real estate is ideal for hiding and securing illicit funds.

Say you're a Russian oligarch or an international arms dealer or just a plain old small-time dictator from a two-bit country that might revolt any day now. Buying an expensive condo in Manhattan or London is the perfect place to park your freshly laundered blood money. First, it allows you to move a lot of cash quickly; imagine how much trouble twenty million dollars—or pounds or euros—is to move and hide in your luggage. But one loft in Soho can easily house it all. As a private transaction between individuals or their corporate avatars, it draws less attention, and it won't trigger tax exposure until it is sold. And if Putin changes your status from crony to enemy or a rival cartel seizes your coca plantations or the rebels crash your palace, you can just hop a plane to Heathrow or JFK.

As a result, many of the luxury towers that now crowd the airspace over Manhattan are empty most of the time. No one really lives there. The owners don't work in town or send their kids to the city schools. They don't shop at local stores. And they don't pay city resident taxes, so police and fire protection, sanitation, and road repair are all free. They are basically ghost towns—or rather ghost banks—steel-and-glass vaults built to hold the dirtiest money from the most dangerous and hellish sources in the safest, most comfortable of addresses, as if floating above us on a cloud.

For his own anonymous lair, Felix had chosen a duplex loft in Tribeca over a doorman building uptown, once again sacrificing luxury for security. But the former industrial space turned out to be lovely—tastefully furnished, spacious, accessed via an elevator that he unlocked with a key from the street and in which he had never encountered a soul. Tonight he'd ordered in sushi, a massage, and, as a special treat sent over from a colleague, a boy and a girl, both teenagers freshly smuggled in from Ukraine: blond and pretty, cowering together and even holding hands like Hansel and Gretel. (Although Felix himself was exclusively heterosexual, he did admire the mindboggling spectacle of Vlad—his "muscle," to use the very appropriate American slang term—stripped bare, playing with his boy, while Felix enjoyed himself with the girl.) Who needed room service after all? In New York these days, everything you desired could be ordered online and delivered straight to your door.

26

After a long sleep and a slow breakfast, Joe and Yelena went by Gladys's and took one of the larger diamonds from the ice tray where they were hidden. Then they headed to Brooklyn. Yelena needed to change into something more functional if she was going to act as Joe's backup, and she insisted on arming up, too, although Joe explained that it was pointless. She just shrugged. She took her assignment seriously.

This was Joe's first look at her place, though it didn't tell him much about Yelena that he didn't already know: It was a large, very clean but very bare space. There was a luxury mattress on a platform box with expensive sheets and pillows. A rolling rack against one wall thickly hung with fashionable but mostly black clothes. Billowing white curtains. White towels in the bathroom and a small number of fancy-looking products. A big, flat-screen TV. Like its owner, the apartment was chic, sleek, beautiful to look at but unlikely to divulge any secrets. The most personal thing was the trunk, Russian army surplus, which contained all her weapons. She didn't lock it. She knew only too well how little use that was. She changed quickly and they took the train to Fulton Street, where they entered a gigantic glass office building so full of comings and goings among almost interchangeable firms and employees that it was basically anonymous. They gave their fake names to security and rode up to the fortieth floor.

No doubt Sherm paid considerable rent, especially given his special need for privacy, but he was not paying for the view from this high floor. His office was a windowless, sound-, radio wave–, and Wi-Fi-proof steel-lined box the size of a small one-bedroom apartment. You knocked on an outer door, and a camera set in the peephole regarded you. If you were the person expected—Sherm's was appointment only—then you were buzzed in to a tiny foyer where you shut the door behind you. When that door locked, a green light went on and the inner door unlocked. Next, you entered the waiting room. Here a muscled-up black fellow sat behind a counter with nothing on it but a screen and keyboard. There were filing cabinets behind him.

"Good afternoon," he said. "Please turn over all weapons, cell phones, and other electronic devices. They will be returned when you leave."

Joe took out his cell and laid it on the desk. He grinned at Yelena. Eyes rolling, she drew the pistol from her shoulder holster and laid it on the table. Then she put down her phone.

"Your backup?" the man asked.

With a sigh, Yelena removed the small revolver she had in an ankle holster.

"And the knife in your boot." When she looked at him sharply, he added: "I can see it all on the scanner."

"You wouldn't expect a girl to go knifeless?" she asked with a smile, then shrugged and drew a long, lethal combat knife from a sheath concealed in her boot.

"Now I feel naked."

"That won't be necessary," the man said. He transferred their items to a file drawer. "Now you can go in," he said, pressing a button that unlocked the third inner door. They entered.

The room was comfortable if simple. Thick carpeting and fabric on the walls in muted grays. A table with two chairs on either side, also padded with gray, and one chair on the side between them. The two seats nearest Joe and Yelena were empty and waiting for them. The two across the table were occupied by a dark-haired man in a stylish black suit with a closely trimmed black beard and, overflowing the chair next to him, the biggest human that Joe had ever seen. He was massive on every scale: arms like the legs of oxen dwarfed the arms of the chair; his tree-trunk chest stretched the fabric of the knit polo he wore. It would be impossible to hug him, should you ever want to do such a thing; your arms wouldn't even make it around his shoulders. His legs, thick as telephone poles, were uncomfortably wedged under the table. It was hard to imagine him ever being comfortable in normal human environments—cars, planes, bathtubs, beds. And topping it all was a massive, bumpy, completely bald head, like a prehistoric dinosaur egg, with beady eyes under a low, heavy brow, a flat lipless mouth, and a drooping black mustache nestled beneath a lump of a nose.

Sitting on the single chair was a little old man in work clothes, a black apron, and thick glasses that made his blue eyes bright as they darted about like twin fish in a bowl. This was Sherm. And leaning against the wall, like the only adornment in an otherwise bare space, was another muscled black man in a T-shirt and sweats who happened to be a cousin of the one out front. He'd be pretty intimidating if he didn't look like a doll beside the mountain breathing in the room. But the AK-47 he held across his chest made up the difference.

This was Sherm's place: essentially he was an appraiser and middleman, hosting sales and exchanges between people who didn't trust each other but couldn't go to the law.

"Hello, hello, how are youse," Sherm called, in an old-time New York accent, eyeing Joe with a barely perceptible twinkle. "Sit right down. You must be Carlo and . . ." He hesitated, looking questioningly at Yelena.

"Just call me Carla," she said.

"Fine," Sherm said with a shrug. "This is Felix." The bearded man nodded. "And that is Vlad." Vlad didn't move at all. Joe and Yelena both nodded and took their seats. Sherm went on: "So youse all know how this works. This place is safe. No one is being recorded. No one is armed, except Timmy over there. So let's get down to business."

Yelena reached into her bra and pulled out a small folded tissue that she laid on the table. Sherm unfolded it.

"Ah," he said. "The ice." From his apron pocket, he drew a small headlamp, which he fitted over his forehead before switching it on, and a magnifying loupe, which he pressed to his eye after removing his glasses. He peered deeply into the diamond, and the bright, tight light beam seemed to shatter into rainbows as it struck the teardrop-shaped stone. Sherm looked up, forehead momentarily blazing before he switched off his lamp. He smiled, showing brown and gold teeth. "This, my friends, is a diamond." He sat back, replacing the loupe with his glasses. "Maybe three carats. Very nice."

Joe folded the tissue and gave it back to Yelena, who tucked it back in her bra. He smiled at Felix. "There's plenty more where that came from."

Now Felix smiled. "I'm impressed," he said, his accent posh Brit with a French undertone. "I had my doubts as to whether you'd be able to arrange payment. But from what I hear, you operation was . . ." He paused. "Extremely professional. I'm glad to be doing business with you."

He offered a hand to shake, but Joe held his out, palm up. "I'm glad you're glad. But there's one more piece of business to take care of."

"Yes, of course," Felix said. "Forgive me. Vlad?" he asked the giant, who reached into his shirt pocket and handed him a small plastic baggie. The bottom held a gram or so of off-white powder. Felix tossed it across the desk and Joe caught it.

Joe shook the contents down and then opened it. He licked his pinky and then dipped it just slightly, coating the very tip. He tasted it, and immediately that warm bitterness filled his mouth.

"Tastes like dope to me," Joe said, resealing the baggie and putting it on the table in front of Sherm. "But you're the expert."

Sherm peered into the baggie with the same concentration he had focused on the diamond. "Ah," he said, smiling appreciatively. "The Persian." He put his jeweler's gear away and took out a small case from which he removed a clear plastic container, a vial with a dropper, and a tiny measuring spoon. He scooped heroin into the little spoon and dropped it in the container. Then he added several drops of the liquid and slowly shook the container until the powder dissolved. In seconds, the liquid changed color, first yellow, then a dark brown. He smiled.

"Shit is on the money, my friend. I'd say over ninety-nine percent pure."

Now Joe put his hand out. "We have a deal," he said to Felix, and they shook on it. Sherm started to hand the baggie back, but Felix shrugged. "Keep it, Carlo. As you say, I have plenty more where that came from."

Joe tucked the baggie in his pocket, ignoring the dirty look from Yelena.

They made arrangements for the exchange the following night, a straight face-to-face on a street in Dumbo, in Brooklyn near the river. Joe and Yelena left first. Their weapons and phones were returned, and the outer doors locked behind them. Next Felix and Vlad came out. As soon as Felix got his phone he made a call. "Hello, my dear," he said. "Yes, we are just leaving." He winked at the guy behind the counter, while Vlad got their guns.

As they exited the building and headed down the block on their way to fetch the Corolla and drive to Brooklyn to check out the location, a woman watched Yelena and Joe from the deli across the street. She sat at the counter by the window, a toasted plain bagel with light butter and regular coffee in front of her, face in her phone like everyone else. Neither Joe nor Yelena took any notice. Why would they? Only Yelena had glimpsed her once before, in passing, and then she had been a blonde. Now she had black hair cut in bangs and dark, round glasses, a black jacket over a white T-shirt and black jeans. As they walked by, her phone rang and she spoke into her earpiece.

"Hello Felix," she said. "I am watching them now. It's the same two."

"Are you sure?" Felix asked.

"They killed my husband," she told him as she casually stood and strolled out, following them from a distance, leaving her untouched food. "I am unlikely to forget."

Upstairs in Sherm's waiting room, Felix spoke into the phone, "Yes, dear, I understand perfectly." He rolled his eyes at the guy behind the desk, who smiled back conspiratorially while Vlad handed Felix his gun and then checked his own, standing like a pillar in the inner doorway. "All right then," Felix said. "See you soon." And he shot the counterman in the chest.

At the same time, Vlad, who'd been blocking the inner door, turned back into the office and opened fire, dropping Timmy, Sherm's guard, before he had time to even raise his rifle. Felix walked back in, approaching Sherm while Vlad stood watch. Sherm had not even moved. He was in shock.

"But, but why?" he asked, finally, as Felix walked up and pointed his gun at his head. "They're gone. There's nothing here to steal."

Felix smiled. "Names," he said.

Sherm blinked at him questioningly.

"For Mr. and Mrs. Carlo," he explained. "Their real names."

Sherm shook his head. "No names here. That's the rule. I know what youse say is all."

Felix nodded at Vlad. As Sherm peered nearsightedly up at him, Vlad cupped his head in his hands, cradling it like a newborn's, fingers splayed over the smooth skull and sparse, fine hair. Then he began pushing his thumbs into Sherm's eye sockets, exerting slow and deliberate pressure as Sherm began first to squirm, then to struggle wildly, then to scream helplessly as the giant's thumbs gouged out his eyes and dug deep, and pain became the only thought, the only truth that occupied the interior of his mind.

"Names," Felix demanded. "I know you recognized the man. Who is he?"

"Joe!" Sherm cried, eagerly. Vlad relented and Sherm gasped in relief. "Joe Brody." He cradled his face in his hands.

"Good," Felix said. "Thank you. And the woman?"

"I don't know," Sherm sobbed. "Yelena something maybe? She's Russian. I don't know her. Please. I swear."

"Shh . . ." Felix stroked Sherm's thin hair. "That's okay, old man. I believe you," he said. Then he shot him in the head.

As they left, Vlad sealed all the sound- and airproof doors behind them, assuring that the three corpses would be safely hidden for a long time.

Heather had dressed in black to blend in with the other sleek Downtown women, but in fact she was in mourning for her husband, Adrian Kaan, whom Joe had killed. Almost as enraging for Heather, he and Yelena had made his martyr's death meaningless by preventing the biological terror attack he'd planned. After lying distraught on the island beach where she'd planned to be celebrating with him, newly pregnant, she resolved to seek vengeance on behalf of her fatherless child and to continue on his path. She'd reached out to his overseas network, offering to take his place as their contact in New York, and they had in turn connected her to Zahir.

Zahir's first assignment for Heather was to find a buyer for his dope in New York.

During their years living underground and more recently when posing as black marketeers, she and her husband had learned their way around, so she knew that Little Maria was the lady to call. She also understood that Maria would find out, quickly, the source of this sudden manna from heroin heaven. Maria was no saint, but it made sense she would turn them down rather than cross long-term suppliers. There were plenty of other players or wannabe players who would not be too particular about touching stolen dope or about the taint of terrorism. After all, the shit was good. For the right price, they'd bag it up with Osama bin Laden's picture on it. So when word got out, she knew it was not a problem. In fact, for her, it was a solution. Insisting on the diamonds as payment, letting it be known the heroin would fund terrorists overseas, all of this was, she hoped, most likely to flush out her own quarry, the murderer they called Joe and his Russian bitch.

Now, while Felix and Vlad covered their tracks upstairs at Sherm's, Heather called Armond, Felix's driver and errand boy, the kind of fanatical romantic they kept on hand to do the grunt work. There had always been a couple of them around Adrian, kissing his ass. To her they were typical adolescent males, desperate for acceptance and importance, and she had been manipulating foolish men all her life. Armond would drive the car, fetch the food, stand guard like a faithful dog. And if needed, he would be the one strapped into a vest full of dynamite and sent onto the subway one day to take out the infidels and blow himself straight to paradise.

At the moment, though, his task was simpler: follow the woman, the Russian. Heather wasn't in any doubt about where she and Joe were going now. They'd go to Brooklyn and check out the location of the next meet, like anyone with half a brain—as she told Armond, who had perhaps a quarter of one. And she wasn't worried about where they'd be later: they'd be at the meeting spot again, tomorrow night. So she told Armond to drive straight to Dumbo, pick Yelena up at the meeting place when she and Joe arrived, and then tail her back to her home, without the risk of her spotting Heather—or Felix and Vlad.

Then she texted Zahir, whom she knew only via phone and email and had never seen. The message was one word: *Tomorrow*. Then she went to make her own evening plans.

27

Joe and Yelena walked the block. On both sides, old buildings loomed over the narrow street, some of it still cobblestone, the rest patched-over asphalt. It sloped down to a fenced-off strip of municipal and industrial scrub and then the river. It was a good spot to meet, close to major thoroughfares but with little foot traffic and deserted at night. Even now the only cars that went by rumbled into the parking garage on the corner, a converted five-story building. The rest of the block was mixed residential, walkups and nondescript lofts. The closest storefront was a coffee shop two blocks away. They walked in and out of whatever was open or easy to open—the car park, the larger apartment buildings—and circled a few blocks. No one paid them any mind.

"A lot of good places to hide and shoot us from," Yelena observed.

"Yeah, but why bother?" Joe asked. "They want to unload that dope and get their diamonds. Why risk a shoot-out? It just draws heat. Even around here someone would call the law eventually."

"Then what about us? We have the same problem. We want the dope and the diamonds. But no cops."

"Right," Joe said. "So we need to be sure the deal goes through. And everyone gets away."

Yelena frowned. "Help them get away? You're always trouble, Joe. It's lucky for you that you're fun, too."

"Me? You're the one who starts bar fights." He took out his Beckett book and then felt in his pockets.

Yelena grinned back. "That's what I meant by fun." She handed him the mechanical pencil she'd used when cracking the strongbox. "Here." She watched as he started sketching a rough map of the scene on the paperback's inside cover. "It's my favorite," she added. "Don't steal it."

When he'd finished the sketch and returned the pencil, Joe asked Yelena to begin sourcing weapons and she hopped in a cab. He contacted Cash and had him bring in Liam and Josh to help steal and prepare the fast, reliable cars they'd need for his plan. He got in touch with Juno, who was home in his mom's basement working on Gio's job, and handed him another technical dilemma to solve. He parked the car in a safe, legal spot a block away from the meeting place. Then he went home on the subway to defrost the diamonds.

Back in Jackson Heights, Joe took out the ice tray in which he'd left the diamonds. He twisted the tray and the cubes broke, dropping into the colander he'd set in a bowl of warm water. As the ice melted, the invisible diamonds appeared, a small hill of iridescent, insanely valuable and rare pebbles. He went to his room to undress and shower—he hadn't been home in a while—then thought better of it and went back to the kitchen and taped a note to the strainer for his grandmother: DO NOT TOUCH—OR USE IN DRINK. She was out at her new job, shilling for one of the card clubs, but better to be safe than find out his grandmother had swallowed a diamond and have to deal with resolving that problem.

Then he turned on the shower and went to undress while the old pipes warmed up. He emptied his pockets—wallet, keys, a jangle of loose change. And there it was, the little baggie of pure dope. He held it to the light and looked at the powder through the transparent plastic, as magical in its way as the diamonds: these substances whose power to create desire—pleasure and beauty, lust and addiction, and, of course, always greed and wealth—ruined lives and nations and left a trail of blood and suffering everywhere they touched. He didn't open the baggie. But he didn't throw it out either. He put it back on his bureau and took a long shower. Then, when he got out and dressed, putting on the same jeans and a fresh T-shirt, he found himself staring at it again. Then he had an idea. He found his book and removed the card that the Vietnam vet, the painter, had given him outside the VA. He called.

"Hey Frank," he said, when he picked up. "This is Joe from the VA, remember? We met the other day?"

"Hey, Special Forces, sure I remember. How's life?"

Gladys loved her new job. It combined two of her greatest skills, grifter and card shark, into one easygoing gig, her version of the part-time job a different flavor of retiree might take greeting folks at Walmart or sitting behind the front desk at a senior center. She was a shill for the casino, working the poker tables at a card club set up in the basement under a food court, which was itself under a shopping center in College Point. Her job was to play, to draw in the civilians and keep them at the table, chatting and making friends while also generating excitement by winning the occasional big hand. Seeing a sweet, slightly dotty grandma who'd been making modest bets on poor hands suddenly hit it big got the suckers riled up and kept them from quitting when they lost. Telling jokes, asking about their families and ordering drinks for the table when she scored kept them from quitting when they won. The game was straight. Gladys didn't cheat, but she was an expert player with decades of calculating odds and reading marks behind her, and most of this crowd could be relied on to lose sooner or later and still go home happy enough to come back. They were steady return customers— Asians from the area, groups of older players, Jewish, Italian, and Irish from Long Island and Latinos from the Bronx and Upper Manhattan—so the house's reputation as honest was important, and any real sharks would be expelled and convinced, via baseball bat if need be, not to return. Gladys won or lost just enough to keep things lively while also keeping it fun, clipping the sheep a little while also making them feel warm and fuzzy: she was half shepherd, half wolf.

But it was during one of her frequent smoke and Jack and Coke breaks that she met Yolanda. She was here with a group: a friend had rented a van to bring a circle of ladies from Washington Heights. But while her friends mostly stuck to the slot machines, Yolanda liked blackjack. She'd done well, too, and was ahead by almost a hundred bucks. In fact, she usually won, and it made a nice addition to Social Security and the pension she got from working for the MTA. But she couldn't let her daughter know, any more than she could know about the Kool 100 she bummed from Gladys.

"Why not?" Gladys asked. "She a religious fanatic?"

Yolanda laughed. She liked this feisty white-haired woman a lot, and she was impressed with the stacks of chips in her tray. "Not that bad. Or who knows, maybe worse. She is FBI."

"No kidding?" Gladys said, drawing on her Kool then cooling it down with a sip of her drink. "I happen to know another gal who works for the FBI. Also Spanish. Very cute. I like her. Honestly, I wouldn't mind seeing her with my grandson. Rather than this Russian he runs around with. She's nothing but trouble."

"Oh, yeah? You got a photo?"

Gladys took out her wallet and showed a picture of Joe, smiling across the table at her last birthday dinner.

"Very handsome!" Yolanda said, searching through pictures on her phone. "Here's my granddaughter, Larissa. She's in her ballet outfit."

"What a doll," Gladys said. "I could eat her alive."

"And here," Yolanda said, trying to find her favorite. "Let me show you my daughter, Donna. Who knows? Maybe we can set her up with your grandson. I don't like the guys she brings around either. And her ex-husband is a real schmuck."

Donna was almost done for the day when Janet called her from the lab, saying she found something big.

"What's up?" she asked as she walked in to find her peering at something tiny through her microscope. "That doesn't look so big."

"Oh, but it is," Janet said, looking up and smiling through her own glasses. "It's huge. Come see."

Donna looked. She saw some kind of dark-colored fiber. "Okay, what is it?"

"Hair," Janet said, with a satisfied smirk.

"Hair?"

"Synthetic hair to be exact. Fairly high quality."

"You found fake hair in the box? In the stuff they burned?"

"Yup. Which to my highly trained deductive mind suggests—"

"Fake beards." Now Donna smiled. "So they weren't Hasidic after all. They were in disguises. You're right. That is huge. Great work."

"Thanks," Janet said. "And look, I cleaned this up." She took Janet to the long table on which the rest of the evidence from the box was laid out. The twisted bit of stainless steel now shone brightly under the strong lights, its silver disk reflecting upward.

"Is that from a stethoscope?" Donna asked.

"Exactly. Got it in one. The rest melted."

Donna stared at it thoughtfully. "So maybe it wasn't an inside job at all. Maybe someone cracked the box. Using that."

Janet frowned doubtfully. "I see what you mean, but the combination lock on that box was top of the line. To crack it at all is super impressive. There's only a handful of people that good around. But to do it in less than ten minutes,

193

bouncing around crappy, potholed New York streets, with the police chasing you?"

"They'd have to be a pro."

"They'd have to be a freaking artist."

"But it's possible?" Donna asked.

"I guess. In theory. But I'm not sure how probable it is."

"Think about it though, Janet. From the thief's point of view. Your goal is the diamonds. That means robbing the armored truck and breaking the box."

"Right."

"So moving the box to another vehicle, something that heavy, and getting away clean before all hell breaks loose or actually escaping in the hijacked truck in Midtown traffic are not options. And dragging enough heavy equipment onboard to cut the thing, then having the time before they come stop you. Also impossible."

"So they cracked it. You're right. It's just like Sherlock Holmes says."

"What does he say?"

"You don't watch the show?" she asked in amazement.

"I haven't had time. It's on my watch list. What the hell does he say?"

"Once you eliminate the impossible, whatever's left, however improbable, is the truth."

"See," Donna said. "Me and Holmes agree."

Janet pulled her vape pen from her pocket, checked to be sure no one was looking, and took a thoughtful drag. She exhaled fragrant steam. "So that was their plan all along. They never meant to get away with the truck."

"Exactly," Donna said, nodding. "They just drove around in circles, giving the safecracker time to open the safe. Then they ditched the truck someplace where they knew it would take us time to get to it."

"On purpose!" Janet added. "Not by accident like Jack thought." He was the senior agent in charge, who'd assumed they'd lost control and crashed into the subway, then fled.

"Right," Donna said, tone rising in excitement. "And they burnt their disguises and stuff not so much to hide evidence as to clean it, make it useless to forensics. No offense. I mean for IDs."

"No, you're right," Janet agreed. "No DNA or prints survived that. And they had to ditch the costumes when they bailed from the truck—"

"So they could just walk away. Fade into the crowd," Donna finished her thought. "Who knows? Maybe take the subway home."

"Brilliant!" Janet shouted, high-fiving Donna. "I mean, you know, deviously clever in an unlawful way. But who is there around who can even come up with a plan like that?"

"That son of a bitch," Donna muttered, her eyes narrowing as the wheels turned in her head.

"Your ex-husband?" Janet asked in confusion.

"No, a different son of a bitch. Thanks Janet!" she yelled as she ran out.

28

Frank let Joe in and shook his hand, holding the cane in his left. He was wearing the same paint-spattered work pants and boots, but now he had on an old blue pin-striped dress shirt, also speckled in paint and missing several buttons through which Joe could see gray chest hair. One buttonhole, Joe realized, was fastened with a paper clip. His glasses hung on a cord around his neck, and he had on a light-blue cotton hat with a floppy brim bent from being rolled and stuffed in pockets. It was clear he'd made an effort to wash his hands but there was still paint along the edges of the nails. His hand felt strong but supple, like an expertly broken-in baseball glove, worked past roughness into smoothness again.

"Hey kid, come in," Frank told him. "Want coffee? I've got some on the boil."

"Sure," Joe said. "Thanks."

Frank crossed the space, loping easily on the cane, and disappeared through a curtain along the far wall, leaving Joe alone to look around. Joe had never visited a working artist's studio before and he realized with a certain embarrassment that he expected the walls to be filled with paintings like the ones he'd seen on the internet. Though of course those were finished works, framed and on display in museums and other collections. In reality, the studio was not at all like a gallery. It was more like a busy, chaotic workshop with living quarters attached.

Frank's studio was in Harlem. He had half a floor of an old building with a view of 125th Street's swarming action below. The main space was mostly open and raw: wooden floors patched with tin, including a square of linoleum marking a space where dividing walls had been torn out and roughly spackled over; bare walls painted white but splattered with color especially at the height where a man might absently wipe a brush, the layers built up over years or decades, so that it looked like a multicolored growth now; a pillar in the center so crusted it resembled barnacles caking a sunken ship; the ceiling open, with lighting fixtures, vents, and bundled cables looping through the beams. A number of canvases, some quite large, shoulder height and arms' width, were slotted into a rough structure made of two-by-fours and covered in a plastic tarp. A few others were turned to the wall, though Joe could see paint at the edges and telltale drips on the floor. Mostly there were art supplies: cans and tubes of paint stacked on metal storage shelves and rolling metal tables like you'd see in a restaurant kitchen, rolls of canvas under a long, paint-covered worktable made of scarred wood, cans of brushes, rags, chemicals, boxes of charcoal, pencils, pads, paper, along with torn magazines, newspapers, books, and discarded mail. In the center of the space were an old kitchen chair, a stool, an armchair with the stuffing bursting out, and a broken-down daybed that Joe recognized from some of the nudes he'd seen online. There were adjustable lamps and an empty easel. Off to one side was a curtain, and through the part he could make out another area with furniture and a carpet on the floor: the living quarters no doubt, occupying the second, smaller part of the space.

Frank came back clutching two steaming mugs of coffee by the handles in one hand and a container of powdered creamer tucked under his arm. "Ran out of milk," he said. "But I found this shit." He put it down on the worktable and handed Joe a mug.

"I'll take it black," Joe said.

"Wise choice," Frank said. "I don't even understand what's in that stuff. It just changes the color. Have a seat." He waved his cane over the Spartan choices. Joe picked the kitchen chair, holding his mug in both hands. Frank sprawled in the busted armchair, resting his mug on the arm and leaning his cane beside him. The coffee was very good.

"So thanks for having me over. On such short notice, I mean. I hope I didn't interrupt your work."

Frank shrugged. "You did but that's all right. I am always working unless something interrupts me. Sleep, hunger, people. This one was welcome. I didn't think you'd call."

Joe nodded. "Well, thanks anyway."

"Uh-huh," Frank said and took a swallow of coffee.

"Nice place."

Frank looked around, as if trying to decide if he agreed. "I've been here thirty years. I took it because no one else wanted it, so I could do what I felt like. Now they'd pay me a fortune for it. But where would I go? I'm land-poor, like some aristocrat. The Earl of Harlem. They got earls back in the old Harlem, over in Europe?"

Joe shrugged. "Maybe not anymore."

They drank coffee. Traffic noise reached them from below.

"So what did you want to talk about?" Frank asked.

"How do you mean?"

Frank shrugged. "It's a long-ass way to come for a free coffee."

Joe smiled. "True. No milk even."

"Right. This is a bullshit café. Not even a cute barista. So then?"

"I'm not sure how to put this." Joe hesitated. Frank waited in silence. "But I feel like some of your pictures, they remind me of things."

"Uh-huh."

Joe laughed. "I guess I should be more specific. The war paintings. The ones of Nam, or I assume that's what they are."

"Yes, indeed."

Joe looked down now and spoke into his mug. "They seem just like things I dream of sometimes. Like exactly. Like you painted my dream." He glanced back up at him. "Is that crazy?"

Frank looked him in the eye. "You're asking if it's crazy that those paintings are of your dreams?"

Joe nodded.

Frank shook his head and sipped coffee. "Not crazy at all, brother. That's exactly what those paintings are. Nightmares."

* * *

They sat in silence for a minute. Now it was Joe who was waiting while Frank looked down, first at his fingers, as if examining the source of the paintings, then into the mug. "I was a tunnel rat. You know what that means?"

Joe nodded.

"VC had those damn tunnels dug in all over the place. Like a Charlie subway, complete with rats. They'd send me down with a flashlight and a forty-five. No use bringing anything else but a Ka-Bar knife, too tight down there. You couldn't even stand up. Had to crouch. Sometimes you had to crawl. I'd creep along, in the dark, hearing the rats scurry around. Sometimes they'd run over my hands or my legs. It was fucking hard not to just open fire when that happened. I hate fucking rats. Even though I'm from here. I'd be down there for hours. I'd have to piss down there. Sometimes I could barely breath, the oxygen was thin or there'd be corpse gas. More than once I came across a body or parts of one. I was supposed to be like surveying. Really I was just a rat in a maze myself. Like, send the nigger down the hole and see if he gets shot. Then put a pin on the map. Anyway, this one day, or night, what the fuck's the difference, I am creeping along in the dark, and I hear a rat. So I freeze, hoping it will just clear off. And nothing happens. But I can like feel it there, close. And I realize I am holding my breath, because, did I mention rats freak me the fuck out? But now, holding my breath I feel like I can hear something else breathing, something alive. So I lift my flashlight and my gun, slowly, slowly, and then, all at once, I hit the light. And right there, right up close to me, like close enough to breathe on, is another fucking face. Charlie. Must have been a kid about

200

my age then. I was nineteen. Round little baby face. NVC uniform and cap. And in his hand, a gun. So I fired. I mean my piece was already pointing right at him, I just had to squeeze the trigger. I shot the face, that baby gook face, right in the center, boom, I pulled that trigger until that head burst all over me like a rotten pumpkin. Got in my eyes, my lips, nose, everything. Then I turned the light back off. And I crawled the fuck back out of there in the dark."

He stopped. He sat in silence for a moment and Joe stayed perfectly still. Then Frank lifted his mug and took a sip. He frowned. "Damn. It's cold." He drank it anyway, then rose, setting the mug on the worktable. "So twenty years later"— he gestured at the paint-splattered walls with his cane—"I painted it. I painted it, and I kept on painting it, over and over, until finally I stopped seeing it in my fucking dreams."

29

When Donna and Blaze Logan got to Club Rendezvous, Joe was not working. Donna wasn't surprised; she'd told Blaze it was fifty-fifty at best but that she thought they might cough him up if she pressed. That's why she invited Blaze. Added pressure.

Blaze had made Donna for a straight girl right off, but she liked her, liked the way she'd handled herself under fire, and there was nothing wrong with having a beer with a cool colleague who happened to be hot as well. So when Donna called her and said how about that beer tonight, she said sure but was not surprised when she added: "There's a catch."

"I figured."

"I'm looking for a source who I think might be holding out on me. But it's a long shot, so I'd rather not bring in someone from the bureau yet."

"Uh-huh."

"I need someone to watch my back," Donna went on to explain, "but who can also keep their mouth shut. And who it might be nice to have a couple beers with, too."

"You mean a friend."

"That's a good word for it."

"Sure, Donna. I can pick you up."

"Oh, and one other thing." She hesitated. "It's a strip club. Female strippers I mean."

"So you figured invite the dyke along."

"No, not like that. But I figured at least you wouldn't freak out on me about it."

"Take it easy. I'm kidding. I'd love to knock back a few and watch some booty bounce. Let's go."

So here they were, nursing their beers at the bar, the only two unaccompanied female customers in the place, but no one was really paying any mind. And Donna wasn't sure what to do next. She'd been in a rage when she suspected—no, knew for sure, in her gut—that Joe was behind the diamond heist, that perhaps he had even come to see her as a way of feeling her out, fishing for any info she might have heard about his plans. After calling Blaze, she'd texted her mom to make sure she could pick Larissa up from aftercare—a disturbingly clinical name for an after-school session of crafts and snacks—and then on the ride out to Queens, she let Blaze do the talking—bitching about life as a marshal—because she didn't want to tell her too much. As a result, now that she was here, her anger had cooled. She asked the bartender if Joe was around. He said, "Joe who?" She told him Joe Brody. He said nope and that was it. She didn't have any next move planned.

But Blaze didn't seem to mind. She sipped her beer and watched the dancers. Donna ignored hers and thought about the last time she had been here, speaking with Joe in the back booth, and about their other encounters: when she had

203

arrested him as a stranger or when he, masked and unknown to her, had spared her life and apologized for hurting her. She thought about their talk on the steps the day before, the comfort and easy intimacy that seemed to flow naturally between them. Like on a great date she thought and then burned with shame at the thought, as though embarrassed in front of herself. She was a grown woman, a federal agent, a mom. He was a liar, a thief, and probably a killer, the worst possible choice of anyone she knew. Even "knew" was an exaggeration. Their relationship was business, not personal. He committed crimes and she solved them. He lied and she found the truth. He ran and she chased. And when she caught him she would take him to prison, not to bed.

Now she realized the source of her anger: betrayal. She felt betrayed by Joe, and the stupidity of that—of thinking there was anything to even betray—just made her angrier. The anger was for herself, but she found it easy to redirect toward a more productive target.

"Keep an eye out," she told Blaze. "I'm going to try something."

"Oh they're out," Blaze drawled as a lanky blonde pranced onstage, languidly winking at Blaze. Donna took a long pull from her beer, then instinctively reached in her bag for her mints, so that just in case things got official there wouldn't be alcohol on her breath. That was her, the good girl, even when rousting a strip joint. As she crossed the busy room, she took her badge out, too, in the leather fold with her ID, and then rested her other hand lightly on her holstered gun. She walked down the back hall, past the restrooms, and around a corner.

"Hey, miss, you can't go there," a passing busboy said.

She showed her badge and kept walking as he backed away. She banged on a door marked MANAGER and, when no answer came, kicked it with her boot.

"What?" a gruff voice asked. She went in. A white guy with a white beard and a big round gut under his shirt and tie looked up from behind a desk heaped with papers, like a fallen Santa, holding a bottle of Tums in his hand. He grimaced at her. "Auditions are Wednesday afternoons," he said.

"I already got a job," she said, holding up her badge. "FBI agent."

"You pinching me?" he asked, more annoyed than afraid, then gestured at his desk as if she were adding more chores to his pile. "For what?"

"I just want to talk to Joe."

He shook his head. "Don't know him."

"You don't know one single person named Joe?"

He shrugged noncommittally.

"Joe Brody. The bouncer," she said.

"Oh, him," Santa said, leaning back in his creaking desk chair and popping a couple of Tums. He chewed thoughtfully. "He ain't been around for a while."

"Get ahold of him. I'll wait. I'll be checking your customers' and employees' IDs in the meantime."

"What?" Now he came to life, standing and focusing on her. "Why?"

"I've got a federal marshal with me. We got a tip there might be someone here with a warrant out."

She turned and went.

"Wait. Wait . . . ah, fuck me," he said as she left. Then he ate a couple more Tums and reached for the phone.

When Yolanda got the text from Donna about being home to meet Larissa, she was already on her way back into the city. However, she was in a van full of ladies who had all just been gambling, she was a little buzzed from those drinks, and she had her new pal, Gladys, with her. They had decided to go out for dinner as a group. Now she elbowed Gladys, who was in the seat beside her, trying to decide if she could sneak a smoke by blowing it out the window, which was the kind that only opened a few inches outward from the bottom.

"My daughter just asked me to be home for when Larissa gets back. She's out on an important case. You mind if we just order in? There's a good Spanish-Chinese place down the block."

"Sure. I want to meet that sweet little grandkid of yours."

So Yolanda texted Donna back. She didn't want her to know about the gambling or the drinks, so she just wrote: *OK. Be careful. Love, Mom.*

When Donna came back from the manager's office, she picked up her beer, finished it off, then told Blaze, "Follow my lead," before striding over to the DJ and badging him. "Cut the music," she told him. "And give me that mic."

He obeyed. The music stopped abruptly and the dancers onstage, all more or less naked, stopped and blinked into the audience, trying to see what was happening, looking suddenly lost in their pools of light. The audience grumbled and a few voices called out. Donna walked up the steps to the stage.

"All right!" one voice shouted. "Take it off!"

"Sit down and shut up," Donna said into the mic, a bit shocked at how loud her voice was. "I'm Special Agent—" A terrible screech of feedback screamed from the speakers and the audience groaned and booed. One of the dancers, the tall blonde, stepped over.

"Stand over here and don't wave the mic so much," she said helpfully.

"Thanks," Donna told her, then into the mic: "This is the FBI." She held up her badge. Out beyond the lights, there was a sudden movement toward the door. "Turn on the house lights! I am here with the US marshals. We will be checking IDs, looking for outstanding warrants."

The movement became an exodus. There was a general rush for the exit, but as the lights flashed on, Donna saw Blaze quickly stepping into position, badge out, and blocking the way, so that only the first handful got out.

"Let's make this as orderly as possible, folks," Donna continued. "Please everybody, move toward the bar or take your seats. After we check you, you can leave and when we're done the show can resume." Santa, the manager, was standing in the doorway to the hall, watching with an expression of pure misery. Donna looked right at him. "But who knows how long that will take?" she wondered aloud.

The customers grumbled but more or less complied, returning to their seats or drinks and pulling out wallets as Blaze approached. Donna handed back the mic. "Excuse me, ma'am. You want to see ours too?" the naked blonde asked her.

"No. You just stand by."

She nodded and huddled with the others as Donna hopped down from the stage. She began at the other end of the room from Blaze, checking IDs, making a show of running them on her phone, idly wondering if at least one or two people in here would pop. She got a lot of dirty looks but no back talk. Then she approached a ringside table, VIPs or wannabe VIPs, with bottles of Moët and Hennessy on the table and two guys, one black, one white, sitting back, dressed in expensive sports gear and gold, neither holding out ID.

"Okay, let's go," Donna said. "Let's see some ID."

The black guy, who was tall and elaborately muscled, scowled at her. "Don't you know who that is? He's Li'l Whitey, the rapper." She glanced from him to the slender young white boy beside him. He looked like a sniveling dirtbag to her.

"Never heard of him," Donna told the muscle, while her right hand moved toward the extendable baton she had in her hip pocket. "But little and white does describe one of our wanted fugitives. So cough it up."

"And what do you say if I don't feel like it?" Li'l Whitey asked, still leaning back with a sneaker on the table.

"I say stand up and turn around with your hands behind your head. You first," she told the black guy. He put his hands up and slowly stood, then made a sudden break for it, trying to ram his way past her like a running back. She stepped aside and tripped him, letting his own momentum bring him down, which it did, with a grunt. She grabbed his arm with her left hand as he fell, to take control as he landed, and put her knee in his back. Then she saw him pulling a gun, a snub-nosed revolver, from his pants. With her right hand, she brought the baton up and let it extend, then flicked it hard across his wrist. He howled and dropped the gun.

Li'l Whitey, meanwhile, jumped up and ran for the door, but Blaze caught him across the face with an elbow as he passed. He dropped to his knees, clutching his nose in both hands. "Aw, fuck, my nose," he cried.

Panic erupted as some of the crowd tried to run or at least take cover while others seemed to be closing in. Donna and Blaze both drew their weapons and stood back to back. "Next time I pick the bar," Blaze whispered.

"Deal," Donna replied, bracing herself.

Then Gio Caprisi walked in.

Donna didn't see him at first; she heard him. "What the fuck is going on here?" a voice called out. "Everybody sit down and shut up!"

The effect was immediate. The crowd fell silent. People sat down or stepped back. Only Li'l Whitey and his pal remained on the floor, moaning softly.

Gio was in a suit as usual, but his tie was loosened and he needed a shave. He had two thugs standing beside him. The manager rushed over and whispered to him, while pointing at Donna. Gio nodded at her. "Good evening, Agent Zamora," he said, then crouched over Li'l Whitey, lifting his face by the chin.

"Jesus, it's you again? Don't you ever learn?"

"I want a doctor," he whined. "And my lawyer. And my manager."

"Yeah. Hold your water a minute." He stood up and called to Donna. "You holding this one for anything?"

"Nah, he can go," Donna said, reholstering her gun. She nudged the other guy with her toe. "But this one has a weapon."

Gio frowned down at him, as he cradled his arm. "You brought a weapon in here?" he asked. "That's two people you're in trouble with. And I'm much worse."

"I think she broke my wrist," he said.

"Good," Gio told him.

Blaze stepped up, holding his wallet; she'd been running his ID. "He's got a warrant. Assault. In Florida. And weapons. So he's a federal fugitive now. My meat, unless you need him."

Gio gestured for her to help herself, as though he were the one she was asking. Blaze rolled her eyes and turned to Donna.

"Take him," Donna said. Then, as Blaze started to cuff him, she added in a lower tone, "Glad your night wasn't a total waste."

"Now then," Gio said to Donna. "How can I help you?"

"I want to speak to your bouncer, Joe," she said. "Urgently."

"Joe? Joe's on a leave of absence. Personal reasons. He hasn't been here for what?" He turned to Santa. "Almost two weeks?"

"Yeah, that's right, boss. I told her—"

Gio put a hand up to silence him, then took out his phone. "I'm calling, okay?" he said, showing her the name Joe on his phone. He listened. "Voice mail," he told her. "At least he has that now." He raised his hand again and spoke into the phone: "Joe. This is Gio. Agent Zamora from the FBI needs to speak with you. Urgently."

"Tell him it's about some lost rocks."

He shrugged at her. "It's about lost rocks, she says. Call me." He hung up. "Now then. If you're going to hold us, then I really should call a lawyer next." He looked around at the restive crowd: the customers, the DJ and bartenders, the girls still onstage. "And maybe order pizza."

"Just make sure Joe gets my message," Donna told him, following as Blaze led her prisoner away. "Good night, Mr. Caprisi."

"Good night," he called after her. "And Agent Zamora?"

She looked back from the door, where Gio's two men had stood aside for her.

"Next time you need something, just call," he said. "You've got my number."

When Powell decided to spend the evening sitting on Club Rendezvous, his expectations were modest. His snitches had told him that the spectacular diamond heist yesterday had been the work of local pros and that it all had something to do with the heroin that known terrorists, including a character known only as Felix, were smuggling into the United States. Powell thought that watching Gio's club might turn up something interesting. He did not expect it to be his ex-wife.

When Donna arrived, accompanied by a stout, short-haired woman he didn't recognize but could instantly see was with law enforcement, his heart started pounding. But was it his spook sense twitching, telling him he was getting closer, or was it just his emotions, the mix of love, hate, desire, and frustration he felt every time he saw her or even thought of her? It was quite possible, after all, that they had some other legitimate reason to visit a known OC hang out.

But when Gio himself, the boss, pulled up—with two obvious heavies in a separate car right behind him and they all hurried in—he knew. Somehow, the plot was thickening, and his ex-wife was in it up to her neck.

30

Fuck it. Leave him.

That was Carol's first thought. She'd made it through the concert, focusing on Billy Joel, using the music as a kind of cover, hiding her own overwhelming emotions, giving her a reason not to talk, not to move. At times her feelings were swallowed up in the larger waves that surged through the crowd, her mind silenced by thousands of people singing "Piano Man," while at other moments the songs seemed to express just what she was feeling. After all, this was the soundtrack to her life, too: why not have "Honesty" or "She's Always a Woman" playing for her internal, private drama? And then there were the times when she wanted to stand up and yell: *Fuck this! Fuck this middle-class suburban bullshit! Shove this whole thing up your ass!*

At the hotel that night, she could barely look at him, but then, in the dark, her rage and pain and fear morphed into desire and they fucked like they hadn't in years. She even wondered if she could have conceived again later, the feeling was so intense, that sense that something deep and profound and life changing had just happened. The next day she contacted a woman she knew, the ex of a hedge funder, who'd gotten out with her house—bigger than theirs but on a less choice piece of land—and her kids and asked, "for a friend" about her lawyer.

Then, a couple days later she realized: Who was she kidding? She was a therapist, a psychologist, and all day she lectured people on healthy and unhealthy attachments, on what made relationships good or bad, but in the end she thought maybe she really knew nothing. Maybe no one did. Love was a mystery, a fever, a curse, and a blessing. It was a spell, good or bad, and it wasn't up to you to break it or to choose whose you fell under. Maybe the ancient myths got it right in the first place: Why not fall in love with a tree or a donkey or a reflection in a pool? Why not become changed into a star out of loneliness, a flower out of passion, obey a yearning within that took the outer form of a beast? She had been fooling herself with that lawyer shit. She hated him, but she was not ready to let go.

So then kill him. That's what she thought next. He stayed out late again, claiming he had a business dinner at a Korean place. It was true that the next day his shirt smelled of barbeque smoke and cigarettes, but she also smelled cheap perfume and sweat and the combination sent her into a murderous rage. She doubted that she even came close to being capable of it, but the thought came to her as an actual idea, something she found herself considering from practical angles. She knew there were guns around. She knew he had enemies or at least people who might get blamed long before she—the innocent little wife who worked with kids and took yoga—ever would be. She had no doubt she could

214

catch him off guard. That was one of the bitterest ironies: he trusted her completely in his way. He would never imagine her capable of harming him. She couldn't really believe it herself, not even when she heard herself talking about it in her own head. She could see herself killing in self-defense, of course. Or killing the way a mother killed: protecting her children, guarding her family. But to point a gun at her husband and shoot him down, out of rage or pain or to solve her problems? No. That was deliberate, premeditated murder. The truth was she was simply not a killer. He was.

So in the end she decided to do it her way, not his. The therapist's way. She would confront him with the truth, stage the drama, expose the secrets, and see what happened next. That was why she went to the crap drawer in the kitchen where the rings of extra keys were, took the spare he had marked "office," and added it to her ring. That night he'd left again, in a rush, muttering about an emergency at some club. Was he going to see *her* then, the smoky blonde with the cheap perfume? No, she doubted it. It did actually sound like Nero he was talking to on the phone and he did seem genuinely annoyed by whatever he heard. She would wait. She would watch. She would follow. She would choose her moment. And then she would catch him—and her, his mistress—in the act.

The last thing Donna expected to find when she got home was that her mom had a friend over. For one thing, her mom didn't have friends over. She had friends, Donna supposed—the neighbors she chatted and sat with out front, other retired coworkers she met for lunch once a year, her group of old ladies who went to movie matinees or whatever in a van— but never once could Donna remember coming back to find her mom just chilling, having a drink, and eating fried rice with a pal.

So when she walked in—already talking as she came through the door, explaining what a crazy night she had, following down a tip in Queens, and did Larissa get to sleep okay and was there any of that Chinese food she smelled left—she was pretty taken aback to step into the living room and see her mom laughing on the couch with an older white lady. And she was really shocked when the lady looked up and smiled and said, "Hi, Agent Zamora, we were just talking about you," and she realized it was Gladys Brody, Joe's grandmother.

At first Donna said nothing. She just looked at the two smiling women with a blank expression, as though she had been woken from a strange dream.

"Sit down, honey," her mom said, reaching for a plate. "You look hungry. There's plenty of food."

Gladys took a beer from the paper sack at her feet and cracked it open. "She looks thirsty, too. Here you go, hon. I bet you could use this."

"You know what," Donna said. "You're right. I could." She took the beer from Gladys and the heaping plate from her mom, and she sat down.

"That's the second one of your girlfriends to come in and start a fight," Gio was saying as he drove with Joe beside him, heading from Queens to Bed-Stuy. When Joe checked his phone after leaving Frank's place for home, there were messages from Gio and Juno, so Gio picked him up himself to tell him about Donna's visit to the club. "I'd hate to have to eighty-six one of my own bouncers, but it's bad for business if the customers at a strip club think the girls might kick their ass."

"She's not my girlfriend. Neither is Yelena, actually."

"Good. I should hope even you aren't crazy enough to start banging a Fed. But she was pissed, man, and in that special way, you know? Like personal. And what the fuck? What's that shit about rocks? She's letting us know she knows about the diamonds."

"Yeah," Joe said. "But why?"

"And how? I want to know who in my crew is sharing our private business. At least now we know for sure the snitch is ratting to the Feds. She knew and my guy in the police didn't."

"We'll see what Juno found out when we get there," Joe said. "He says he's ready to report."

"It's about time."

"Just relax. You make him nervous."

"What's he got to be nervous about? I'm the one who's nervous."

"Just stay calm and try to be nice."

"I'm always calm and nice," Gio pointed out as he moved the car swiftly into a spot on Juno's block.

"That's true. You are," Joe admitted. "I think that's what scares the shit out of people."

* * *

217

"Three."

"I see your three and raise you another three."

"I fold."

"Okay, I'll pay to see what you're holding." Donna dropped three more pennies in the pot. They had raided Larissa's piggy bank and replaced the coins with cash. Now, as her mom watched, Gladys turned up her cards. A flush.

"Damn," Donna said. "I was sure you were bluffing."

Yolanda laughed and sipped her beer. "You can't out bluff her, honey. She's a pro."

"Just watch and learn, kid," Gladys said, sweeping the small pot of pennies into her growing pile. "These are the cheapest lessons you'll ever get."

"Wait, are you cheating?" Donna asked, embarrassed even as she said it, for being such a cop.

Gladys laughed. "Hustling, not cheating. There's a difference. Cheating is a crime. Hustling is just playing the player along with the cards." She ruffled the deck. "Not that I can't do both," she added with a wink, handing Donna the cards. "But I don't have to cheat to beat you. Your deal."

Yolanda laughed louder and Donna felt herself blushing as she shuffled and dealt. "What's your grandson up to tonight?" she asked, with an offhand air.

Gladys shrugged. "I don't ask. I learned a long time ago not to try and control him. Just leave a window open. He'll come back when he's hungry. That would be my advice."

"Advice?" Donna asked.

"For anyone trying to catch him," Gladys said and tossed a penny in the pot. "Ante up."

Donna and Yolanda both anted, and Yolanda, who was a little buzzed for maybe the first time since Donna's wedding, slapped her daughter's knee. "You better hope she's not after him, Gladys. My daughter's a special agent, FBI, and she is damn good at her job."

"So's Joe," Gladys said, from behind her cards. "Another thing you have in common." She tossed some pennies in. "I bet a nickel."

Juno tried to make his crib as much like an office as he could. It was his office, really, where he created beats, recorded rappers, and did the hacking and cracking that paid his bills, but it was also his bedroom and his mom's basement. So receiving Gio Caprisi there made him a mite uneasy. He made the bed, hid the dirty clothes, closed the drapes that separated his area from the washer, dryer, and ironing board, and tried to lay out the various lists and reports he had printed like at a legit corporate conference, with copies for himself, Gio, and Joe, along with bottles of water, arranged on the coffee table between the broken-down couch he'd inherited when his mom redid the living room upstairs and the busted armchair he covered with a leopard-skin-printed bedsheet.

He needn't have bothered. Joe of course had been there before, and Gio didn't even seem to register the surroundings, nor did he touch the papers or the water. He just sat down, looked Juno dead in the eye and said, "So? Who's the rat?"

"Okay, well, to answer that, let me show you what I did." He pointed at the screens on his long desk and hit a few keys.

"I created a program that searched through all the messages and calls from all the accounts and devices you gave me, then cross-referenced that with the dates and times of when that guy in Europe got busted or the diamond heist or when you say you heard there was talk. Looking for patterns and shit."

"And?" Gio asked, his eyes still on Juno and not the rows of numbers or graphs. "Is there a pattern?"

"Yup. A triangular one. Three people, or three entities anyway. One inside the group you gave me, let's call that A, and two outside, B and C. Back before the Europe guy gets got, A and B are talking back and forth, then C contacts A, then transmissions between A and B pretty much stop. But A and B are both talking to C all the time, and the traffic definitely spikes around your target times."

"Enough with the letters, Juno," Joe put in, seeing Gio's frown. "Let's hear some names."

"Okay well, B, the first outside man, the account is anonymous but it traces back to a guy named Patrick White, if that means anything."

"Motherfucker," Gio said. He was calm now and smiling. "I had a feeling about that."

"C was tougher. A lot tougher. Like bizarrely tough."

"What does that mean?" Gio asked him.

"It's standard to hide your identity, of course, with proxy servers and blind accounts or fake names, but this C's security is heavy-duty. So heavy-duty that even I couldn't crack it, and I can crack anything."

"So you don't know who he is?"

"No, but I know what he is. Only the government has encryption software this new and advanced. Way beyond even the best corporate. And not local cops either. This is big-time."

"FBI?" Gio asked.

"Maybe . . ." Juno said, thoughtfully.

"CIA," Joe said.

"Yeah," Juno agreed. "That's more like it. This is like top secret spook shit. CIA or NSA or whatever."

"Fine, then that's the law," Gio said. "So what about the rat inside my house? Who is A? Or is he hidden, too?"

"A was clever. Multiple proxies. Dummy email accounts that self-destruct after the message is read. But he was not cleverer than moi." He checked his papers. "One sec, sorry. There were so many names. Here it is. A comes up as one Paul Rogers." Juno looked up with a grin. "Y'all know that dude?"

Juno never saw it coming. Gio attacked, lunging across the room, knocking the coffee table over and scattering the papers and water bottles. Only youth and the survival instincts of a nerdy, skinny kid growing up in a rough world gave Juno the reflexes to leap up over the chair and, in a blink, scurry across the room and up the stairs. By then Joe had reacted, too, and was holding Gio back in a tight hug.

"It's not his fault, Gio," Joe was murmuring into his ear. "He just did what you told him to."

Gio nodded, breathing hard, hands up and just as quickly as it came, the storm passed. "I know," he said. "I know. I'm okay."

Joe released him carefully and called out to Juno. "It's okay, Juno, don't worry."

There was a beat before Juno's head appeared, peeking down from upstairs.

"It's safe to come back down," Joe said. "I promise."

"Sorry, kid. I didn't mean it," Gio said, as Juno tiptoed back down. "Look," he added. "I'm sitting down." He and Joe both sat back on the couch and Juno returned, stepping gingerly over the mess and perching on the edge of his chair.

"Now," Gio asked, in a very soft voice that Juno found creepy rather than comforting. "Are you absolutely fucking sure?"

"Sure they talked? Yes. A . . . I mean Paul Rogers." He paused cautiously for a second but when Gio nodded, went on: "He talked to White. Then after the bust in Europe, the G-man and Rogers connect. But that's as sure as I can be without reading and hearing all the convos. I don't know what they said."

Joe spoke: "Is there some way to check it? Like can you send them both, Paul and Pat, a fake message that seems to come from C? See how they react?"

"Yeah. That could work," Juno said, forgetting his fear and getting excited. "I could create an alias, like a cloned account, the way spammers do when it seems like your dead grandpa is trying to sell you Viagra."

"Just do it," Gio said, standing up abruptly. Juno flinched. "And remember, only you, me, and Joe know about any of this. Ever."

"Yes, sir, Mr. Gio. I mean—"

"Let me know when you know. You need a ride?" he asked Joe.

"No, Juno and I have more work to do."

"Right." He pulled a fat roll of cash from his pocket and tossed it in Juno's lap. "Good work, kid. And thanks," he said as he went upstairs and out. He had recovered his equipoise. He seemed terrifyingly calm.

After Juno settled down, with many assurances from Joe that Gio would not kill the messenger, he showed Joe what he had come up with for the exchange and Joe gave him the diamonds to prepare. Then he checked on the other guys, who had taken care of the cars. Then he tried Yelena. Since he was in Brooklyn and they had to pick up weapons from her source in the morning, he thought maybe she'd want him to stay over with her. But she didn't reply and, after a while, when he finished with Juno, he went home. To his surprise, his grandmother was out, too. He knew she had a new gig hustling cards at a club, but she was never out this late. He made a sandwich, ate it, and went to bed.

31

Yelena Noylaskya was born in a Russian prison—in other words, in hell. Her father was unknown and her mother, a career criminal—prostitute, madam, thief, and drug dealer—died behind bars, leaving little Yelena to be state raised. Born into crime, as the tattoo of a Madonna and child covering her back symbolically declared, she quickly adapted to life in her jungle and learned to be predator rather than prey. A prodigy at burglary, she also grew up to be lethal, with or without weapons, and the tattoos on her hips, a dollar sign and a skull, told this, too. Finally the stars she wore, tattooed on her upper chest beneath each shoulder bone, showed the high regard and position of honor she held in the Russian underworld. But, despite her success as a criminal, she had always been known to the authorities—they raised her, watched her grow, kept tabs on her—and eventually they pulled her back into their web, showed her a heap of evidence, some of it even true, and offered her a choice: She could return to prison and end her life where it began. Or she could be set free to hunt again, this time in America. If she agreed, she would be turned over to the SVR, the Foreign Intelligence Service, successors to the KGB. They would provide assistance in the way of visas and so forth, along with additional training in spy craft. She would be their eyes and ears in New York, keeping them apprised of the doings of the Russian Mafia among other things. She was the one they reached for when they heard that the wanted terrorist, Adrian Kaan, was in New York and plotting an attack.

During her first caper with Joe, her real mission had been, ideally, to steal a sample of the virus for the Russians while also helping to insure that Joe and the others succeeded in taking down Adrian, whom they feared as much as the CIA did. Instead, the virus had been destroyed along with Adrian and his cell. Good enough. Her bosses in Moscow were satisfied and they didn't ask any questions. Case closed. She was safe. Or at least she felt safe sitting in her local café, reading a newspaper in Cyrillic, until Heather sat down across from her.

"Good evening, Yelena. Do you know who I am?"

Yelena's eyes flickered with surprise for just a split second, then went calm again. She sipped her tea.

"You look vaguely familiar."

"I should. You and your friend Joe ruined my and my husband's plans recently. And then you helped kill him."

"You're here for revenge?" Yelena asked. "Then why aren't you shooting instead of talking?"

Heather shrugged. "Don't be mistaken. I am very good, but you are better, I think. You could kill me in a fight. But you won't do it here and now, will you?"

Yelena shrugged noncommittedly. "We'll see."

"And then there is Joe to consider," Heather continued. "And our mutual plans for tomorrow. So for now I am just here to talk."

The waiter appeared and Yelena ordered two teas in Russian. He brought them in glasses. Yelena took a cube of sugar from the bowl and put it between her teeth. "So talk," Yelena said.

Heather dropped a cube in her tea and stirred. "The people I work with have connections to US intelligence, but they also speak to Russian intelligence. Money is the universal language, don't you think? Like religion and love." She licked the spoon. "Anyway, my friends told me about your friends in the SVR. But I was thinking, what if I talk to them myself? What if I tell them that it was you who cracked the vault at the perfume lab, you who had possession of the virus for days and who could have stolen it or taken a sample anytime? What would happen? My guess is they'd bring you home and that would be the last anyone saw you."

Yelena sipped her tea, letting it melt the sugar between her teeth. Heather went on.

"On the other hand, if your friends in Brooklyn, maybe even some in this café, found out that you were spying for Moscow all along, then New York would be even more dangerous for you than Russia."

"Sounds bad for me," Yelena said. "But you have a solution."

"I do. Give me Joe."

"Give him?" Yelena listened carefully, sipping tea as Heather spoke.

"I need the deal to go through tomorrow. So nothing goes wrong till then. And as long as we get away clean with our diamonds, you and your pals can have the dope to sell for yourselves. But once we make the trade, you are going to kill Joe for me, while I watch. That way I will avenge my husband's death. And I will also have the pleasure of watching you kill the man you love."

Yelena laughed abruptly, her tongue full of sugar. She swallowed. "I don't love Joe. We work well together. In several ways. That is all." She shook her head. "You are a true romantic, I see. A drama queen. All this love and revenge. You're still a very American woman after all." She put her empty glass down. "As for me, I don't love anyone but myself."

Heather smiled and sipped her tea. "Then I was wrong. We have no problem after all."

In the morning, Joe met Yelena for breakfast. She had syrniki, farmer's cheese dumplings with jam and sour cream and tea. Joe had a Turkish coffee. A text from Cash came while they were eating: *Found 3 fixing.* He'd spent the night with Liam and Josh, hunting for cars that suited their purpose—fast, reliable, and as inconspicuous as possible. When they spotted one, they'd break in, ideally by using a device Cash had that searched and found the remote frequency to unlock it, but picking it if need be, then driving it back to Reliable Scrap, the wrecking yard out near Jamaica that he used as a cover for his car-theft operation. Normally, when he and his cohorts took a vehicle, it was driven back there, chopped up immediately, and vanished into the gigantic maze of junk and auto parts. Other cars, special orders, were hunted and stolen on request, provided with new VIN numbers and fake paperwork generated by

Uncle Chen, and shipped to his clients overseas, mostly wealthy mainland Chinese.

Cash and the others had found three cars they liked—a black Audi sedan, a dark-blue two-door Saab, a sleek, green four-door Lexus, all late models, but nothing over-the-top flashy—and were out at Reliable this morning, tuning them up, adjusting shocks and fuel injection systems, and, of course, switching out the plates with other parked cars. As long as the state matched, people rarely looked at their own license plates, so it was unlikely to be reported soon, and a stolen car with legit plates and no visible damage to the locks or windows could easily pass unnoticed, unless a cop took the trouble to run it through the system for some reason. They would not be in these cars long enough to worry about that. If they were stopped during this caper, it would be too late to worry; they'd have bigger problems.

"I tried you last night," Joe said to Yelena as they headed out. Joe paid at the register and dropped a tip on the table.

"You should have left a message," she told him. "I turned my phone off to go to sleep early."

"It's just as well," he said. "I crashed early, too."

They walked a few blocks to the Grandmaster Chess Shop. As the little bell over the door tinkled, a dozen heads turned, found nothing of interest, and returned to the boards over which they were bent. The small room was packed with tables holding chess boards, chairs, shelves full of chess sets and related items, books, timers, portraits of Russian chess heroes. The glass counter displayed some especially valuable sets. Three games were in progress, with more people looking on: all men and all old. They sipped tea as a samovar wheezed in the corner. The air was thick with smoke. A younger man with a thick, black beard, thick, black-framed glasses, and a lot of colorful tattoos was moving the dust around with a filthy feather duster. The old man behind the cash register ignored them, smoking his pipe and reading a Cyrillic book of poems. People referred to him as the Grandmaster, but whether he had really been a champion once or just worked in this shop, Yelena had no idea.

While Joe watched, Yelena went to the counter and chose a pewter knight from a set. It was very unusual, intricately designed to resemble a Mongol warrior.

"Excuse me," she asked the Grandmaster. "I want a knight like this," she told him. "But larger. A special order."

He put his book down and removed his pipe. "That would only come as a set," he said, smoke oozing out of his mouth like cartoon speech bubbles while he talked.

"Fine," Yelena answered. "Show me the samples."

He nodded and stood. "Mitka," he called to the young man who silently took his place behind the counter, and then to Yelena: "This way." She and Joe followed him through a door marked PRIVATE and into an overcrowded storeroom. It was twice as dusty as the front and ten times as packed, with shelves to the ceiling full of more chess stuff. Clenching his pipe between his teeth, he pulled back one of the shelving units, revealing a hidden door, and slid it open.

"Shut it behind you," he said and led the way through. Joe pulled the shelves back into place and shut the door behind him. They stood in utter darkness while the Grandmaster hit a switch and the fluorescent lights buzzed on. Now they were in a much cleaner, sparser room, with a table in the middle and more crates and boxes on metal shelves. He put his pipe back in his mouth and relit it as a vent in the ceiling sucked away the smoke. "What do you need?" he asked between puffs.

"Four handguns, automatics, preferably Sig 9s, Berettas, or Glocks," Joe said. The Grandmaster began pulling down boxes and laying them on the table. "Two automatic assault rifles, with scopes. Ammo."

Pipe clenched in his teeth, puffing like a choo-choo, the Grandmaster efficiently unpacked a selection of weapons and laid them on the table. "Rifles," he muttered through his teeth. "Pistols. What is this?" He dug in the bottom of a crate. "Ah, knives, too, if you like them." He opened a box in which a row of wicked combat knives were displayed. Joe chose a small throwing knife with a four-inch triangular blade and hefted it in his hand. He handed it to Yelena.

"A gift," he said.

She smiled. "*Spasibo*."

"Ammunition," the Grandmaster said and laid down boxes of cartridges. "Want to test?"

"Please," Joe said and he and Yelena began loading the weapons.

"This way." The Grandmaster opened a door across from the one they had come through. This one led downstairs, where a shooting range was set up, complete with targets. Soundproof tiles covered the ceiling and walls. He handed them ear covers and safety glasses and put on his own. "Go ahead," he said as he shut the door. "No one can hear us down here."

Side by side, Joe and Yelena fired, trying the different guns, making choices. Neither spoke, except to point out minor defects: a pistol that pulled left, a rifle that needed cleaning. Then they would turn together toward the paper men and rapidly shred them.

"We'll take these," Yelena told the Grandmaster. "With ammo and extra clips." He nodded, smoking. Then, with a sly grin, she added, in Russian: "And I need a couple of special items, too, if you can."

32

They met in the dark street. Joe and Yelena drove the Lexus, Joe behind the wheel, wearing a white button-down and jeans, Yelena, all in black, holding the velvet sack with the diamonds in her lap beside her gun. An hour before, Liam and Josh, driving the Audi, had installed themselves on the rooftop of the multistory parking garage, prone with rifles, and had noticed an armed man in a hooded sweatshirt in a similar position up the block. That was to be expected; they would both take the same precautions against a double cross, and Joe assumed that Felix's sniper had spotted his men as well. Juno and Cash were in the Saab, parked discreetly out of sight around the block, monitoring police frequencies and waiting. This part of Joe's plan was, he hoped, not expected, and they'd been careful to park well away. Even if for some reason they were seen, there was no reason to assume they were a part of this deal, which was going down out of their view.

Joe and Yelena cruised down the narrow street, abandoned now after work hours and lined with sleeping trucks. He stopped halfway and blinked the lights. Immediately, another car pulled out, blinked its lights back, and stopped, facing them about twenty feet apart. Felix drove, while Vlad held a large duffel stuffed with sealed kilos of heroin. As agreed, Joe and Vlad got out, holding their items for exchange, while Yelena and Felix followed close behind, each with a gun drawn: a standoff. If either one tried anything, the odds of both dying were high and impossible to predict, which was the closest they could get to safety.

"Nice to see you again, Joe," Felix said with a grin. "No point in pretending now."

Joe smiled back. "Hello, Felix."

"I assume Carlo is dead?" Felix asked.

"I assume so, too. As I hear Sherm and his boys are."

"Really?" Felix asked. "That's too bad. But maybe not so bad for us. Now we are both untraceable."

"Then let's take care of business, before some dog walker wanders by and you feel obliged to kill them, too."

Felix laughed and nodded at Vlad, who unzipped his pack. In the glaring headlights, Joe could see the bricks of heroin. He loosened the cord on the pouch and held up the diamonds, which seemed to dance on his palm as the streetlight bounced over them.

"Beautiful," Felix said, as Vlad zipped his bag and set it on the ground before Joe. "It's been a pleasure, Joe."

Joe pulled the cord tight and handed over the diamonds. "Anytime, Felix. Take care." Yelena watched, gun still drawn, while he hoisted the bag, which was a lot heavier than it had appeared in Vlad's arms, onto his shoulder and loaded it into the rear of the car. Then, just as Felix was getting back behind the wheel, a blond woman stepped out from where she'd been crouching beside a truck.

"Joe," Heather called, and Joe turned to her, trying to recall her face. He stepped aside to give Yelena a clear shot at her. "Yelena," Heather said then and smiled. Yelena had turned her gun on Joe.

In a flash Joe reacted. He went for Yelena's throat, choking her with one hand while the other reached for her gun. But she fired twice point-blank into Joe's chest, and he dropped, blood bursting through his white shirt. He collapsed in the headlights, head twisted. Blood trickled from his mouth.

"So long, Yelena," Heather shouted as she ran for the car where Felix and Vlad waited, diving into the back seat. Before the door was shut, they were reversing rapidly back down the block. Yelena watched, unmoving, as if stunned by the retreating headlights, while Felix jerked into a three-point turn, threw it into forward, and was gone. Immediately, she dropped her gun and kneeled over Joe, staring at what she'd done.

"The sniper's gone," Josh's voice spoke in her earpiece. "All clear."

"Here, too," Juno said.

"It's clear," Yelena whispered. Joe opened his eyes, then smiled up at Yelena, teeth bright red. She helped him sit up and he spit out a broken capsule and a mouthful of red goo.

"Yuck," he said. "That tastes like crap. Couldn't you get cherry flavor or something?"

"This looks more realistic," she replied. "You have to suffer for art."

The button-down shirt he wore was shredded, and you could see the thin metal plating Yelena had strapped to his chest with leather bands. Next she had filled condoms with blood for homemade squibs and taped them on. When she fired the blanks into him, she had pressed the barrel right to his chest. Although there were no projectiles, the charge was enough to blow the squib and burn a hole in the shirt, creating a realistic gunshot—or realistic enough for their needs.

Now, as Felix drove away, Juno and Chase would follow, tracking them with the tiny crystal transmitter Juno had hidden among the diamonds, which now showed up on Juno's laptop screen. The range was only a block or two, but they would not start moving until Felix passed them at the corner, and they did not have to maintain visual contact. Liam and Josh would trail from even farther back, ready to step into position when Felix and the others went to ground. Meanwhile, Joe and Yelena would stash the dope and then meet the rest of the crew for a final surprise assault to retake the diamonds.

Yelena lifted Joe's shirt from the back and unstrapped the plate. He grabbed the gun and, as they rushed back to their car, both were grinning. They had pulled it off. Everything was going according to plan. If they were two very different people, they might even have hugged. Then the law arrived.

PART IV

33

That morning, at the CIA's field office downtown, Agent Powell got a call on the secure line. It was Pat White. White had been a CIA asset for years, ever since the agency had run across evidence tying the New York mobster to money and weapons supplied to the IRA and to arms smuggled through those channels, some leading back eventually to PLO camps and Hamas training sites as well as far left groups in Europe. Rather than turn this over to the FBI and other counterespionage agencies for investigation and prosecution stateside, the CIA had recruited him and, since White, despite his international reach, rarely left his patch on the West Side, he worked with the New York office and Powell, in time, became his handler. White fed Powell intel—the time and location of a meeting between the heads of a Mexican drug cartel and Central American paramilitaries, the new identity just acquired by a Chinese industrial spy—and Powell protected White, warning him of sting operations to avoid, feeding domestic agencies info on his rivals, and even tipping him off about defectors in his own ranks, like Harry Harrigan, who was promptly disappeared.

Then, a few weeks ago, Powell had started pressuring White to find a weak spot in Gio Caprisi's organization. White bucked. Gio was not an enemy. If anything he'd been an ally or at least a genial colleague, and the gang war that might erupt were Gio to go down and leave a power vacuum could do him much harm and little good. But Powell was adamant. He told White that Gio himself was not necessarily the primary target. He was looking into FBI corruption and the possibility of a former Special Forces solider who'd pulled black ops for the CIA and others, now gone rogue and working for the mob.

In the end, Pat had to come across. So far, he had used his position masterfully to protect and increase his power. Despite the small size of his crew, the pacification of his old stomping grounds, and the general dwindling of the Irish mob in New York, he had remained a force to be reckoned with. But he was walking a tightrope, balanced between two underworlds: spooks and gangsters. If the truth came out, he would tumble into the net and be the next rat caught and killed.

So, the way Pat saw it, he had no choice. He was in his usual booth at the diner, in the back by the window, reading the *Daily News* sports page and eating the runny sunny-side up eggs, extra crispy bacon, and slightly burnt toast with real Irish butter that Gerald made for him special and served to Pat himself, walking from the kitchen in his apron with his plate and leaving the thermos pot of coffee. Although the river was a block away, the sun seemed to bounce off the water and ride the breeze to light his window. His sports book had come out way ahead on the game last night, so he was in a fine mood when Liam, his "nephew"—actually the son of a cousin back in Ireland—reported in as instructed to keep him in the loop and told him that the final exchange of diamonds for dope was going down that night. He ran through the plan with him to be sure it was safe and sound, then told him what a fine boy he was and wished him luck and to be sure and mind what Joe told him. Then he grabbed his pack of Pall Malls—he still had the unfiltered straights in the soft pack ordered special when his people smuggled in untaxed cigarettes from out of state or from the Indian reservations—and headed out for a smoke in the alley, where he called Agent Powell and told him what he wanted to know. He loved his nephew and hoped it turned out okay for him, but he felt no guilt or remorse. The way he saw it, he had no choice.

Donna was late to work, just ten minutes but still she was usually like clockwork, walking in with her first latte of the day on the dot. But that morning the trains had been even more of a nightmare than usual—she found out later someone had tried to jump—which she should have taken as a sign: the day was going to be fucked. She was hungover for one thing. She rarely got drunk and never went out drinking on a work night—but then she hadn't, had she? The party had come to her. And she'd ended up playing poker and getting slowly bombed with her own mom. And with Gladys, Joe's grandmom, which still felt more like a dream than reality—or maybe one of those things you were relieved to realize was only a dream when you woke up. Again, there was nothing illegal or even unethical about it. Joe was not wanted for anything or officially being investigated, never mind Gladys. Nor was there anything specifically wrong with her move at the club earlier: just a couple of federal law enforcement officers rousting a known OC hangout, trying to shake out information. They'd even bagged a fugitive in the process. But if she were honest with herself, she had to acknowledge the pattern: one way or another, there was something about Joe that made her cross lines. And that worried her.

Her coffee tasted like crap. It wasn't Sameer's fault. He'd mixed her the same magic potion he did every time in his plexiglass cart out in front of the office. It was the inside of her mouth that tasted like a sewer into which a poisoned rat had crawled to die. She could feel the fur on her tongue. So she was washing a couple of aspirin down with a bubbling glass of Alka-Seltzer when Andrew stopped by and let her know that her shit morning had just turned into a shit day. And night, most likely.

Andrew and Donna were friends and backed each other up in meetings or on the street. So when the CIA local field office reached out to their office's head field agent as a courtesy to bring them in on intel that the CIA had received about a possible exchange going down between the diamond thieves from the Midtown heist and terrorist-linked heroin traffickers and Andrew realized that the information had not crossed Donna's desk as it should have—that it was as if she were specifically being avoided—he felt he had to stop by and let her know what was up.

"They're working directly with NYPD," Andrew told her. "Basically their boss just told ours to cover his own ass and not look like he's ignoring protocol. So now I'm being sent along as liaison, chaperoning their date. But I haven't been told shit about when or where or who. Too classified for us mortals." He made quote marks in the air: "Security concerns." The implication was clear: hints about a leak in the FBI and a shadow of doubt cast over Donna.

"Son of a bitch," she muttered. She tried to repress a burp from the Alka-Seltzer, then remembered it was only Andy and let it rip.

He frowned distastefully. "Which one? There's too many around here to keep track of."

"My ex-husband. Son of a bitch numero uno. If it's sketchy, even for the CIA, and it somehow screws me, then he is in on it. Believe me."

"So what will you do?" Andrew asked, sitting on the edge of her desk, eyeing her barely touched latte. He'd been late today, too, thanks to the jumper, and he hadn't had time to stop. One loser ruining the morning commute for how many thousands? And he hadn't even jumped. "You drinking that or what?" he added.

"No, go for it," she said, and he gratefully drank. "There's not much I can do," she went on, following her thoughts. "Yet."

Andrew grinned. "Sounds like you're scheming up something."

"Always. Just keep me posted later, all right?"

"You got it, sister."

"And watch your own ass, too. I don't want any bite marks or bullets in it."

That morning, when Gio told Carol that he had several important business meetings set up for that night, that he'd be in the city and then working late in the office, Carol decided it was time. So, without even blinking, she told him right back that she had an important conference that night, too, discussing some at-risk patients with psychiatrists and educators. Was she getting to be as good a liar as he was? In any case, he bought it, kissed her, said he was so proud of her for doing such good work, and suggested that maybe they could have his mom just come by and cook for the kids. They were too old for sitters but this would just be a visit from Nonna, cooking their favorite gnocchi.

The thing that really got Carol, that made her start crying for a second in both rage and sadness when he left, was that he was right. That was just the right way to handle it. He was almost certainly a cheater and a liar. He was without a doubt a racketeer, a thief, and a gangster, and she knew in her heart he was a killer. But he was also a great dad.

That morning, when Detective Fusco showed up for work, he got a rude surprise. Well, actually, it was not all that surprising. He had been on Gio Caprisi's payroll—and under his thumb—for years. A compulsive gambler, he'd racked up debts, then traded information in payment, and he was now so compromised, so implicated that he could never untangle himself without risking his career at the very least—more likely prison—or if Gio got to him first, his life. Dirty or not, he had been a cop too long to have any illusions about who he was dealing with. Gio "the Gent" Caprisi was charming and seductive all right, like a cobra. The last snitch Fusco had ID'd for him ended up in a dumpster, chopped to pieces. There was always room in the trash for one more.

The irony of it was that Fusco was good at his job. He was a highly capable detective with a clearance rate way above average, so when he was offered a spot on the Major Case Unit, an elite team handling serious crimes like bank robbery or kidnapping—or big-ticket diamond heists—he took it as his due. He'd earned it, despite everything. Gio, of course, was thrilled. His boy was in the big league, and his new job put him directly in the flow of information coming to and from the Feds. But Fusco knew all along he was playing with fire, and that morning when the call came from his boss, he had the feeling they'd just drenched him in gasoline and asked for light.

The CIA had intel about a deal going down: the hot diamonds—from, as the news put it, the "spectacular daylight robbery in Midtown"—possibly being traded for a heroin shipment brought in by smugglers with terrorist connections. A team was being hastily pulled together from Major Case, OC Task Force, and the FBI and CIA as advisers. Why Organized Crime? The assumption all along had been that the diamond heisters were pros, the best of the best, and while there was no question they were "organized," thieves of that caliber were rarely in gangs or crime families. Rather they formed a sort of independent guild unto themselves. But the dope was different. There was no way to distribute that amount of heroin without access to a network, most likely either the black gangs in Harlem or Brooklyn or the Hispanic crews who controlled the dope trade in the Bronx and most of Manhattan. Anyone who tried to set up shop on the streets they owned wouldn't live long enough to get rich.

Also, and this was what made his stomach flip, the CIA was telling them that there was "uncorroborated and nonspecific but semireliable chatter" that the operation involved members or associates of the Caprisi crime family. And then there was the bit that scared him shitless: they also claimed to have intel that one or more compromised law enforcement officers from an unspecified agency might be involved.

That was bad. That was Fusco's ass, basically. Even if he wasn't the "officer" in question—and how could the CIA of all people know about him anyway?—it still scared him since if Gio went down and his family underwent a major prosecution, he was very likely to be caught in the undertow. One phone call, one meeting, one image on a security camera somewhere, and he was fucked.

On the other hand, what if Gio Caprisi—his curse and cross, the vampire who fed off his blood—what if he really vanished, was swept off to life in prison or witness protection or wherever they put him? Then maybe Fusco's own crimes would vanish, too, flushed down the same drain. Even his gambling debts would be canceled if Gio was canceled. It wasn't like a student loan to be traded and passed around. There was a real possibility that maybe, in this one night, all Fusco's problems could be wiped.

So when he and his team got their invitations to the party that night, he hesitated. Call Gio and warn him: yes or no? All day long he asked himself that: yes or no? And while he was a good cop and an excellent detective, Fusco, clearly, was a lousy gambler. He knew it. And even as day turned to night and the team headed to the location, a dark, quiet street in Dumbo, and began to get into position, he hadn't decided which way to bet. The game plan, dictated from above, was to hang back and let the exchange happen, then seal the block and trap the players. Squad cars and plainclothes were set up on the surrounding streets, ready to move in. Fusco was actually in his car, parked out of sight, waiting with the agents that the CIA and FBI had sent along to "observe and advise." A stiff prick named Powell, a typi-cal spook, riding shotgun in Fusco's car, adjusted the radio and AC like he owned it, with a cooler but less confident young FBI agent named Newton in back with Henderson, a close-to-retirement hack from OC Task Force. He finally decided: go with your gut. And his gut said call Gio. They say the house always wins? Well, Gio was the house. So, at the last possible second, he announced he had to smoke, then stepped out of the car, ducked around a corner, and called. Then he texted *URGENT 911*. Then he called again. But Gio didn't pick up.

34

And so that's why that evening, as Joe and Yelena were heading back to their car grinning big, he with the blank gun and his shirt soaked in fake blood, she holding the plate she'd made, and Juno and Cash were pulling out to follow the stones, and Liam and Josh were rushing downstairs to get to their car to trail them, with everything having gone off like clockwork, precisely according to plan, without even a (real) bullet fired, it all instantly went to shit as the law came crashing in.

Juno's warning came just as the cop car appeared. "Yo five-o!" he barked into their earpieces right as the police car, which had been cruising silently, hit its lights and sirens as it came around the corner fast behind Joe and Yelena's car, blinding them in the headlights.

"Don't move. This is the police," a voice announced redundantly over the loud speaker as they squeaked to a stop, bouncing on their shocks, and spilled out from both sides drawing their weapons. Yelena dove for the car. She was unarmed but had left an AR-15 on the back seat, and she grabbed for it now. Joe immediately opened fire.

The gun was full of blanks of course. They'd filled the magazine, unsure how many shots Yelena would need for the trick, so now he had seven empty rounds left, which he blasted straight at the faces of the cops as he, too, sprinted for the car.

The cops, however, did not know they were blanks. Therefore, they reacted in the way any sane animals would, seeing a man aim a pistol right at their faces and pull the trigger: they freaked out. They recoiled in terror from the muzzle flash bursting right in their eyes. One fired, wildly, hitting nothing but a wall down the block as he ran back to the patrol car for cover. The other dropped to the ground, almost as if he'd been hit. Joe emptied the gun at them and got behind the wheel of the car.

Meanwhile, Fusco's unmarked car had pulled in behind the cop car, but by then Yelena had her rifle and, rising through the sunroof was firing real bullets into the windshield of the cop car and over the heads of the newcomers, who scrambled for cover. Joe slammed on the gas and they bounced off over the cobblestones. Over the radio, Fusco and Powell berated the cops with the shattered windshield, who were still ducked and covered and who were blocking the narrow street. Finally, realizing they were alive and unhit, the traumatized cops got back in their patrol car and got rolling. Fusco followed, with Powell roaring beside him, and Henderson on his walkie in the back, trying to call for backup. Andrew, meanwhile, was deep in thought. He had the weirdest sense of déjà vu, almost as if he'd seen this woman before. And there had been speeding cars and bullets that time, too.

At that point, just a handful of seconds after Juno's yell, Joe and Yelena heard more yelling on the earpiece, from Josh and Liam, and then, from around the upcoming corner, more shots and more sirens.

"Josh is hit. Josh is hit," Liam called, and as Joe and Yelena reached the corner, the black Audi shot by, driven by Liam and pursued by another cop car, its siren wailing. Joe joined the chase.

As soon as Josh and Liam saw that Felix and the others were in motion, they rushed downstairs to retrieve the car they'd left parked at the curb and catch up to Juno and Cash, who were tracking the diamonds from a discreet distance. But right when they were running out of the street door, a police car came flying around the corner. The uniforms inside had been sent to intercept the black BMW containing Felix, Vlad, and Heather, but seeing two men with rifles getting into a sleek black car, they figured this was it, jolted to a stop, and, yelling their warnings, opened fire. Josh fired back, giving Liam cover while he got the car going, then ran and jumped in beside him as he rolled out. That's when he got winged.

"Josh is hit," Liam called to the others. He peeled out, while Josh pulled his door shut, grimacing as blood seeped from the hole in his shoulder. The bullet had gone clean through. He hunted in the glove box for something to press against the wound and found a pack of Kleenex, which were immediately soaked.

The cop car sped after them, siren blaring, and a moment later, in the rearview, Liam could see Joe and Yelena come around the corner and fall in behind them, with another police car and the unmarked car chasing them.

"How bad?" Joe's voice came over the earpiece.

"I'm okay," Josh grunted.

"Through the shoulder but he's bleeding bad," Liam said.

He made a right and then a left, zooming through the mostly empty streets, trying to avoid the tangle of dead-end blocks up ahead that he knew would trap them in Vinegar Hill. As a result he found himself turning onto a wider, busier street. And there was Felix, tooling along with Vlad beside him and Heather in back, looking at them and their parade of police in sudden confusion and alarm. Assuming they were coming after them, Felix gunned the engine. Liam, out of necessity, sped up to stay ahead of the cops, and Joe and Yelena came next, with the other cars chasing them in turn. As they passed the corner, another patrol car fell in line, merging into their lane. Liam rode Felix's bumper, with his lengthening tail behind him. Meanwhile, a block over, on a parallel street, Juno and Cash, who had been trying to keep a low profile so as not to alert the quarry, now had to speed up to keep the diamonds in range.

"Liam, do you know a doctor you can go to?" Joe asked over the earpiece.

"I do," Liam said. "But I don't think he'd appreciate me bringing the law with me."

"You still on the rocks, Juno?"

"Yeah, man," Juno answered. "You know Cash is cool behind the wheel. But if we keep up like this they're gonna make us, or we're gonna get pulled over ourselves."

"Right," Joe said, glancing over at Yelena, who was checking her guns to be sure they were all loaded with real bullets. He checked both side mirrors and glanced in the rearview at the cops on his tail. "Let's see if we can give you both some breathing room," he said. Then he signaled as he changed lanes.

They were Downtown now, in the wider streets near Borough Hall, surrounding the municipal buildings and courts, which was convenient. Traffic was sparse at night, plus, if they were caught, there wouldn't be far to go. Joe swerved right, taking the Lexus over the curb and across a large plaza bounded by the courthouse on one side and trees and benches on the other. The two cars behind him followed, while the others continued after Liam, splitting the party in two.

Now Joe floored it. With no traffic ahead of him and the wide plaza to himself, he pushed the engine and was quickly speeding past the others, who were still jockeying on his left, along Cadman Plaza.

"Okay, here I come," he told Liam, then glanced at Yelena. "Get ready," he told her.

She pulled her seat belt tight and braced herself, the rifle in her lap. "Ready," she said.

Joe veered left, cutting through the benches and across the sidewalk, then between parked cars and back onto the road. As Liam changed lanes to give him some space, Joe aimed his car right at the cop car behind Liam and hit it, full speed, clipping the right front corner with the front left side of his car. The impact sent the cop car spinning out of control, and it slammed into a bus stop on the corner. Liam and Felix both shot through the intersection, amid honks and screeching brakes. Traffic stopped. Liam sped off, passing Felix, who turned down a side street unpursued—or so he thought—except for Cash and Juno, who were tracking him from a block away, cruising like a shark in shallow water. Joe went into a controlled skid, ending up angled across the lane, blocking the line of police cars behind him as the light went red. He stopped.

With a jerk, the cops behind him stopped, and a kind of shiver ran down the row of cars as each one hit its brakes. Everything came to a halt. The car Joe had hit was up on the curb, wedged into the demolished bus shelter, its right side crumpled, its disoriented occupants still trying to get out. The lead cop car sat in confusion, its occupants peering at Joe's headlights through their shattered windshield, and behind them the others shouted into their radios, unable to see what was going on. That's when Yelena opened fire.

She leaned her rifle out and began blasting at the first cop car, blowing away both tires and piercing the grill and radiator, just as she had already obliterated the windshield. The frantic cops inside ducked as they struggled to take their belts off and unholster their weapons while crouching under the dashboard. Joe hit the gas, and as the light turned green, he tore out into the intersection, while the cops in the first car sighed with relief at being free of bullets and those behind them tried frantically to pull around the sides.

Then Joe made a U-turn, a wide loop around the intersection and, bouncing over the curb, cut through the plaza once again. He was going right back the way he'd come.

In the unmarked car at the rear of the parade, Powell was losing his mind. He punched the dashboard and yelled at Fusco to back up, which he was trying to do, though the traffic that was collecting behind him made that difficult. Fusco shouted over his radio for the patrol units ahead of him to turn around and continue pursuit—and get out of his goddamn way—but that was made harder by the crippled cars in front. Meanwhile, was anybody still giving chase?

"All units, come in," Fusco called over the radio. "Anyone still in pursuit of green Lexus four door?" There was silence. "Hello? Come in . . . Speak the fuck up!"

"Negative," came the sheepish reply.

"Sorry, Detective."

"We put out an alert. We got the plates."

"Fuck me," Powell muttered as Fusco, having backed and filled a few times, finally got loose. They raced across the park and on to the trail of the Lexus with the other cops now free to follow behind. "They went that way," he told Fusco, who already knew and ignored him. In back, Andrew watched the show calmly, while Henderson hung on to the strap, grunting and cursing as Fusco drove over curbs and made wild turns. His back and kidneys did not need the pounding.

The other suspects, in the black Audi and the BMW, were long gone by now, away clean. There was an alert out, but it was unlikely to help: they had vanished into the vast sea of city traffic. More units called in, converging on the area, tightening the net, but the only fish left to catch was the slippery Lexus, which seemed to be returning to where they'd all started. It wasn't a smart move: they'd be cut off by the river and the dense traffic heading over the two bridges into Manhattan with a small army of police officers closing in.

"Can you trap them?" Powell asked.

Fusco shrugged, hands on the wheel, eyes forward, navigating the streets while his siren screamed. "Looks like they're going to trap themselves," he said, still not entirely sure of what he'd have if he did catch them or if he wanted it.

"You back there!" Powell twisted around to shout at Andrew. "FBI. Why don't you do something?"

"I am," he answered evenly. "I was told to observe and advise. So right now I am observing you lose your shit." He returned Powell's glare. "And I advise you to get the fuck out of my face."

35

Joe and Yelena had boxed themselves in. They'd had no choice. They had to help Liam get loose so he could take Josh for medical care. And they had to shake Felix free, with Cash and Juno on his tail, relaxed enough to settle down and lead them to the diamonds. So Joe had drawn the heat deliberately, first slowing things down to give them a head start, then looping back the way they'd come to take the pursuit off track before the net closed in too tightly. Now the others were breathing easy, and they were getting choked off.

"I'm thinking we should ditch this car," Joe said as he sped through the streets. There were cops in his rearview and he could see sirens at the intersections as more police moved in. Yelena was busy transferring the dope from the duffel to two smaller backpacks. She tossed the empty bag out of the window.

"Let's park," she said.

Joe turned back into the street where they had met Felix to start with, but this time he was coming up the wrong way with cops behind him, and there were more flashing lights coming down to meet him. They were blocked in.

"Hold on," he said, and Yelena braced herself. Skidding as he turned, Joe cranked the wheel and entered the parking garage.

Before, when Liam and Josh had used the roof as a sniper's perch, it had been easy to access. They just walked in the main entrance as if they were picking up their car and left via the stairway and a street exit, which was unlocked from inside in case of fire. The only thing the building was really guarded against was someone stealing a car or avoiding payment. Breaking in with a car hadn't occurred to anyone. Now Joe sped past the shocked attendant and crashed through the barrier, splintering the wooden arm.

He drove up the ramp, following the rise of the curve and leaning on his horn to clear the way, though the structure was quiet, with the parked vehicles in for the night. He could hear the police sirens behind him. At the second level, when he saw the elevator he cut the wheel right and stopped, parking the Lexus the long way across the elevator doors and also blocking the ramp. He removed the keys from the ignition and leaned out his window to press the elevator Call button. As the police arrived, Yelena leaned out her window and took aim.

"Try not to kill anyone," Joe said. She gave him a dirty look. "Please," he added.

"I haven't killed anyone all day," she pointed out, then opened fire, spraying the police cars and the parked vehicles. The cops scrambled for cover as her bullets rained down, creating a huge storm of noise and breaking glass. A couple tried to return fire but they were just shooting blind. Joe watched the elevator's indicator light.

"One more floor," he said. She kept shooting. Joe aimed his handgun at the doors as they opened, just in case, but the elevator was empty. "Let's go," he said and opened his door, pushing out the two backpacks and then sliding through. Yelena followed, continuing to fire over the hood of the Lexus while Joe pressed the top button and the elevator doors slid shut.

They waited. It was unnerving riding the elevator in silence, as though on their way to the office, but unless paratroopers had landed there was no way the cops had made it to the top floor yet. Joe had left the Lexus so that it blocked the ramp and they were in the only elevator, so the police would be humping it up the stairs. Still, they slid the backpacks onto their shoulders and aimed their guns outward as the doors slid back.

No one was there. Joe held the Open button while Yelena grabbed the trash can that stood beside the elevator and set it to keep the doors from closing.

The top floor was mostly empty and open on all sides, with a bunch of maintenance and repair equipment piled in a corner, which they had seen when checking the place out the day prior. Joe ran and grabbed a mop and pushed it through the handles of the stairwell doors. That would slow them down a bit, though they had to assume that officers on foot would be running up the car ramp, too, in a few minutes.

While he was doing that, Yelena was dragging an extendable aluminum ladder over to the concrete barrier that ran around the open sides. Joe ran to help. Beneath them was a narrow alley, an airspace really, and then the roof of the building next door, one story shorter. Holding the ladder together and extending it to its full length, they set the bottom onto the roof below, with the top propped against the parking structure.

"You first, kitty cat," Joe said.

Yelena smiled. "Scared, Joe?"

"Absolutely," he said, bracing himself to hold the ladder steady. Yelena climbed onto the wall and then, on her hands and knees, began to crawl downward, moving carefully but swiftly across. The ladder bent under her weight a little, but Joe held it tight, leaning his weight on it while glancing over his shoulder. The elevator doors bounced against the trash can.

Yelena hopped gracefully off the ladder and onto the roof. Taking hold of the ladder on the other side, she waved for him to join her. Joe took a last look back. He could hear pounding on the stairwell door now. So he went.

He climbed onto the wall and then, very carefully, he set first one hand and then the other on the side rails of the ladder. He tested it by pressing and, though it gave slightly, it held steady as he began to inch forward, moving one hand then the other, until his knees were resting on the crosspieces. Then he began to crawl. He felt wind and space around and beneath him, and the ladder seemed to bend under his weight, but he kept going, equally worried about falling to the concrete below and the cops arriving from above. He'd be an easy target here. It would almost be a game to shoot him off.

Yelena smiled up at him. "Good," she called out. "Keep going. And don't look down."

"Thanks," he said. "I'm afraid to look up, too. If you see a cop now, it's okay to shoot him."

She grinned. He kept going. When he crossed the point where the ladder rested against the edge of the lower roof, he immediately rolled off. Together, they pulled the ladder down onto the lower roof and left it hidden in darkness and shadow. They could hear cops yelling now and see flashlights moving around in the garage, searching cars and corners, but no one had yet looked down.

Yelena dashed to the door that led to the building stairs. It was locked, with no keyhole on the outside for her to pick. She shook her head at Joe and pointed at the back side of the building. He waved her on, keeping watch while she ran over, then followed. They clambered onto the fire escape. Now they were out of sight of the parking structure, as well as hidden from the police gathered out front on the street. The fire escape led down to a small cement backyard, only accessible through the building. Another trap. They began quickly but quietly to move down the steps of the fire escape, checking the windows. The first window they reached was dark and barred with a heavy security gate that looked as if it had not been opened in years. But the next was lit and open, with the gate pulled back, no doubt to accommodate the gray cat curled on the fire escape, enjoying the night air. At their approach, the cat jumped back through the window. Yelena went in right after it, her gun drawn, and pointed it at the head of the young woman who sat on the couch. She was in sweatpants and a Columbia T-shirt, redheaded and pale, probably even paler than usual at that moment. Joe came through fast as well, moving immediately to check the rest of the small apartment: a tiny bedroom, an overstuffed closet, a bathroom, and the main room, which comprised living room, kitchen, and dining.

"Clear," Joe said, as he put his gun away and went back to the window. He shut it, locked the gate, and drew the curtains. Yelena remained focused on the young woman, gun steady.

"Don't worry," Joe told her, grabbing her remote and silencing the TV show she was watching. "I won't let her shoot you as long as you behave, okay?"

She nodded, petrified.

"Now," he asked her, "is there anybody else coming over here tonight? Boyfriend? Girlfriend? Did you order food?"

She shook her head. "No," she croaked, voicelessly, then cleared her throat and tried again. "No one's coming. I was going to order Seamless but I don't have to." Her lip trembled. "Take anything you want. Take my laptop and money. Just please don't hurt me . . . or . . ." She gasped for air, as though drowning in her own fear. " Please don't rape me."

Yelena scowled. "Rape?" she asked, breaking her silence. "You think I look like a rapist?"

"No, no, I'm sorry. I'm sure you're not. I mean, couples don't usually rape do they? I don't know!" She started crying. "This is my first time!"

"Calm down," Joe said, gesturing for Yelena to put away the gun. "Nobody's going to do anything to you. And we won't rob you either. I promise. You're going to be okay."

She nodded, still petrified. "Um . . . are you okay?" she asked him then, staring in horror at his torn and blood-stained shirt.

"Don't worry. That's not his blood," Yelena explained and the girl paled again, eyes wide.

"She means it's fake," Joe reassured her. "Like Halloween. It's a long story."

Her face rapidly registered hope, then confusion. "Then what do you want?"

"We just want to hang out here awhile," Joe said. "You see, right now, outside, cops are swarming all over the place looking for us. So we can't go out. We need to stay out of sight until they clear off, and then we will clear off, too. They might search this building. They might even knock on your door, but as long as you do what we say, everything will be fine. Understand?"

"You're like fugitives or something?"

"Right," Joe said, removing his backpack and sitting in a chair. "We're criminals making our getaway."

Yelena shrugged her pack off, too, and put it near Joe's, then perched on the couch. The cat crept up onto her lap. She stroked it behind the ears and it purred as she smiled sweetly at the terrified girl. "We are like Bonnie and Clyde," she told her. "Isn't that fun?"

36

As soon as Liam was clear from the police he slowed down. He knew he should probably ditch the car, but Josh was bleeding quietly beside him, slipping into shock, and he didn't have time to stop. Instead, he quickly turned a few corners and joined the flow of cars heading up the ramp toward the Brooklyn Bridge, trying to lose himself in traffic the way a runner might hide by slowing down and walking with a rush hour crowd. It worked. The only heat he drew was angry drivers honking at him for shouldering his way in, but now he was freaking out over the traffic that had been his shield. They inched over the river, like a worm crossing a fallen log. He glared furiously at the dark rear window of the Jeep in front of him, like it was a TV screen about to light up with an important message, then turned, every few seconds, to check on Josh. Head back, eyes closed, profile silhouetted against the city light and river darkness. Looking at him, Liam felt, to his surprise, and to use the word that he spoke to himself, silently, tenderness. It was like the end of a gangster movie, an old one, where the heroes, maybe best friends from childhood, maybe sworn enemies till now, face the end together, one dying in the other's arms, with so much unsaid and yet nothing needing to be said at all.

It was a silly thought he knew. Romantic. Yet weren't criminals, in some sense, romantics? Even if they themselves would puke at the idea? Even if most of the ones Liam actually knew, having grown up around them, were dumb, brutal bastards, thick as planks or mental. They were playing with fate, rolling the dice on their own freedom, betting their lives that it would come out all right, while knowing, in the long run, the odds still ran against them like in gambling or love.

Then again, criminals were hardcore realists, too, and as a cold-blooded, clear-eyed cynic, Liam also knew: someone had talked, someone had tipped off the law. That's why he was here now. How else could the cops have popped in at exactly the right time and place? Someone had grassed. And that someone needed to pay in blood for the blood his friend was spilling now.

So when the phone in his hip pocket buzzed and it showed an unknown number and Liam answered, asking "Yeah?" the voice, clearly Gio's, asked only: "This phone safe?" Reassured by Liam that it was one of the burners he and the rest of the crew had bought for the job, he went on to say: "Liam I have some hard news for you." Liam listened, saying nothing in response but: "I understand. Tell me what you need." And he knew. It really was like the end of a gangster picture, the wicked twist. Yes, someone had talked, and it was he. He, Liam, had betrayed his mates and set up Josh to be shot, because as it turned out, talking to his grand old uncle Pat was just the same as talking to the filth.

The traffic moved. Some light somewhere had changed, opening the clogged roadways, releasing the backup. Or some accident or incident had been cleared, someone else's tragedy or comedy playing out on another stage, the best or worst night of some stranger's life, merely a pain in the ass for the rest of us.

Liam crossed the river. Descending into Manhattan, he drove swiftly over Centre Street and across Chambers toward the clinic whose doctor, a do-gooder serving the underserved all day, made his real money serving do-badders by night. He was waiting and ready. Liam would get his partner there alive and make sure he was all right. Then he would make this car disappear. Then he would visit his uncle.

Josh was moving. His eyes were closed but his head turned and his lips worked silently, like he was having a bad dream. Liam reached out and squeezed his hand.

"You're alright, Josh," he said. "We're getting you help. You're going to be fine."

Josh's eyes fluttered. He tried to speak. "Liam?"

"I'm here Josh. Don't try to talk. Save your strength. You're going to be fine. We're almost there." He squeezed Josh's hand again, harder. "I'm here with you."

Josh smiled then, his full, pretty lips soundlessly forming the words "thank you," and he squeezed back. They held hands the rest of the way.

37

Cash and Juno made a good team. They were roughly the same age, grew up in similar neighborhoods, and succeeded through similar means. Half street, half geek, smart and quick, but never as athletic as their older brothers or as tough as the local thugs, they survived by developing skills that the people around them came to value and admire: Juno the tech wizard, Cash the ace car thief and driver. And both took pride in being the best.

So now they operated like pros and got along like pals, even agreeing on the music to which they nodded in unison as Juno tracked the diamonds on an iPad he held in his lap and Cash smoothly and seemingly effortlessly glided them through the streets, making sure never to fall too far behind and lose the signal or press too close and get made. In fact they had not actually seen the car containing Felix, Vlad, and Heather since the scramble with the cops. They'd hung back, keeping out of sight but always within a one-block radius.

This took some doing. Cash had to run an obstacle course, negotiating stopped buses, slow traffic, backing trucks, and clueless drivers, dodging errant bikers and jaywalking pedestrians, catching lights and navigating one-way streets and construction zones, all while avoiding any behavior that might get them pulled over. He did it cool, too, nonchalantly, one hand on the wheel, head and shoulders loose, but eyes in constant motion, checking the mirrors and scanning the road ahead, reacting to what was about to happen a beat before it happened, not a beat after. That was the key.

Juno's blinking dot took them to Queens and stopped, finally, in Astoria, on a block off Steinway Street. This was one of the city's main Arabic communities, once dubbed Little Egypt, but now packed with Middle Eastern and North African shops, cafés, and restaurants run by Lebanese, Moroccans, and Syrians among others.

Moving slow and careful now, Cash and Juno closed in on the signal, which seemed to be emanating from a large building on a corner. They circled the block, passing the black BMW they'd been tracking all this time, now empty and parked by a hydrant. The front side of the building was revealed to be a big Middle Eastern restaurant and nightclub with a constant flow of customers bustling in and out, cars and taxis dropping people out front. A neon sign read CLUB LAYALI. Cash pulled over in a spot with a view of the entrance. They waited. Cash smoked a cigarette and stretched his tight shoulder muscles out after the long, tense ride. Juno turned the music up and watched his dot. Fifteen minutes went by.

"I think they're settled in for now," he said finally.

"Maybe they're getting dinner," Cash suggested. He was starving himself. He never ate before a job and now the idea of chicken roasting on skewers was making his stomach growl. "Maybe we should go in and check?"

"Joe said just sit on them and call. I ain't moving in with just us."

"Not move in. Just get closer. He said cover the place, too. But without Liam and Josh how can we? They could go out the back right now and we'd lose them. Or head back to their car."

Juno nodded. "Okay. Let's park and go inside, just to try and pin down where they are in the building. Meanwhile I'll text Joe the address."

"Great," Cash said as he pulled around the corner and parked illegally behind a construction dumpster. "I'm fucking starving."

"And I've got to piss so bad I can taste it," Juno added.

So they went in and while Cash waited for a table, Juno went to the men's room. The place was huge, even bigger than it seemed from outside. A converted warehouse, there was a long bar, a central floor full of tables, draped booths along the walls made to look like private harem chambers with people sitting on pillows and smoking hookahs, tile and arched doorways everywhere. On a stage in back, a band played traditional instruments and women were belly dancing for a louder, drunker crowd at bigger tables. The ceiling was high, with fabric hanging down to look like a tent, and there was a balcony running around the mezzanine with more tables, quieter and more romantic, mostly couples eating by candlelight and gazing down at the action.

The men's room was down a flight of stairs, and for a while Juno lost his tracking signal, but coming back down the hallway after using the bathroom, the iPad in his back-pack buzzed and he checked: the diamonds were close, very close, seemingly right under his feet. Curious, he paced the hall: restrooms, a janitor's closet, and at the rear, a door that when pushed, opened to reveal a dim storeroom, filled with cartons and packed shelves eight feet high. He stepped in slowly, shutting the door quietly behind him, face down in his tablet. The signal was still beneath him. In fact he had already passed over it somewhere in the hall. Clearly there was some sort of subbasement, but Juno couldn't see any stairway or other entrance. Then the lights came on, and a voice behind him said: "You're standing on it."

"Sorry?" He turned. It was a middle-aged Mediterranean-looking man with a closely trimmed dark beard in a gray suit and blue shirt.

"The trapdoor to the basement," he said. "You're stand-ing on it."

Juno smiled, flashing his innocent fool look. "I don't know what you mean. I was looking for the men's room. They said downstairs . . ."

The man raised his arm. He was casually holding a gun, not really aiming it at Juno, just showing that he had it. "Now, now. Let's not get off on the wrong foot. The party is just starting." Juno raised his hands and the man gestured at his sneakers with the gun. "Lift that mat and I will show you how to get to the VIP lounge. It's invitation only."

Upstairs at the table, Cash was waiting eagerly for the appetizers he'd gone ahead and ordered, unable to wait for Juno to finish taking a leak. So when his phone buzzed and it was a text from Juno telling him to come downstairs right away, he cursed under his breath and stood reluctantly, still looking around for his food. He needn't have bothered. Vlad, who was watching him from across the room, had already canceled the order.

38

Donna was making the best of it. After not getting invited to the big bust, her first impulse to was to brood like a high schooler dissed by the cool kids, but instead she regressed even further and took her daughter to an animated movie with gummy bears and licorice, a rare treat, smuggled in her purse. As a result, her phone was on silent when Andrew's texts and calls came in—another rare treat, since for once she was definitely *not* on call. By the time she checked, in the lobby, there was a whole series of messages describing the drama that had been unfolding while she watched cartoon animals on the screen. So she let Larissa play a driving video game—another special treat!—while she called Andrew back. He was half-alarmed and half-gleeful. The op had gone completely sideways and they had ended up capturing nobody, nor did they recover any diamonds or seize any dope. Instead they triggered a shoot-out and a high-speed chase through the streets of Brooklyn, resulting in a couple of busted-up police cars and a giant black eye for everyone present except, for once, the FBI. They were just observing.

The NYPD were catching most of the hell from the city, and in turn they were blaming the CIA for crappy intel. And the bureau, which now claimed they should have been handling it all along, were mounting up to assist with the building-to-building search. "If I were you I'd get down here," Andrew said. "Not that there's anything much left to investigate. Still it's fun watching them whine. You might even get to see your ex-husband eating shit."

Donna knew he was right. If nothing else, she should show her face, offer to help with the crisis, even if it was all a big waste of time. But it was too late to get a sitter and her mom, much to Donna's unease, was hanging out with her new best friend, Gladys Brody. Poker lessons. Donna sighed. She'd known about her mother's little secret vice for months, and if she could go from losing to winning without breaking the law any more than she was already, Donna supposed that was an improvement. And she couldn't deny she liked Gladys. She was fun. A lot more fun than her mom's usual sidekicks, who mainly talked about their ailments. So she understood the attraction. It was her own attraction to the Brody family that she found hard to figure.

It all added up to a big bowl of mixed feelings when she called her mom and said she was heading to Brooklyn for a work emergency and could she drop Larissa by? Her mom said absolutely. They were going to bake some cookies and change the game to hearts.

39

Their hostage was named Ami, spelled like that. Her mom was a Francophile, and she was pretty cool once she got over being completely terrified. She even gave Joe one of her boyfriend's shirts—a garish Hawaiian number she was eager to let him think got lost in the laundry—so that he could take off the bloody one and wash off with paper towels at the sink. She noticed he had a good body, lean and muscled. Her boyfriend was an ex-athlete who still played football on the weekends, but he was both bulkier and somehow softer. On the other hand, this guy had a lot more scars. He also found a coin, a quarter, in the front pocket of the aloha shirt, and laid it on the kitchen counter, which just felt odd to her somehow, like he'd kidnap her at gunpoint to hide from the cops but he wouldn't take her change.

Her boyfriend, she explained when asked, was a digital marketing consultant out of town for work. No, they didn't live together yet. She designed websites, freelance right now, though she was thinking about going full time somewhere, maybe a start-up. She almost asked them, out of habit, if they needed their websites redesigned but stopped herself.

Or did criminals have them, too, on the dark web, with code names and masks, like Anonymous? Even if they did, it wouldn't be these two, who clearly had no idea what a digital marketing consultant even was.

"Like tweets?" the man had asked.

"Among other things," she'd said and let it go. He had a flip phone for God's sake, on which he laboriously texted with one finger.

And the woman, Ami didn't know what to make of her. She was foreign, Russian or Eastern European, and seemed never to have heard of *Game of Thrones*, which is what Ami was watching and what she was told to continue watching once it was clear they'd all be stuck there awhile. The woman sat on the couch with Ami and watched TV with the volume low. The guy moved a chair over by the door, where he could hear footsteps and peek out the peephole. He couldn't see the TV from there so he reached into his pocket and pulled out a folded-up copy of the *Times* crossword puzzle, then asked the woman for a pencil. She reluctantly handed him a mechanical one.

"Don't forget to give it back," she said. "It's my favorite."

"I gave it back last time, didn't I?" he said and then frowned at the clues. They went back to TV.

"This is a show for children?" the woman asked finally. "With knights and dragons?"

"No. I mean, it's fantasy," Ami told her. "But for adults."

This idea seemed to confuse her, until a few scenes later some incest action started to unfold. "Now this is fantasy for adults," she said. "But then why not just watch porn?"

Finally Ami searched the listings and found an old episode of *Project Runway*. This she liked, immediately joining Ami in critiquing the clothes, which led them to a general discussion of fashion. In fact they were kind of bonding, talking about what a genius Rei from Comme was, when suddenly the guy shushed them and turned out the lights. The woman grabbed the remote and turned the TV off, then held Ami's hand in the dark. Instinctively, Ami squeezed back, as though they were friends hiding together after smoking pot in the dorm or something. Then she realized—or remembered— these were criminals on the run and the woman was keeping her under control and would silence her with violence if need be.

Then a knock came, hard and with authority. "Hello!" a gruff male voice called. "This is the police. Anybody home?" He knocked again. Her eyes adjusting to the darkness, Ami could now see that both the Russian woman and the guy, who stood still as a statue by the door, were holding guns. Finally, she heard knocking on the neighbor's doors, followed by some distant murmuring. Then silence. The man turned on the light.

"All done," he said and smiled reassuringly. He put the gun away in his belt, and she noticed that he'd clipped the woman's pencil to his (or her boyfriend's) shirt pocket, and she was about to say something, like teasing him about it, but then decided to just shut up. Then his phone must have vibrated, because he checked it and nodded at the woman. She got up and checked the window, peeking through the curtain first, then opening the gate to look out, while

Ami held the cat. You couldn't see much. She was in a rear apartment. Next she took Ami's keys and went up to the roof while the guy watched her, smiling the whole time and telling her they'd be leaving soon and she'd done great so far, in the same tone her dentist used before drilling.

The woman came back and smiled, too. "All clear," she said, and they put their backpacks on. Relief was flooding through Ami at this point. She felt this whole thing turning from the scariest night of her life to an amazing dinner party anecdote. But then the guy reached into her purse and got out her license. He gave it to the woman, who snapped a photo with her phone—an iPhone, much better than his—then gave it back to her. He spoke in the same even, friendly tone.

"Now we know who you are, where you live, everything. Enough to find you, no matter where you go. You know enough about us to cause some trouble but not that much. So I'm going to strongly advise you, Ami Hendricks, not to mention tonight to anybody, not ever, not even to your boyfriend. Because if you do, either we or our friends will be back, and that won't be a pleasant visit like tonight. Understand?"

She nodded. Instantly, she was in stark terror again, realizing how close she had been to danger all along. These people looked and talked like they were friendly, normal people, but they were something else. She saw her cat, yawning wide, fangs showing, then rubbing against the woman's legs, and she remembered something she'd read somewhere: you think your cat loves you because it cuddles with you, it's cute, and it purrs, but it would kill and eat you if it could.

"Good," the man said and he smiled. "Now you can go back to your show."

He opened the door.

"Thanks and have a good evening," the woman said, walking out.

"You, too," Ami answered, reflexively, and they were gone.

40

When Pat walked into Old Shenanigan's, only the manager nodded at him, respectfully but discreetly. That was how he liked it. Although he controlled this place, he was strictly a silent partner, and he liked being able to come and go without being noticed, as opposed to other spots, like the private social club or the diner where he held court. But here, if anyone did say anything about the old guy in the cap and raincoat who just walked through the EMPLOYEES ONLY door, they'd be told to forget it. He was checking on the construction or taking inventory of the booze, someone unimportant doing something boring. In this way he had a safe, secure place to meet where he knew no one he didn't want to could see or hear.

So he was completely thrown when he entered the torn-out men's room he used for private one-on-one talks expecting to meet Liam and flipped on the light to find Gio Caprisi standing there, holding a gun.

"What the fuck?" Pat barked, his sense of ownership and generalship overpowering the immediate rush of confusion and fear. "What are you doing here?" He took a step forward, but Gio pointed the gun at him.

"Hold it," he said, and Pat realized there was another guy there, hiding behind the doorway. Nero, Gio's sidekick, stepped up behind him and frisked him, removing the revolver from his ankle holster.

"No wire, boss," Nero said, stepping around front to point his own gun at Pat, too.

"Wire? Fuck you, Gio, coming to my place and making implications—"

"Drop it, Pat," Gio said. "Don't waste your last few breaths on bullshit. We know you've been selling us out to the CIA."

Pat slumped. Suddenly, he felt like what he was, an old, tired, bent man facing the end. It was almost a relief, yet every nerve in his body still jumped and twitched, demanding he run or fight or bargain or beg for his life. "Look Gio, I can deal you in. This CIA thing works like a charm. Protect us. Sink your enemies. Just put the guns down and we'll talk."

Gio smiled. "Sure, let's talk. In your nice private soundproof room. Too bad you have to die in a toilet though. But that's what we do to lying, snitching pieces of shit. We flush them."

In a flash, the rage that had fueled Pat's whole life came back and he stepped toward Gio, fists up. "Fuck you, you guinea faggot cocksucker. You think no one knows—"

Gio fired. The first shot went through his lung and stopped him. The second pierced his heart. Then Nero started pulling the trigger, too, and by the time he fell—a crumpled, lifeless heap with a cap on top—his body held a dozen bullets. Liam stepped into the room from the dark corner down the hall where he'd been waiting. He regarded the corpse.

"Much obliged, Gio," he said, quietly. "It had to be done, but I don't know if I'd have had the stomach. He used to bounce me on his knee. Then again, he also taught me to shoot people."

Gio switched his gun to his left, then held out his hand. "Consider it a symbol of our new friendship."

Liam shook his hand. "I'm happy to hear you say that, Gio. And honored. And I know I speak for my brothers, too."

"Please send them my regards. And my sympathies." He turned to Nero. "Stay here and help him clean up. And get rid of this, too." He handed him the gun.

"But, Boss, where are you going?" Nero asked. "Don't you want me to come?"

"I've got another meeting tonight," Gio said, walking out. "A personal one."

Nero watched him go, holding guns in each hand, while Liam started dragging a construction tarp in from the hall. He shrugged and shoved the guns in his pockets and went to help. They still had a lot of work to do tonight.

41

Joe and Yelena drove to Astoria.

When they left Ami's building, after moving stealthily down the stairs and peeking carefully out at the now-empty streets, they immediately began to walk normally, like a tourist couple holding hands and sauntering down the block with their packs on. It was silent. Life had returned to normal. They crossed the street, turned a corner, and found the Toyota Corolla where Joe had stashed it. It had a ticket from street cleaning, which he peeled off the windshield and threw in a dumpster along with the Lexus keys. Then he grabbed the Corolla keys from where he'd hidden them under the bumper. He opened the door for Yelena and dropped the backpack full of dope on the rear seat, then got in and they drove. Joe rolled his window down as she lit up a smoke.

They rode in silence as Joe steered them onto the BQE, heading to Queens. Finally he spoke: "You know you're going to have to leave town for a while. Heather Kaan will tell someone about you after we take her diamonds, if she hasn't already."

"Only if she lives," Yelena pointed out and tossed her cigarette out. It sparked as it jumped along the road behind them and died. "But, yes, I have to go. It's not smart for me to be here or in Russia, not for a time."

"Where will you go?" Joe asked.

"First on a vacation. Caribbean maybe? Or a Greek island no one even knows the name of. Why?" She smiled at him. "You want to come, Joe?"

"Maybe." He grinned at her. "Send me a postcard." He looked back at the road. Wind and the low hum of tires filled the car. He gestured at the backpack on the floor by her feet. "You should take those," he said. "Sell it. You'll need the dough."

She looked at him carefully, then unzipped the bag and, with the knife Joe had bought her, opened the tightly wrapped plastic bundle to pull out a kilo, a vacuum-sealed brick of pure smack. She held it up to him.

"You're saying this is all mine, Joe? To do with what I wish? You're giving it all to me as a gift?"

"Why not?" Joe said, with a shrug. "It will do you a lot more good than me, that's for sure."

"Okay then," Yelena said, and she slit the bag open, shaking it out the window. It vanished instantly in the wind, and then she let the empty bag go. She looked back at Joe, defiantly, as if challenging him to object. He said nothing and drove.

"I don't like this stuff, Joe," she said finally. "Not for my mother and not for you."

"Okay," he said quietly, then said nothing more as she cut open and dumped the rest, both backpacks, a small,

282

multimillion-dollar dust storm on the highway. When she was all done and had wiped and replaced her knife, Joe looked over at her and smiled. "Maria is going to be pissed."

Yelena shrugged. "I don't like this woman either."

Joe laughed. "Yeah, she's not at the top of my Christmas list." Then: "Send me your overseas account number. I will wire your share of the money from the stones."

She waved him off. "I will send it to Juno." Then after a beat she asked, in a different tone: "Have you ever been to jail, Joe?"

"Sure. But never a serious bit."

"I have. I will not go back." She patted the gun at her side. "I will go this way instead."

Joe nodded. "You will hold court in the street."

"Explain this? I don't understand," she asked.

"It's a saying, among criminals, who vow never to be taken alive. They'd rather just have their trial in the street and settle with the law there, instead of going up in front of a judge."

"Yes." She nodded in approval. "I will hold court in the street. But I will be the judge."

42

Joe and Yelena drove past the address Juno had texted—it was Club Layali, some kind of Middle Eastern restaurant—then parked in front of a hydrant down the block and walked back, entering through the front door. The manager greeted them with a smile.

"Good evening. Welcome. I am Mohammed. Table for two? Perhaps a quiet table upstairs?"

Joe looked around, taking the place in. "You know, I think we will check out the bar first. Then maybe sit down and eat."

"I love belly dance," Yelena explained.

"As you wish," the manager said with a smile and a gesture of welcome. "If you need anything at all, please just ask for me."

"We will. Thanks," Joe said, as Yelena led him by the hand to where the drinking and dancing were going on in the rear of the huge space. But instead of joining the fun, they wandered to the back and then followed the restroom sign downstairs.

"Juno said the signal was coming from underground," Joe said. Then: "Meet you back out here?"

Yelena nodded and went into the ladies' room while he checked the men's. There was nothing of interest. Together they walked past a janitor's closet and a disused old phone booth to another door. Trying it carefully, Joe found it unlocked, and he stepped in slowly. She followed. It was a storeroom, crowded with cartons and shelves but too small to contain any other doors or stairways.

"What do you think?" he asked her. She shrugged.

"Well, look who's here," a voice said. It was Heather, stepping from behind a stack of crates, holding a gun on them. Immediately Vlad stepped out from another angle, also pointing a gun. Heather smiled at Joe. "What a surprise. I didn't expect to see you again." She kept the gun on them while Vlad frisked them both and took their weapons. "What's that?" she asked and he handed over Yelena's knife.

"Cute," she said and pocketed it. "Now Yelena, pull that mat up. And Joe, you open the trapdoor. You're just in time for our going-away party. It's in the private lounge downstairs. Your pals are already here."

Mohammed watched the white couple cross the restaurant— the tall, thin, dark-haired American man and the blond Russian woman—frowning to himself when, instead of going into the bar like they said, they went downstairs to the restrooms. And when they did not return, he knew it was bad. He knew that the people who had come in and taken control of the club that afternoon were trouble when the clearly terrified owner had ordered him to say nothing and to stay out of the storeroom tonight, taking out any

285

supplies he might need first. He didn't know their names or their plans, but he knew it was something he wanted no part of. None of his concern. Then these two walked in. And he knew this man's face and his name.

He was Joe somebody. They called him Sheriff or the Bouncer. Who knew why? All Mohammed knew was what people said: he had killed Adrian Kaan and the others in his terror cell. He had stopped an attack, a big one, using biological weapons. He had saved many people: New Yorkers and tourists. He had also saved Mohammed, his family, and his friends a lot of pain and suffering. Because when the terrorists attacked, killing Americans in the name of Allah, who did the Americans come to take vengeance on? Them. Ordinary people. Real Muslims, who understood that Islam was peace, that it was haram, a grave sin to kill, that Allah wanted them to live in love and understanding with all people, that faith was freely chosen, and that it is through kindness and compassion that one serves the highest will. Who rejected violence, having been its victims, and the reign of horror in the lands controlled by the ignorant fanatics who committed barbarities in Islam's name, mainly upon Muslims. Who just wanted what every immigrant in New York wanted, what half of Queens wanted: to live and work and raise his family in peace, without the horror of history following him here. New York was a free city; here, truce was declared.

So when that man, Joe, whoever he was, went downstairs with his Russian girlfriend and never came out, Mohammed did what he had to do. He took a break, went outside, lit a cigarette, and with trembling fingers he called someone he knew who knew people, an older man, an Egyptian who'd lived here for decades, who helped restaurants and clubs like this open, get licensing, get connected with suppliers and garbage pickup, who smoothed things with the inspectors and settled disagreements with the Greeks who also ran this neighborhood.

When he got the call, the Egyptian was smoking a hookah upstairs from a private club where men were drinking tea and gambling over backgammon. He thanked Mohammed and told him he'd done the right thing and to forget all about it now. Then he called a black Muslim from Harlem he knew and from him got the number he needed. "I want to leave a message. It's very urgent," he told the voice that answered. And when the voice asked, very politely, "May I ask for whom you are calling?" he said a name that he had known and heard for years but had never had any reason to say himself. "For Mr. Gio Caprisi."

43

Gio arrived at his office. He parked downstairs in his personal spot, although the lot was empty at that time of night, except for Paul's car, his Porsche, the indulgence for which Gio teased him. Then he took the gun he had stashed under the seat and stuck it in the back of his waistband.

Gio would never so much as cross a street carrying a weapon that had been used in a crime. And the gun he had now was clean and untraceable, with the serial number filed off. If by chance police were to suddenly jump out from behind the potted plants and grab him here, then the most he'd be guilty of was possession of an unlicensed firearm, and even that, by the time his lawyers got done with it, would end up at worst as a fine. Probably the cops would end up having to come to him and apologize.

That was Gio. That was how he did things. He was careful and he was smart and no one fucked with him. Until Paul. Paul had made him reckless and stupid. And now Paul, whom he had trusted and loved, had fucked him over. And for that he would die.

Gio unlocked the door and walked upstairs instead of waiting for the elevator, and when he got to the office it was unlocked and the lights were already on. Paul was waiting in his private office to go over some banking reports and, no doubt, Paul assumed, to be together after as well. To do what they did together, what they shared, and what no one else knew. The idea that the one person in the world he'd trusted with this side of himself had betrayed him made him physically ill, and he had to swallow bile as he opened his private office door. Then he put a big smile on and said hello to Paul.

"Hi Gio," he said as he walked in. "You're late. I tried to get as much done as I could."

"Yeah, sorry," Gio said. "I got stuck at my last meeting. Though actually, I wanted to skip work tonight. I wanted to do something else."

Paul smiled. "You want to play? Me, too. I was thinking about you all this time. And about Gianna."

"No," Gio said. "I want to try something different tonight. I want you to be Paula. I want to see how pretty you look in one of those dresses."

"But . . ." Paul look confused. For the first time some kind of shadow came over those clear blue eyes. "I mean I've done drag before, of course, but we never . . . I didn't know that was your thing."

"I just want to try it," Gio said and sat. "I want to watch you undress and change into a girl. I want to just look at how beautiful you are."

Paul smiled, flattered despite himself. "Okay," he said. And he started to disrobe. Gio held his hand out for his shirt, and as Paul removed each article, he carefully smoothed and folded it. When he was nude, Paul went to the closet and got out a dress, choosing the blue sequins. He stepped into it and pulled the straps up over his shoulders. Gio had to admit, even without a wig or makeup, he looked a lot better in it than he did, a lot more like a real girl. He showed himself to Gio, even did a little twirl.

"Like me?"

"Yes," Gio said. "I love you." Then, clearing his throat, confident now that Paul was not wearing a wire, he asked him: "Did I mention why I was late?"

"Yes," Paul said, a bit self-conscious now, sitting down and crossing his legs that were covered in blond hair. "A meeting that ran long?"

"Right. Exactly. Though it didn't really go that long. I took care of it quickly. It was with Pat White. You know him, don't you?"

Paul shook his head. "I don't think so."

"No?" Gio asked. "I thought you did. I was worried the news about our meeting might upset you."

"Me? Why?"

"Because he's dead. He's full of bullets. I killed him and right now he's getting bagged up and thrown out like trash."

Paul stared. Gio had never discussed this side of his business with him before. Paul was just a numbers guy, a money launderer. He knew nothing about where the money came from or what Gio had to do for it. Nor did he want to know. And now Gio had confessed to a murder.

"Gio, I . . ."

"What about a guy named Powell, a CIA agent, do you know him?"

"No, I . . ."

"No? That's weird. Because you just answered an email from him and it sure sounded like you knew him. And Pat, too." He'd been staring hard at Paul, deadening his expression and speaking in a flat, neutral tone, but now he had to look away for a second. Paul was crying.

"Gio, please, let me explain. I did it for us. I'd never do anything to hurt you."

"For us?"

"It was Pat White. He set me up. You're right. I knew him. He was a client. I've been moving money for him for a few years, and he fed me to Powell. So when Powell came to me, he already had me cold. But he offered me a deal."

"So you traded my life for yours."

"No. Never." He was shouting now. He was angry, indignant, standing up. "I made a deal for us both. If I cooperated, fed him information like Pat did, then you and I could both be allowed to disappear."

"WITSEC?"

"Better. Much better. It's the CIA. They can give us new identities, new passports, even new birth certificates, real ones. And he said we could keep the money, too, the overseas accounts. Don't you see?" Paul knelt, still crying, and crawled over to grab Gio by the legs. "This is our chance. To get out. To be free. To live together. In the open. Like real lovers. To have our own lives. Baby," he said, looking up at Gio. "This is our chance."

Gio smiled. He couldn't help it. There were tears in his eyes. He stroked Paul's hair. He was actually relieved at the realization: he could never kill Paul. It didn't matter what he'd done. He loved him. That was it. He cleared his throat.

"You have to go, Paul. You have to leave tonight. And never come back." He stood up and crossed to the cabinet behind his desk, then got out a glass, poured himself a big shot of scotch, and drank it down. Then he took out the gun that he knew he'd never use and laid it on the desk. Paul stood, pacing around.

"Okay, fine. We'll go. Fuck Powell. What can he do now? We'll get our own papers; there's plenty of money."

"No, sorry, kid. That's not going to happen."

"What do you mean?" He stopped and faced Gio.

"I can't go. I can't leave my family. You know that. And you know it's all over for you if you stay here. So you have to go. Take the money. The accounts in Switzerland, they're yours. My gift."

"No, please, Gio," Paul said, his voice cracking. Gio crossed the room and held him, held him up, and kissed him. Then he let go.

"You have to go, Paul. Now. And don't come back. Please. Not ever. Because then I really will have to kill you."

Paul started to speak, but then he looked into Gio's eyes and he saw that this was the truth. He seemed to slump, to surrender. Silently he changed back into his street clothes while Gio watched without moving. Then he stepped toward the door. At the last minute he turned back to look at Gio once more, smiling at him while his eyes shone with tears, and suddenly a look of terror broke across his face. Gio turned just in time to see Carol, his wife, coming through the door from the bathroom. She grabbed the gun Gio had left on the desk and shot Paul through the heart.

Even after she'd stopped shooting and Paul was clearly dead, flung back on the floor, Carol was shaking so badly that Gio was afraid the gun would misfire, that she'd kill herself or him.

"Give me the gun," he said softly, and, as if she had forgotten about it, she looked down and let him take it from her hand. He put the safety on and slid it back into his waistband.

"I'm sorry," she said. "I'm sorry."

"No," Gio said. "It's me. It's my fault . . . all my fault . . . I can explain."

She shook her head. "No. You don't have to. I heard. I know."

"Carol, I can take care of this; don't worry. I can clean this up and then we can talk and then if you want me to leave, to move out, I'll understand."

She put her fingers over his mouth, still shaking her head. "No," she said. "You don't understand. I heard. About that man you killed tonight. About the CIA agent. About the money. I couldn't just let him walk out. Don't you understand? I had to do it. I saw that you loved him. I knew you could never do it, so I had to. I had to protect our family." Then she kissed him softly on the lips and went to sit on the couch, where she began to sob. Gio stared at her, as if he had never seen her before. Then his phone buzzed. It was Nero.

"Yeah?"

"Boss, it's me."

"I know. The phone told me. What is it?"

"I just got an urgent call about Joe."

Gio listened, then he hung up and while his wife wept and his lover's dead body bled out, he tried to think. For a moment he felt paralyzed, weak, like maybe this was finally too much, even for him. Then he did the only thing he could think to do. He called Special Agent Donna Zamora.

44

Heather liked Yelena's new knife.

They were in the subbasement, an old storage room, left from back in the early 1900s when this was a warehouse serving the waterfront and hidden later when this chamber was used by bootleggers during Prohibition. The room was deep in the foundation, the walls were raw stone and cement, the ceiling low, the air damp and lit with dusty bulbs behind wire mesh. There was a rough worktable of old, thick planks and, anachronistically, a few metal folding chairs. There was a large cage the size of a small room, where they used to lock up the expensive booze. It was old but strong, with iron bars and a big, old-fashioned lock. Now it held Cash, Juno, and Yelena. Felix stood leaning against the bars, holding his gun. Armond and Vlad were both gripping Joe, though one of Vlad's arms, the size of an elephant leg, would be enough to hold him; Armond was really just helping to keep him still for Heather, who was planning some delicate work.

As soon as Heather and Vlad got them downstairs, Juno and Cash had started yelling their apologies. But Joe saw the cuts and bruises on their faces and the phones and iPad on the table, along with the velvet bag containing the diamonds and the rusty key to the cage.

"No worries," Joe reassured them. Felix held a gun on Yelena while Armond unlocked the cage and pushed her in. She glared silently. Then, at Heather's signal, Vlad and Armond took hold of Joe, gripping him by the arms. Immediately, she kicked him in the solar plexus with the toe of her boot, and when he lurched forward, she spun and landed a roundhouse kick to his face. He flew back, but the two men held him, and he stood, blood seeping from a cut lip.

"How pretty," Heather said. "Is it real blood this time?"

"Taste it and see," Joe told her.

She leaned in, slowly, while the men held Joe still. She held his face in both her hands. She looked deep into his eyes. Then she kissed him, abruptly and hard, and bit his lip, squeezing it between her teeth. She let go, smiling wildly.

"Sweet," she said. "No wonder the Russian bitch likes you."

"Come on," Felix said. "Let's just kill them all and go. This is a waste of time."

"This is my time, Felix," Heather told him. "You and your boss can have the diamonds. I don't need your money. I told you that. This is what I want. Just a few minutes or who knows, maybe an hour with our friend Joe." She picked up the knife. "Can you last an hour, Joe? How long did they train you to hold out under torture before you talk?"

Joe licked the blood from his lips. "I'll talk now. What do you want to discuss?"

"I want to hear you beg. I want you to beg me to let you live, knowing I won't. I want you to beg me to let you die." She began slicing the buttons off of his shirt.

"Hey, I just got this shirt."

"Sorry. Just testing the blade. It's really very sharp." She ran the tip over him, like a pointer. "What should I cut off next? An ear? A ball? Maybe I will cut your eyes out and make Yelena eat them. Or maybe just slice the eyelids off and make you watch while Felix here does what he likes to do to girls. What do you think, Joe? What should I cut?"

"I'd say cut my hair. I've been meaning to for weeks."

She laughed. "That's funny, Joe. You're a funny guy. I like you. Hey . . ." She pushed his shirt back and exposed the star branded on the side of his chest. "Here it is. I heard about this. So they really did it. Made you their little sheriff?"

"That's a birthmark."

"You know, I think I'll cut this off first. Or no, I know what I'll do." She got very close to him, close enough to kiss again, and pressed the knifepoint into his chest so that a drop of blood swelled like a small red berry at the tip. "I will carve my husband's initials into your flesh, so that as you suffer, you will know why." Joe winced as she slid the blade over his skin, drawing a large A. The blood was just beginning to flow when Donna came down the stairs.

"Freeze," she yelled. "FBI."

Donna didn't really expect anyone to freeze. She expected them to move. Nor was she sure if she was really there in her official capacity as an FBI agent. But she needed the woman with the knife, whom she recognized as Heather Kaan, widow of the terrorist, who was carving up Joe, to move. She was too close to Joe for a clear shot. So Donna yelled, and the woman spun around to face her, stepping a crucial foot or two from Joe, and with the path cleared, Donna took her shot and killed her, just like she'd been trained to: with a bullet right through the heart.

By then, everyone was moving. The moment Donna fired, the two men had let go of Joe and dashed for cover, and Felix, standing by the cage, had raised his own pistol to shoot at Donna. She swerved to take him out next, but by then he'd dropped his gun. Yelena had leapt up, grabbing the top of the cage, and swung her legs through the bars to close around Felix's throat. Now she had them crossed under his chin, with her thighs clenched around his neck, pressing the carotid arteries. And from the way his eyes bulged and his arms flailed, it was clear that she was squeezing the life out of him. Donna swerved back toward the other men, but it was too late. Vlad, moving with surprising agility for a beast of his bulk, the way grizzlies run down hikers and snatch salmon from rapids, had loped over the small space, grabbing Donna and flinging her across the room like a child. She flew back, knocking her head against the wall, and dropped to the floor unconscious.

Joe had moved, too. The second he heard Donna's voice he had stomped Armond's instep with his heel, causing him to flinch and let go. Vlad's grip was too strong to break, but when Donna fired and Vlad moved, Joe was able to drop to the floor. Heather fell, dropping the knife, and he grabbed it up as he rolled out of the line of fire. It was, as Heather had pointed out, very sharp and perfectly balanced. A well-made tool. Holding it loosely and with his forefinger along the spine to guide it, Joe launched it in a short arc that ended between Armond's shoulder blades, a few inches below the base of his neck. Armond fell to his knees and pitched forward, gurgling.

Using his momentum, Joe now sprang back to his feet, but it was too late. Vlad was already coming for him after knocking out Donna, drawing a Glock from his waistband, the gun like a toy in his massive paw as he raised it to fire. Rising on one foot, Joe kicked straight out, clipping the gun, and sending it flying from Vlad's grip, but that was all he could do. By then Vlad was on him, wrapping his arms around him, closing Joe in a bear hug and slowly but surely crushing him, as the giant's arms coiled about his neck and chest like twin boa constrictors.

Joe couldn't breathe. He couldn't see, face pressed as it was into Vlad's shoulder, his bicep like a vise sealing off Joe's windpipe, while the other arm, clamped under his rib cage, crushed his diaphragm. Vlad squeezed Joe close, holding him tight like an eager suitor at a ballroom dance, lifting him to his toes as they waltzed. Joe tried kicking, but Vlad had his legs planted correctly, far apart and solid, like stone columns, and it was hard for Joe to do more than thump his feet weakly like a bored kid on a plane, annoying the person in front of him. His arms were up in front of him, elbows bent, pinned uselessly between his own body and Vlad's. All he could move were his wrists, like little flippers that he flailed pointlessly, as though he were a drowning man, weakly waving for help. Which he was. He was sinking into unconsciousness and then death, drowning in the giant's embrace.

From the cage, Joe's friends were watching him die, and they couldn't do a thing. Cash and Juno were on the ground frantically trying to reach Felix's gun, which had fallen out of reach. There was no way. It was too far, but they kept trying, as though their arms might suddenly grow. Yelena, too, could see him fading out, feet dangling, being hugged to death, but she herself was strangling Felix, and if she let him go too soon he'd get the gun. She could see the old, heavy key to the cage on the table with the diamonds, and the sight was infuriating. She knew she could pick this lock in minutes, seconds maybe with the right tool, but she didn't have seconds or tools. She had nothing. She could do nothing but watch Joe die.

Joe, too, felt like he was watching himself die in his own mind, which was yelling at him to do something, anything to save himself, to buy himself one more precious breath. Moving his fingers on his left hand, he felt Yelena's mechanical pencil where he'd clipped it to his pocket, pressed now between his body and Vlad's. Slowly, with his index and middle fingers, he drew it out, then closed his other fingers around it, taking great care not to let it slip. Then, millimeter by millimeter, he began to turn his wrist, using the tiny bit of movement he was allowed to raise the pencil higher. He shifted his right hand, too, and, reaching with all his strength, managed to get his hand on the side of Vlad's head. Not that he could do anything to injure that massive block. But he gripped the flesh on Vlad's neck tightly with his fingers and stuffed his thumb in his ear, for leverage. Annoyed, Vlad shook his head, like an ox shaking off a flea, but Joe held on. He was close now, face-to-face. He could feel Vlad's breath. Then, with his right hand holding himself steady and the fingers of his left hand wrapped tight around the shaft of the pencil, thumb on the eraser, he drove the point into Vlad's right eye.

At the last moment, Vlad saw the pencil coming and instinctively flinched, but that only gave Joe another quarter inch of free space to work with as the tip of the pencil punched through the outer membrane of the eyeball and sank into the socket with a sickening feeling, like a toothpick piercing a grape.

Instantly, Vlad released his grip, and Joe gasped for air, but now he was the one hanging on as the giant tried to throw him off. Joe grasped him tighter, with his whole right arm clutching Vlad's neck and his legs wrapping his hips, like a baby gorilla hugging his mother. Vlad pounded Joe's back with his fists, and the pain made him grunt like he was being beaten with mallets, but he clung on, and as he got the whole of his upper arm free, he bent from the elbow and rammed the pencil home with all his strength.

Vlad howled—a high, piercing screech—and began to flap his arms wildly, as though desperate for flight. Joe fell back, staggering and wheezing as he watched the giant flail. Like a fish on a hook—a shark flopping on a deck or a speared marlin thrashing at the end of a line—he flung himself around the room, knocking the table over and flattening the chairs, limbs working convulsively, sending his huge body careening mindlessly like a runaway train, nerves still driving him despite the pencil sticking out of his brain.

Barely able to move, Joe limped across the room to where the others in the cage now watched in silence. Only the giant roared and screamed, making terrible high-pitched sounds like a baby or a dolphin. He didn't sound human anymore.

Joe picked up Felix's gun and fired, putting a single bullet through his other eye. The giant dropped. Then Joe swung to Felix, taking aim, but saw immediately that it wasn't needed: Felix's eyes were bulged now and full of broken vessels. His face was blue, his tongue squeezed between his purpled lips. He was dead. Yelena unclenched her legs and let him go. He fell.

"Jesus fucking Christ," Cash murmured quietly.

"You two are hard fucking core," Juno added, finishing the thought.

Still cramped and aching, Joe got the key and opened the cage. "You guys better get going," he said to Cash and Juno. "Make sure to get your phones. We'll hook up later."

They stood there, still staring at the dead bodies: Vlad on his back with the pencil poking up and Felix slumped against the cage. "Let's go," Joe said, louder, as he rushed over to Donna. "Time to move."

"Right, sorry," Juno said. And then to Cash: "Let's go, man."

They grabbed their belongings and Cash quickly said, "Thanks Joe," as they went. He crouched over Donna and checked her pulse and breathing. She was okay, just knocked out. Yelena retrieved her gun.

"You can have your pencil back now if you want it," Joe told her. "I know it's your favorite."

"Keep it to remember me by," she said. "I will keep the knife you gave me." She drew it from Armond's back and wiped it carefully on his shirt. She smiled at him. "It really is a very nice knife."

"I'm glad you like it," Joe said. She headed to the stairway.

"Yelena," he called. She paused and looked back, but he didn't know what to say.

"I will see you again, Joe," she said finally.

"I know it," he answered.

And she went. Joe watched her move swiftly up the steps and she was gone. For a second he felt the urge to go after her, but of course he could not. There was too much to do here, and then Donna started to moan and mumble in his arms.

"Hey, sleepyhead," he said softly, bending over her. "Time to rise and shine."

Her eyes opened, and seeing him she smiled. "Hi," she said, looking up at him.

"Hi there," he responded, brushing her hair back, his mouth just a breath away from hers.

Then she yelled, "Fuck," and she sat up, as consciousness returned and she remembered where she was. "Fuck, fuck, fuck," she repeated, looking around, and then: "Ow, shit," holding her head at the rapid movement.

"Easy, easy, it's all over," Joe told her.

"For you maybe. Fuck," she said one more time, getting to her feet, one hand braced on the wall. "Where the hell's my gun?"

"Here," Joe said quickly, picking it off the floor by the barrel and handing it to her.

"This is bad," she said looking around, her eyes narrowing at the sight of Vlad and Felix. She shook her head. "I'm not even going to ask."

"Don't worry, Donna. We can handle this."

"Joe, I shot someone. Off duty. For no reason. At least none I can explain. To aid you in the commission of . . . God knows what. How are we going to handle it?"

"That's not the 'we' I meant," Joe said. He leaned closer. "You showed up and you helped me and I thank you for that. Now you're going to have to trust me. Get out of here, get some aspirin, and wait for my signal. An hour, maybe less."

She hesitated, wanting to ask questions but not wanting to know the answers.

"How will I know when the signal comes?"

"You'll know. Now hurry the fuck up and go."

And with that he turned his back on her, found his phone in the mess on the floor, and made a call. Seeing no other choice, Donna went up the stairs and through the club— which was packed now and louder than ever, with no one even glancing her way—and then back out to her car.

"Gio," Joe said when his call went through. "It's me. I could really use some help getting rid of a little problem over here."

"You and me both, brother," Gio said, his voice quiet. "I was thinking about a ride on the boat."

"Sounds good," Joe said, wondering why Gio's voice seemed strange. "I also need you to make a couple of calls."

45

Five minutes later, the phone in Rebbe's house rang. He was sleeping, but they woke him when they heard it was Gio calling with an emergency. Rebbe listened to Gio, and ten minutes after that, long enough to make a cup of tea, Rebbe called Hyman Shatzenberg, the senior brother. He told him that someone who had reliable knowledge of the stolen diamonds' location had contacted him through an intermediary. They were willing to turn the goods over to the authorities in return for a finder's fee of 10 percent, if Rebbe would broker it. Shatzenberg eagerly agreed.

Half an hour after that, Donna's phone rang. She was sitting in a diner drinking coffee. Amazingly, she had been famished and had just put away a cheeseburger and fries, eating with the hearty appetite of one resigned to her fate. The call was from her work line, patched through.

"This is Special Agent Zamora, how can I help you?" she said as she watched the waitress walk by. A man with a heavy Hasidic accent—Brooklyn meets Vladivostok—said he had a tip but wanted to remain anonymous. There was information relating to the diamond heist. Then he gave the address of the crime scene she had just left and told her to check the basement.

She guessed this is what Joe meant when he said she'd know. Paying quickly, she drove back and now went in officially, badging the manager, a fellow named Mohammed, and asking to be led to a supposed basement storage room, with his permission. He gladly agreed and also gladly waited while she went down alone.

In some ways the scene was the same. The huge man still lay on his back with a puncture wound through one eye and, forensics would show, a bullet through the other. Armand's corpse was facedown on the floor. Drug smuggler and suspected multiple murderer Felix Habibi lay slumped dead against the cage, a gun near his body. No other bodies were in sight. Heather Kaan was gone. Joe was gone. All evidence of Donna's own presence was gone.

However there was a small plastic baggie containing heroin flung on the floor near Vlad's corpse. And on the table, which was back upright, sat a velvet bag that when she checked was found to contain diamonds.

Donna couldn't help smiling as she called it in.

Agent Mike Powell was not having a good night. First, an operation that he had personally initiated and for which he'd provided the intel, had gone to hell and the NYPD was dumping the blame in his lap. His insistence that the actual info was good, that the meet did indeed happen as he said, did not seem to be mollifying anyone. It had also been his idea to circumvent the FBI because of "suspected"

306

leaks, and this, too, was being thrown back at him. The FBI was demanding an apology and insisting, moreover, that the whole reason they blew it was because the FBI should have taken the lead. Nonsense, of course, but how could he argue? It was definitely not the moment to reveal that his main suspicion was that his ex-wife was boning one of the diamond thieves. His station chief had been eating shit with a smile all night and he knew, once he'd digested it, a fresh, steaming pile would be waiting on his own desk in the morning.

And now his "assets," transformed like bad stocks into liabilities, had disappeared on him. Pat White had vanished. His phone was dead. His family claimed he had not come home for dinner and no one at his usual haunts had seen him. People on the street were already talking about a shake-up within his crew, a shift of power from him to the Madigan brothers, Tim, Sean, and Liam. People in Powell's office were saying he'd fled, gone rogue, if a gangster who was snitching on his comrades in order to preserve his own power could ever be anything else. He might have gotten spooked, worried his double-dealing was about to be exposed, or it might have been his retirement plan all along—to escape with his offshore millions, beyond the reach of the law and of Mrs. White.

And now, as he redialed his other source, Nightcrawler—his man inside the Caprisi family—that, too, was going straight to voice mail, and his texts were going unanswered. It was possible of course that he would turn up any minute, that they both would, but Powell didn't think so. He thought they were dead. Sitting at his desk, with his bright reflection staring back at him from the wide window, he suddenly felt exposed, as though someone out there were spying on him now, aiming at him. He shut the light. He told himself it was just to get quiet and think for a moment, but in the dark, staring out at the empty street and the silent buildings, all he felt was alone.

Then his phone rang. It wasn't the regular office phone or the secure line. It was his personal cell, though when he looked he saw the number was blocked.

"Hello?"

"Hello, Mike, glad I caught you. I hear you had a rough night and lost some assets. So did I. Valuable ones."

"Who is this?" Powell asked, standing up.

"We've never met, but we have a lot of friends in common. And some enemies, too. It's possible we could achieve a lot together."

"I'm still waiting for a name," Powell said, looking out at the night.

"Fine, then, I will give you one," the voice said. "Zahir."

This time the FBI took the lead, and they showed up in force, along with a team from the NYPD's Major Case squad, headed by one Detective Fusco. As the ensuing investigation would show, the bullet in Vlad's head came from Felix's gun, and no other brass was found on the scene. Felix's cause of death was strangulation, inflicted by someone of incredible strength, quite possibly Vlad himself. The presence of the diamonds and some raw, pure heroin indicated that the group responsible for both crimes had turned on each other. Everyone from all concerned agencies was happy to declare victory and close this one out, except for Powell. But since his asset Paul was the one missing player and now the prime suspect of having absconded with the heroin, if there even was any, he couldn't really say much, even when Pat White's dismembered body turned up weeks later in a New Jersey swamp.

The finder's fee of $400,000.00 was duly paid, and after expenses, split six ways it came to $61,666.66 each. Along with weapons, vehicles, technology, and miscellaneous, the expenses also included $5,000.00 cash that showed up in an envelope with no return address, mailed to one Ami Hendricks. Yelena's share was wired to her numbered account through Juno. Joe, as usual, gave half to his grandmother and the rest to Gio, to stash for him in his safe. Joe said he didn't need the extra money since he had a job, and it would just be a temptation. And Gio didn't question why he had hung on to that heroin sample so long.

46

That night, while Donna was with her fellow agents at the crime scene, Joe was with Gio on his boat. It had been a long night for both men and a hassle getting those bodies onboard, so now they sat in silence, listening to the engine as Gio steered them out to sea. When Gio felt they'd gone far enough, he cut the engine and then finally spoke.

"Well," he said, taking in Joe's garishly colored, buttonless, aloha shirt. "At least you're dressed for a cruise."

Joe laughed. He'd used the boat's first aid kit to clean up his cut and, while he would surely be bruised and aching for a few days, he was otherwise unharmed. He wondered if Dr. Z could help with the soreness from where Vlad had tried to squeeze his guts out of him like toothpaste.

Gio got out a heavy, serrated knife used for gutting fish and together they went back to the rear deck, where the bodies of Paul and Heather were spread on plastic tarps. Joe grabbed some chain and did his best to bind them together, also threading the chain through a couple of cinder blocks, supplies they had taken from a Caprisi-controlled construction site on the way. Joe had left the

Corolla there, too. One of Gio's men would retrieve and dispose of it later.

Now they dragged the bodies to the edge of the boat and, lifting together, flopped them halfway over the side. Next Gio dragged the blade across Heather's throat and the arteries in her arms. She'd been dead awhile and her heart no longer pumped out the blood but, as with chum, the scent would help draw predators and hopefully convince them that this was evidence worth eating. He turned Paul's head up next and hesitated for a moment.

"Let me do it," Joe said, but Gio shook his head, then slashed Paul's jugular open and sawed into his arms and legs. Together they heaved the load over, and with a loud splash, the heavily weighted bodies instantly vanished, sinking below the dark surface. Lastly, Gio tossed the knife.

Now that he could finally let himself relax, Joe suddenly felt his total exhaustion and sat down heavily on one of the padded fishing chairs. Gio went to a cabinet and then came back and took the other chair. He handed Joe a large bottle of mineral water and opened one of bourbon for himself.

"Thanks," Joe said, and they clinked bottles, then drank.

"Mind if we just sit here for a little while?" Gio asked. "I feel like as soon as I step foot on land, life is going to start back up again. I just need a little pause."

"No problem," Joe answered. "It's been a long time since we've taken a spin out here together."

So the two friends sat in silence, floating on the surface of the ocean, watching the first specks of dawn begin to gather, like motes on the far rim of the world. Meanwhile, in the water around them, the sharks were closing in.

Acknowledgments

Thank you to Doug Stewart, my agent, without whose faith and foresight none of this would be possible, and to everyone at Sterling Lord Literistic, especially Szilvia Molnar for her hard work all over the world. I am deeply grateful to my editor, Otto Penzler, who first brought up the idea of a "next book," for his vision and insight, to Morgan Entrekin, for his guidance and support, and to everyone at Mysterious Press/ Grove Atlantic, especially Brenna McDuffie and Kaitlin Astrella for taking such good care of my books. Thanks to my friends for their kindness and early reading, especially Rivka Galchen and William Fitch, and also to Nivia Hernandez and Antonio Chinea for help with my Spanish. As always, all errors are my own. Most of all, thank you to my family, who have put up with me the longest, for their love and patience, and to Matilde, who has already given me so much—even the emergency loan of a Norwegian laptop to finish this novel on time.

About the Author

DAVID GORDON holds an MA in English and Comparative Literature and an MFA in Writing from Columbia University. He is the author of *The Serialist*, which won the VCU/Cabell First Novel Award and was a finalist for an Edgar Award. His work has appeared in the *Paris Review*, the *New York Times* and the *Los Angeles Review of Books*. He was born and lives in New York City.